A Cheating Man's Heart

Derrick Jaxn

First Edition: November 2014

Publisher's Note:

This is a work of fiction. Names, characters, places, and incidents either are the product of the author's imagination or are used fictitiously, and any resemblance to actual persons, living or dead, business establishments, events, or locales is entirely coincidental.

The publisher does not have any control over and does not assume any responsibility for third party websites or their content.

Website: http://www.shopderrickjaxn.com/

Instagram: http://instagram.com/derrickjaxn

Facebook: https://www.facebook.com/officialderrickjaxn

Twitter: https://twitter.com/DerrickJaxn

ISBN: 978-0-9910336-2-1

"Love is kind, love is patient, but even the strongest loves get tired of waiting."

"People that don't leave your mind are usually somewhere hiding in your heart."

"What does it profit a man to gain every girl in the world, yet lose the one who really cared about him?"

"Never hand your heart to someone who's still picking up t he pieces to their own."

—*Derrick Jaxn*

Table of Contents

Prologue

"Ooh! That one," I said, jumping up and down.

"Which one?" she asked.

Sugary residue from my ring pop had dripped its way to my fingers, now smearing across the toy vending machine's glass as I pointed to the watch I'd been lusting over. It sat snugly on the far left corner, seemingly looking at me with the same soulmate connection I felt for it. "The blue Superman one!"

"Okay. Stay right here, and watch me work."

My big sister, Pooh, who was twelve years old at the time, pulled out a handful of balled up dollar bills she'd been saving up over the past few weeks.

We'd taken her bike down to the skating rink so I could go birthday shopping at what we called the Vending Machine Mall located at the very front when you first walk in. But we didn't have a lot of time because Daddy's gift was coming later on and it was supposed to be a big one. He'd barely been able to keep the excitement to himself in the days leading up. My guess was it was either roller skates or some kind of spaceship. Either one would do.

All I know is, I'd been waiting my entire four years of life for this day, so I strutted in like I was a Kardashian, pointed my gift out to Pooh, and let her do the rest. But my heart sank when her first stab at the watch missed.

She put in another dollar and tried again, this time with

her eyes narrowed and a better grip on the joystick , and she got it.

My eyes lit up, and my adrenaline rushed. For every second the mechanical claw took to bring my watch to me, the anticipation for my next gift doubled.

Pooh and I pulled back up to the house on her 10-speed bike just before Momma started up her hatchback and screeched out of the driveway. I figured she must've been trying to get some last-minute groceries for my birthday dinner, hopped off the handle bars and sprinted on towards the porch.

Daddy met me at the door, his brow furrowed and his lips shaping to yell out after Momma before he looked down and saw me. His facial expression warmed in an instant, beaming all thirty-two of his Jamaican pearly whites.

"Birthday boy! I'm sure glad to see you. Did you get it? Huh? Did ya get your watch, son?" he said, bending down on one knee to meet me at eye level.

I took my hand from behind my back and then put it in his face. "Sho' did!"

He laughed and pulled me in tight for one of his bear hugs, "Well, I got something for you. Your teacher says you're already counting by two's and you don't even use your hands like your classmates. I bet you can even count money, can't ya son?"

I shook my head up and down confidently.

"So tell me something. How many cents are in a dollar?"

Without hesitation I yelled, "100!"

He smiled then reached in his back pocket for his old worn-out leather bill fold then pulled out a freshly printed

100 dollar bill. "That's my boy. Instead of a gold sticker, I'll just give you this. Now what'cha think about that?"

I'd never seen a 100 dollar bill before but I did recognize that it was money with the number 100 on it. And 100 was bigger than one through 99 so I put two and two together and the tingly sensation in my chest pushed my mouth and eyes into huge circles of excitement.

"Now, you tell me what you want to get with your prize money, and we're gonna go get it."

"Anything?"

"Anything. Just name it."

I knew exactly what I wanted. I took a deep breath and said, "Milk!"

"Milk?" he asked, looking confused.

"Yes, Daddy. Milk." I confirmed.

At the time, the *Got Milk?* commercials advertised how milk made a body strong. Super heroes were the strongest people in the world, so it was a no-brainer. I wanted some damn milk.

He shook his head then looked at me and smiled again. "Milk it is. We'll pick some up on the way to go get your real gift. Go on inside and change into a clean shirt. I'll be back in ten minutes to get you."

Before I rushed off into my room, flinging the shirt off of my scrawny body and digging into the drawer for a clean one, I checked my new watch for the time. It was exactly 6:00 p.m. and forty-three seconds.

I changed my shirt and with about eight minutes left, I did the only logical thing any kid with too much energy to sit and wait would do; I pretended I was a superhero.

With a bath towel tied around my neck, and my tennis ball-inside-of-the-tube socks nunchucks, I was "withaaaw-ing" all around the living room. Super heroes didn't use nunchucks, but a black one would once he got his milk.

At exactly 6:10 p.m. and forty three seconds, I ran back outside on the porch, ready to leave with Daddy.

But I didn't see him.

I doubled checked my watch then went in the kitchen to cross reference it with the microwave. Both of them had the same time down to the very second.

I ran back outside and decided to practice my counting until he came back. Figured he had to make a stop for gas, or maybe he was stopping to get the milk first so we could save time.

I counted all sixty seconds of every minute out loud until I got to ten.

But nine counts of ten later, I was still waiting on the porch. My ring pop gone, my words slurring from the exhaustion of counting for so long, all while the sun had begun setting.

Momma had come home not long before and started dinner.

"Baby, you all right out here?" she said, wiping her hands on her apron, looking at me through the screen door.

"Yes, ma'am," I turned and answered.

"I think it's time you come on in. It's getting late."

"I can't right now, Momma."

"How come, baby?"

"I'm waitin' on Daddy. He said he'd be here in ten minutes."

She put her hand on my shoulder, exhaling heavily and her eyes aiming down the road. "Come on inside now. You can wait for him there."

Grudgingly, I went back inside--losing count of the minutes and beginning to count the years.

So far, it's been 21.

Hail Mary Pass

Pete put his finger to his temple like he'd just gotten a great idea. "You come home from work, take out the trash, replace a few bulbs like you said you would, and some more manly stuff. Once that's over with, you get out of your work clothes and into your boxers and tube socks just to decompress because it's been a really long day.

"A call comes in from your woman. She tells you she just got punched in the face. By a man. So you rush down to wherever she's at. One hundred miles an hour. Pissed. Already counting the bail money and subtracting it from your account balance because you *know* you're about to go to jail today, right?

"When you get there, you see the douche-bag who did it. He didn't even leave the scene. Matter of fact, he has his hand raised for another swing and pauses when he sees you. You charge and before you get to him, she steps in front and tells you that she's been having an affair with him for the past six months. She just didn't know how to tell you until now...that she needs you to get him off of her.

"What do you do?"

I looked at Pete for a moment, baffled to the point I had to squint. "P., what in the *hell* are you talking about? None of that happened."

"Right, I'm just sayin' though. It coulda."

"But it didn't."

"Doesn't matter. Not like you would've told me anyway. Apparently there's a lot of things we keep from each other," Pete said, sitting back into the diner booth, rubbing one hand backwards through his mullet-styled blond hair.

He agreed to meet me for lunch to catch up on my session with Dr. Holley but had the attention span of a goldfish, especially when a nerve was touched, like the one I'd just plucked by admitting there was a lot more to me than I'd ever told him. That's where his random, subject-changing question came from to begin with.

"How was I supposed to tell you?"

"I don't know--smoke signal, carrier pigeons, Morse code, tin cups on a string, SOMETHING!"

Pete dropped his head into his hands then pushed his hair off of his forehead behind his ears again. "All right, bro. So back to *your* story. You were in this room with a gorgeous woman, good credit, her edges fully intact, yet you made the irrational decision to leave without so much as touching her knee. And then what?"

"Come on, P., you're missing the point. This wasn't some kind of date. She's my--"

"Your shrink, I get it."

"Not my shrink, my therapist." I shot back, to deaf reception.

Pete shrugged his shoulders dismissively. "Okay, your therapeutic shrink. I can meet you in the middle."

I took a sip of my lukewarm coffee, then looked out of the massive glass window beside us that opened into the busy streets of downtown Charlotte, trying to gather my thoughts again.

"Okay, so back to what I was saying. Dr. Holley, she still feels like I gotta chance to find love, it seems."

"You've gotta be kiddin' me. How about you pay me 500 dollars an hour and I'll teach you how to count backwards starting from 10."

"You're not taking me seriously, P. and that's messed up with all the times I've helped you with 'Shonda."

"But that's different. You already know my situation."

By *situation*, he meant the cultural learning curve he's been trying to overcome.

See, Pete is like a short version of Fabio...if Fabio had a bird chest and a pot belly. My pale brother from another is what I've always called him. And he has a mean sweet tooth for chocolate. King-sized chocolate. Rashonda, to be specific. She's an Amazon woman, standing at least six foot two in flats to Pete's five foot six in boots. With two tube socks.

That, plus their background puts a lot of distance between them. So, since I was raised by and with black women, I qualified as what Pete called his "black-woman-whisperer", a term I didn't care for but charged to his head, not his heart.

"Okay, yours is a bit different," I continued. "I don't know why I'm telling you all this anyway. I need to save my breath for the rest of this session."

"Oh, you're going back?"

I shook my head, looking down at my watch. "Yeah, and it's about time I head out. She's probably already there."

"Okay, cool bro, but just one more question,"

"No, you cannot borrow my car," I answered him in advance.

"Dude, for the last time, I swear I'll bring it back safe. I swear."

"No, P. I'll see you later," I said, putting the tip on the table for the waitress.

I grabbed my coat and walked out, feeling his peripheral vision following me so he could break the twenty and keep some for himself. That's my boy, but he has to be the cheapest person I have ever come across, and reckless too.

That's how we met. He had snuck into a night club when I first moved to North Carolina last year,
pushed up on a Panther's girlfriend and purposely backed into me, pretending we knew each other so he wouldn't get his ass beat. And we've been best friends ever since.

I drove back to the therapist's office, taking in the fresh air I'd only been getting when I was out at seminars and media appearances, which was cool...in the beginning. But at this point, I'm ready to experience family picnics, teaching my son how to hold a baseball bat, then cheering too loud at his games until they put me out.

Doing my daughter's hair for the first time, screwing it up while my wife tells me she's proud of the effort. Then seeing my baby girl fake a smile to make her daddy feel better about it, too, before she goes to school and gets ragged on by her snobby ass kindergarten friends she'll grow up to be cuter than anyway.

I want weekly unwind and wine sessions with my wife. Where we hire a sitter, sneak away from the kids, and spend the night enjoying the love we've built. Making love, both mentally and physically, until we've purged every stress and worry that caused us to take each other for granted. But it seems I can't even get past the first date without feeling like

I'm wasting my time.

That chemistry, the spark of something potentially special--I haven't felt that in years. And seeking professional help is my last resort. It's the Hail Mary pass at the end of the season as I try to earn a spot in the playoffs. If it doesn't work, then the whole idea of family and happiness was going to have to retire. For good.

I beat Dr. Holley back to her office with ten minutes to spare until the second part of our session. I could've waited in the car until she'd gotten there, but saw no need to waste gas so I got out and checked her office door to see if it was open, and it was.

I let myself in, walking hand in hand with curiosity as I perused the room.

The femininity was refreshing. The automatic mist fragrance on the wall reminded me of the sample smell-goods that fall out of women's magazines. Her master's degree from Howard hung proudly on the wall amidst lit candles, and then there was a picture of her and a man on her desk.

A selfie with him holding the camera and her face smushed up against his cheeks, both of them smiling from ear to ear, love for each other permeating their pores. She looked at least six or seven years younger in the picture, which was odd because I hadn't seen a ring on her finger. A ring that I felt deserved to be there.

"What are you doing?!"

I jumped when I heard her voice and turned to see Dr. Holley glowering malevolently at me then behind me at her picture.

"Oh, I was just--I mean I was about to--"

"Were you going through my things?"

"No, of course not. But...this guy," I said, pointing to the picture. "Is that your man?"

"First off, it's none of your business, and secondly, no, he is not!" she snapped, snatching the picture and putting it in her drawer.

I didn't know who he was, but something about it touched a nerve when I asked.

"Mr. Fletcher, I think we'd better go ahead and get started."

"All right, cool."

She walked behind me to her chair and flipped open her laptop. With an outward veneer of calm, she remained silent and waited for me to resume the saga of my past relationships in college.

I charged it to the game, then found a sweet spot on the couch.

The memories came rushing in, mentally taking me back to the lake again; Jazmin and Danielle running full sprint towards my car, and the gun placed firmly on my tongue.

Words Unsaid. Cries Unheard.

"SHAWN! OPEN THE DOOR!" Danielle's voice was frantic, a tone I wasn't familiar with.

I eased the gun back onto my lips. A wave of embarrassment wafted over me. *Where in the hell did she come from?* I thought, as I squeezed my eyes with the illogical hope that this could all just start over.

Jazmin stopped short a few yards back as Danielle came straight to the car, yanking at the door handle. She had tears streaming down her face and her hair was sticking to her forehead from the sweat.

"Let me in, please," she pleaded, her voice hoarse from the screaming.

The bloodshot-redness in her eyes penetrated every nerve I had to finish what I had started. I took the gun completely away from my mouth and unlocked the door. She swung it open and clasped her arms around my neck, almost as if I still meant something to her.

"I'm so sorry. This is my fault, I know it is," she cried. "I shouldn't have said those things to you and I'm sorry."

"Danielle, please don't apologize. None of this is your fault."

She hugged me harder, tears beginning to soak the neck of my shirt.

I looked outside the car and saw Jazmin standing in the same place she'd stopped before.

She was bothered by the sight of Danielle and me. It was written on her face, signed by her eyes, eyes that also wanted to cry but stitched tightly with the strength that'd held her together through every other painful situation in her life till that point in which she'd had enough.

She was grateful to see me alive, but she couldn't ignore the reality that no matter how bad she wanted to console me, too, there'd be no reciprocity. Something she was no stranger to; but she was committed to ending that cycle no matter who it meant losing so long as it wasn't herself.

I looked back down at Danielle, her sobs now beginning to mollify. "How did you know I was here?"

She wiped her face on my shirt, then looked out at Jazmin. "Well, first she called me. Said she drove by and the door was wide open and when she went to check, she saw your suicide note. She found my number on one of the bills at the house and I knew this was the first place you'd come, so we got here as fast as we could."

The moment I looked back over at Jazmin, she cut her eyes from me. I wanted to talk to her or at least let her speak, but in front of Danielle, I couldn't find the audacity.

"I'm just glad you're okay, Superman. You scared me," Danielle said.

The tables turned, and I began being the one assuaging Danielle which caused Jazmin to break her silence.

"Are you guys all right now?" she asked, her gaze locked back in on me. It was a look that said, "Is this it? Are you really going to act like you have nothing to say to me? Did you mean anything you ever told me about being there for me? Because here I am, ready to save your life, but you won't even speak up to save my heart."

I cleared my throat, willing to accept whatever came of my next move. I had to talk to Jazmin, even if it was just for a moment but leaving her out cold like that would be unacceptable. I had too much respect for her and she'd gone through a lot to come find me.

But Danielle nixed that with a swift reply.

"Yes, we're okay. Thank you." she responded, dismissively.

Jazmin didn't wait to hear any more. Ruefully, she turned and walked away, her heavy footfalls leaving traces in the dirt. And I didn't stop her. This time, not because I was scared, but because her healing process didn't need to be prolonged any further, even if it meant there was more I wanted to say to her but never would.

After tossing the gun in the lake, Danielle switched seats with me and drove us back to the apartment. The asphalt rushing beneath us, clicks of the turning signals, and amicable silence kept us until we got back.

It had been at least twenty-four hours since I'd eaten, so I was seeing stars. Or maybe that was the sun I was looking at. Either way, it had my head spinning but I managed to struggle up the stair case.

Without speaking or even looking at me since we'd gotten in, she went straight to the kitchen and started pulling out sandwich meat and bread. The fact that she was in business attire told me this wasn't in her plans for the evening, and I began feeling like an inconvenience.

I tried to stop her. "Danielle, please. You don't--"

"Look, just sit there and let me do this."

"I just don't want you to feel like you have to."

"I know I don't have to. But title or no title, we have to take care of each other."

I let her statement marinate.

"Okay. But don't you wanna talk about all this?"

"Not much to talk about. Cheating's not complicated. You did it. It's over. And besides, it was just sex."

She looked at me for confirmation. Confirmation I didn't give her with my lack of any reaction at all.

She paused from the sandwiches, and continued. "It was just sex. That's it...right?"

"Danielle, I love you."

"That's not what I asked you."

Think Shawn.

"Was it just sex?" I repeated trying to stall long enough to gather the courage to tell the truth. "I mean, no. It wasn't."

Silence came again. We just looked at each other. The wall around her heart was mounting and cementing harder and harder by the second.

But I didn't have it in me to keep lying to her. Lying to myself. What Jazmin and I built went beyond just sex and there was no denying that.

"I mean, that's what it is. Am I *in* love with her? No. But I can't say it was just physical either."

She went back to making the sandwiches, pretending she was ignoring me.

I continued, "So that's why, I'm glad we're not together anymore."

She slammed down the butter knife that she'd been using to spread the mayonnaise . "You sure are pouring it on thick, ya know?"

10

"No, I'm saying, this may be a good thing for both of us even though it was bad how it happened."

She resumed her mayo spreading before clasping the two pieces of wheat bread and turkey together. "That's fine. I'm not ready to even think about a relationship and neither are you. Here, eat this. I'll have my friend come pick me up. Try to get some rest."

She handed me the sandwich and walked out. Not even a goodbye hug, as I should've expected.

I began wondering if telling her the truth was really worth it. Just days before, I could smell the kiwi fragrance of her shampoo while she lay on my chest and we cuddled. But at the moment, I might as well have been another piece of furniture she was stepping around. I felt completely invisible again.

But, I Thought You Said
I Was Sexy

I never told Momma about my attempted suicide; it'd worry her sick. But apparently I didn't have to because she always talked like she knew anyway. Woman's intuition? Maybe. Either that or she had super powers like I'd always suspected.

Like when I was younger, Momma used to wake me up every day about ten minutes before my alarm went off, so of course, it pissed me off and I'd give her *that look*. And when I did, she said what she always said, "You better fix ya face before I come fix it for you." And I'd force a smile until she walked out.

But one night, I was having what most would call a dream--to me it was a prophetic vision. I was in my '64 Cadillac Coupe Deville like I was David Ruffin himself, and in the passenger seat was my baby, Phylicia Rashad. We were singing along with the radio off key at the top of our lungs, eating cereal, and everything else that goes on in a perfect day. Then, out of nowhere, the world turned to bright white light coming from my ceiling fan with Momma standing over me saying, "You better fix ya face before I come fix it for you."

But this time, I didn't fix my face. I stood my ground. Phylicia Rashad doesn't make cameos in just anybody's dreams. I was special, and as far as I was concerned, Momma was blocking.

She paused briefly before running back to her room. I was shocked because I never thought of Momma as the type to retreat, but then I realized that she didn't retreat.

She just needed a moment to turn on her stereo.

Whitney Houston's *It's Not Right, But It's Okay* blasted through the house and Momma came out with her robe flying behind her like a cape. She whooped me so bad I started snitching on complete strangers, giving away government secrets, and offering bribes I didn't have.

Till this day, I'll never understand why somebody would bob and weave so much without their opponent ever swinging back. But Momma did, all to Whitney Houston's song. Her super hero music.

But now that she was older, all that changed. Her powers were intuitive and more spiritually inclined. So when she "felt something wasn't right," she acted on it.

She began talking to me about young black men and depression, the hopelessness we felt but was never encouraged to talked about.

Me, I always felt I could speak out and I knew that people would listen. I had family that loved me, especially her and my sisters. But unless someone could change my situation, the "It's going to be alright", and "Just pray about it" mantras wouldn't help. It's like you're starving and someone is telling you, "Just think about food. You'll feel full in no time."

No.

Only one thing will make it all better and that's if it all gets better. If you can't make that happen, you get an E for effort, but no thank you.

To people like me, death wasn't taboo. It was inevitable. Unless you're Tupac, then of course, you live forever. But since the rest of us had to leave this earth one day, I had every intention of seeing myself to the door. Depression was just presenting a not-so-attractive early retirement package.

But that was then.

If all goes well, death will wait until I'm about 80, and only then I'll go out with a bang. Me, my notepad full of bucket list bullet points all crossed out but one, trench coat with no clothes on underneath, on my way to snort a bag of coke that'd make Tony Montana jealous.

Okay, maybe not the bag of coke. But something that was too dangerous to try when I had my whole life ahead of me that seemed like a lot of fun.

In the meantime, I took Momma's advice and started considering new hobbies and a bigger circle of friends. I had to find something else to fill the void after realizing my career in football meant being a sprained ankle away from pushing grocery store shopping carts the rest of my life.

With a limp.

I was still cordial with most of my former teammates but I didn't smoke weed, play video games, walk around musty, remixing Top Ramen recipes with hotdogs all day. So I didn't fit in.

My social slate was clean with everything except memories.

So, I took up the closest thing to it--photography. It was a natural transition for me: a dreamer, a visionary. I also had a special place in my heart for a woman's body. Society had demonized and over sexualized it, but to me, it was a work of art.

As fate would have it, there was a baby boom of aspiring models coincidentally as Instagram was on the come-up. So, I got in where I fit in as the go-to guy for all their online-attention fix needs.

In just a few weeks, I was making more money than I did at the diner I'd gotten fired from, which was fine. Just about anything beats walking around, eyeballing tables for some charitable loose change after multiple runs to the napkin station despite articulating my offer for extra napkins to perfection.

Yeah, wasn't missing that too much.

My photo shoot sessions were sexy, like scenes from *Love Jones*. Music, low lighting, drinks(BYOB of course), and a huge mirror beside the camera took the model's mind off of the shoot, giving her the feeling of superstardom. Front and center. Beyoncé-wind through the hair and everything. That confidence percolated through sensual poses and made for much better shots.

Small talk flowed in between the clicks of my camera, which became the vessel for all of their problems with men, family, and stress in general. The power I felt as their photographer to make them feel both sexy and mentally comforted was addicting.

One drawback was the inevitable attraction that festered after a few shoots. Such an awkward spot to be put in because I was a professional who kept it strictly business. At least I tried to.

"So, your fine ass is single, about to graduate, and all you want to do on the weekend is cuddle up with your Nikon?" Chantel asked, staring through my bullshit I was about to feed her.

She was cocky, but for good reason, and mixed business and pleasure like it was an apple martini.

A long 5'10" with a prominent four-pack, her back, shoulders, and thighs equally toned. She may have been mixed with a little Dominican not too far up the family tree, which would explain the silky smooth, cropped do. Her tight eyes and narrow jawline made her resemble a cocoa butter complexioned Nia Long from *Friday*.

"Well, yeah. I can hold several women in my memory card at a time. No strings attached, no soul searching when I see a herpes commercial; none of that." I laughed, trying to deflect her request to hang out some time.

"But I thought you said I was sexy?" she retorted.

"But I didn't say you were the only one."

"Whatever. I won't push it. Let me know when the final edits are done so I can get them to my agent. If you change your mind about getting out of this lonely ass apartment, you know the number," She put her elbows through the sleeves of her shirt. Slowly. Making sure I didn't miss a thing as her hourglass wiggled a few times, flexing the V shape of her hips and exposing her whiskey-colored nipples.

We had just wrapped up an implied topless shoot leaving me to once again do the rain dance on my penis' pretty picnic. Never a fun event.

"Cool. You know it may help if you start working with other photographers. You're going to have to, eventually, when you're ripping the runway and stuff," I suggested, putting my camera back in my bag.

She came up close to me."Maybe, maybe not. If they want me to model for them, they'll play by my rules. And when I play, I play to win," she said, seductively releasing her bottom lip from the clinch of her teeth.

All she was missing was the forbidden fruit, but if she had it, she would've had me asking for seconds.

But she didn't. So, I grabbed my tripod and pretended I wasn't fazed. She rolled her eyes as if I was out of my mind and walked towards the door.

In the beginning, we never talked outside of the photo shoots. Like I said, I was a professional.

That all changed when she began sending bathroom mirror glamour shots, asking for my "professional" opinion. A part of me wanted to tell her to chill because I was still a man. The "still a man" part sat back and enjoyed the show.

Did I dabble with the thought of reliving my younger days of recreational sex, cheap dates, and excuses as to why I couldn't settle down? Of course I did. But I had to leave that in the past. Not because I'm just this awesome guy, but because I couldn't keep a consistent erection ever since my break up with Danielle, not even when I was alone. It was psychological, I think, but I was either going to wait out my little heartbreak phase or earn a nickname after my limp noodle.

Involuntary celibacy it was.

Jazmin never quite left my mind either. Every little thing reminded me of her: cheesecake, condoms, violence. I know, that's a weird combination.

But I still wish our last words weren't our last words. She

never stopped being there for me even when it meant she couldn't be there with me. She was a friend, and I don't use that term loosely.

But since she moved back to Atlanta after the last time I had seen her, it was time for me to make new ones. Male ones this time.

The difference between me and the rest of my generation is that I didn't yearn for clique-affiliation. I could go anywhere by myself and have a blast, and most times I did. I would most likely be the leader if I did have a group of friends, but leaders have to enjoy being bothered because that's what followers do. And I damn sure wasn't a follower. But the only way to make an intentional effort to get acquainted with more males in a heterosexual way was through one of the biggest cliques on campus--a fraternity.

They operated like friendly, helpful, educated gangs. The signs they threw up, the calls they did to each other, and their colors reminded me of Crips and Bloods back home, except they weren't violent. In fact, they even did organized line dances on occasion. Non-threatening and talented.

I passed by one of their members all the time. I think he knew me from playing football as most people on campus did. His name was Ronnie, but we only addressed each other by head nods and perfunctory *what ups*.

Ronnie was a nerd. Not the kind who whimpered off in a corner afraid to look up when jocks walked by. But the "Steve Urkel meets confidence of Kanye," "fight to the death if you dare not recognize his Halloween costume was from season two of *Star Wars*" type of nerd.

But he was always courteous to me, so talking to him was

worth a shot.

I saw him walking outside the cafe one day and figured it wouldn't hurt to ask him for more info on his fraternity. Little did I know.

"Shhhh," he said, whispering and yelling at the same time. "You're all out in the open with this, dude!"

"Out in the open? You act like this is the CIA or something."

"Look here, meet me in ten minutes on the other side of campus behind the old business building. Come alone and make sure you're not being followed." he said, still checking over our shoulders for spies...I think.

We went to our cars from there. He drove a much newer one than I, speeding off while slamming on brakes to carefully ease over the speed bumps nearby. His paranoia was rubbing off on me.

I followed not too far behind, pulled up to the spot, and before I could open my door he was already hopping in the front seat.

"Okay, so let me get this straight. You wanna be down with the brothers. Am I right?" he asked.

No dumb ass, I wanna buy a unicorn and ride off into the sunset.

"Yeah, I do."

"You sure?" he said with a look of chagrin.

"Yeah. But I'm also trying to find out more about it first. It seems interesting."

"Interesting? No. A Rubik's Cube is interesting. My dear Alpha Kappa Omega is more than just interesting. We are a service to all mankind with a life-long brotherly bond that can never be broken." As I listened to him without an obvious expression of awe, he turned in his seat to get a better look at me, cocked his head sideways and said, "Wait, you really don't know anything about us, do you?"

I stared blankly for a moment, trying not to offend him. The truth would do it. A lie would too. So I just kept silent, and somehow, that did it anyway.

He went to open the car door.

"Wait a minute! Okay, so maybe I don't know much about y'all, but I'm a good dude. And I'm a fast learner."

"What's that supposed to mean?"

"That means that if you give me a few days, I'll know everything about Alpha Kappa Omega. If I don't, we'll act like this never happened. Cool?"

He scratched his chin and looked away for a second so as to think. Already the dynamic was shifting to him being my superior. I didn't like it, he seemed to love it, but I didn't have much of a choice.

"All right, except a few days is too long. I'll meet you at my apartment tomorrow at the West Commons, third floor, door 312. Be there at six p.m. sharp. I may have companions over so be cool until I tell you otherwise. Nobody needs to know about any of this." He reached out for a handshake.

Later on that evening, I scrolled through my phone for new texts, rereading old ones and hoping a new one would pop up while I did so. But a new text wouldn't be good enough. If it wasn't from Danielle, then it was just a false alarm.

For what it was worth, we did manage to stay in touch with an occasional right-after-church talk when we crossed paths. "Hey, how you been? God is good. I can't complain. Nice seeing you." That talk. It's what most couples do when they make an agreement their heart doesn't sign off on as did Danielle and I.

I couldn't focus on anything.

My bed felt like a double king sized reminder of loneliness, and dreams got replaced by memories on repeat through a night of insomnia. Too hot, too cold, too hungry, too full, gotta pee; something was always wrong enough to keep me up at night.

My phone vibrated from an incoming text. I got excited until I saw who it was from.

Chantel: *Hey you. [8:52 p.m.]*

To pay her back for getting my hopes up, I was tempted to do my *three-and-out*. That's where I respond to three messages and then just stop, a technique commonly used by the *ain't-shit* population that I found useful from time to time. But she didn't deserve it so I just closed out of the messages altogether and went to go do my studying.

That was something I didn't do much of when I was with Danielle. She'd get jealous of the attention I was giving my notes, prance around naked, close my binder then say a sarcastic "oops" at the end. But when I woke up the next day, whatever I was reading had highlighter notes in it because she refused to let me fail.

I loved that about her. How she'd never let me get too far off track. That's when you know you have yourself a winner. I'd bet my next paycheck that a "We can have fun but we will not lose focus" type of woman is in every successful man's life.

I did my round of modern-day studying--Google. But it was too much for one night. I got the basics down then split the rest off for the next morning so as not to prolong my sleep struggle any longer.

After double checking my alarm, my screensaver returned to the face of it. It was a picture of Danielle and me. She was sleeping, and I was smiling. Aside from me looking like a complete creep who'd just chloroformed her, it was really romantic.

For the past few weeks, I'd been mentally taking swims into that water under the bridge we called our good times. Never deleted our pictures, never changed her caller ID from what it had always been, *Baby*.

Before I dozed off, I put a few possibilities on how I could cup that water in my hands for another sip in the far corner of my brain and locked it. Promised myself that if one of those ideas broke free by sun-up, I'd give it a shot.

Why Didn't You Say That in the First Place?

Irolled out of bed the next morning, and before I brushed my teeth, I checked my phone. A habit we're all guilty of that needs to end.

I must not have locked that box of possibilities of seeing Danielle again too securely because one of them made its way out and strutted around my mind the entire morning. Teasing me. I don't know if it was the restlessness or if I was just eager to walk face-first into her impenetrable guard, but I was ready to give it a try.

I went into the building her class was held in, inconspicuously finding something to read in my phone as people passed by. Professors never really let class out when they were supposed to so I set a twenty-minute window that I'd wait. If that didn't work, then that possibility of seeing Danielle was going back into its lock box where it belonged.

But the door flung open and out came the slackers who'd been asleep all session, finding life in their pursuit of another time-wasting endeavor. Due to my height, I could see over the crowd they made and noticed Danielle's natural poof a few students back.

But instead of walking by her as she came out of class as usual, I stepped in front of her, interrupting the people walking out behind her too.

"Hey, what's up Danielle? How are you?" I asked, smiling and waiting for her confused expression which soon came.

"I'm fine. What are you doing?"

"I'm speaking."

"Okay...you spoke," she said, uninterested and trying to move past me.

I side stepped in front of her again, mindful of how this might appear stalker-ish to the untrained eye. But there was a method to the madness and I had come too far to stop at close.

"Can I at least get a hug?" I said, stretching my arms out and beckoning her to come to me with my hands. I looked more like an over sized toddler hoping to get picked up by his mommy, but it worked.

She rolled her eyes and gave me a completely platonic hug. Despite that, every nuance about her from the texture of her skin to the smell of her clothing made me ache with hopefulness.

I moved out of her way to let her walk by, trying to hide the excitement of my breakthrough. She didn't run away and she didn't call the cops...yet. So it was a breakthrough to me.

My joyride on cloud nine came to a halt just an hour later at the sight of one person.

Lewis.

He was leaning against the side of the biology building with a few of his basketball player teammates, throwing bait out to the sea of women walking by, hoping for a bite.

I knew it was him because his car was parked inconveniently in the middle of the road to make sure nobody missed his paint job and rims that his parents bought him for Christmas.

I'd been meaning to settle a score with this brother for the longest.

My heartbeat sped up and the hairs on my neck stood to attention. I was still in damned good physical shape, and even if I wasn't, it wouldn't have mattered. My adrenaline was flowing like water from a new faucet. Just walking away would've been the right thing to do, but being right is over-rated. Everyone knows that.

I hadn't shaken the guilt of not being there to stop him from beating on Jazmin. How she couldn't run fast enough, scream loud enough, or beg hard enough to keep him away. How he never had to answer for his actions; he just went on with his life as if it didn't matter how much he'd hurt people. He needed to know what that pain felt like.

I kept walking to my car so I could drop off my phone. I didn't want it to break if we went to the ground which would probably happen once his friends jumped in.

That didn't bother me though. My adrenaline-heightened hands felt like I'd just grabbed hold of a live car battery. Tremorous, and every vein running through them fully charged begging for me to turn them loose.

I closed my car door and started walking towards him, not sure if he even recognized me.

People were everywhere, some walking and talking, others posted up waiting for their next class.

I wasn't sure if cameras, professors, or any campus securi-ty were close. I just needed to cross the street and purge this energy and ill will that was increasingly overwhelming me the closer I got to him.

His two friends saw me and stopped talking to stare. They were both about my height, but frail in comparison. I think my clenched fists gave me away that I wasn't coming for a friendly chit-chat.

Clothing around this time of year for females was either tight, scarce, or both. This meant hormones and street harassment were out of control, which meant Lewis was in his natural habitat.

He cat-called to a freshman girl walking by. "Gah-dayumn, shawty. What dat mouth do doe!" reaching for a dap to his friends for them to join in, the kind of thing that gave all brothers a sordid name. Then their focus directed to me, which stopped him mid-laugh.

He squinted, trying to see if he could recognize me, then looked back at his boys as if to ask if they knew me. They shrugged, leaving Lewis to turn around to me again, but a little too late for an introduction.

I snatched the neck of his shirt with my left hand, and thrust my right one towards his nose with every ounce of strength I had.

It landed.

The force made him slip from my hand and hit the ground.

At that moment, I heard someone yell out, "Woooorld Staaaaar!" before students milled around us from the building and the surrounding dorm lawns.

I pounced on top of him, swinging a few more times before realizing he wasn't fighting back. I thought maybe I had seriously hurt him, which sobered me out of my anger, but only briefly.

"Who are you?! Get off me! Let me go, man!" he screamed.

His voice was feminine. "Ay man, y'all just gon' sit there?!" he yelled, looking up at his boys.

I looked at him, still breathing heavily with a lot of energy left to spare, then up at his friends who were recording the whole thing on their phones. The crowd around us had followed suit, all making sure they got HD footage of the scene.

I looked back down, and since he was healthy enough to talk, I put my hands around his throat.

So much hatred was permeating through my finger tips enclosed around his neck.

I squeezed harder.

He really had no idea all the destruction he'd caused. All the pain. How his actions nearly led to me losing my life, but more importantly the physical and emotional scars of my friend, the only friend I'd had till that point.

Yet he had the nerve to be begging for help.

I glared at him, his face turning a deep dark red now, then for a split second, Jazmin's face flashed across my eyes. I could see the terror she'd had the night he beat her as she ran to get away but couldn't. Her face stared at me with the same fright that was now in his eyes too.

I let go.

He gasped for air.

I put my finger on his forehead and got closer to his face so what I was about to say would reach his ears only.

"Listen and listen close. Stay away from me and my friends, or next time--"

"Yo friends? Man, I don't know you or yo friends."

"Jazmin. That ring a bell?"

29

He looked back and fixed his mouth to answer before I cut him off.

"Shut the fuck up!" I yelled, raising my fist to hit him again. "Her *and* Danielle. They don't know," I said, looking around at the spectators, "but I know. I know exactly what you did."

I stood up from him, contemplating kicking him, but opted out. He didn't have the guts to fight back. Typical behavior of a coward who'd put his hands on a woman.

I walked back to my car, cognizant of my surroundings in case campus security had gotten called and I needed to keep it cool. But even with all the people who had their phones out, no one called the authorities.

I started the engine, trying to figure out what in the hell had just happened. It was out of my character to act like that. Even in my days on the football field, I could always keep my cool but at that moment, I just...snapped. Momma told me my dad had a temper like that.

My phone's alarm went off, letting me know I had 10 minutes till time to meet up with Ronnie at his apartment.

My clothes smelled like outside and I was still sweaty from the altercation. I grabbed a can of air freshener from the back seat and sprayed a mist into the air to fall down on me and my clothes. It was a quick fix, but it helped.

I pulled up at his apartment with about seven minutes left to spare. Trying to remember what door he told me he was in, I grabbed my phone, remembering that I had saved it in there somewhere.

Found it.

Walked up to the third floor and followed the voices.

Knocked on the door and someone opened it right away. I didn't know them. They didn't know me either and welcomed me in anyway.

"Hey, what's up bruh?" Ronnie said from across the living room, this time a lot more spirited than before.

He looked at the girl closest to him and handed her his red cup, then he got up and walked past me, not saying anything, to a room in the back. I assumed that it meant to follow him so I did.

"You're late." he said, with his nasally congested tone as he closed the door. He had a real teenage fast food shift leader *you missed a spot* air to him. It was starting to bug me, but I didn't let it show.

"What you mean? I was five minutes early. It's not even six o'clock."

"Like I said, late. Come earlier from now on or I'll feel like you don't take this seriously. Did anybody see you?" he asked,

"I don't think so. I wasn't looking though."

"You have got to be more careful. If this gets out, it's over with, regardless if I like you or not. You understand?"

"Yeah," I said.

"Go ahead, have a seat." He pointed to his computer chair as he sat at the edge of his bed.

His room was particularly clean with a new-car smell in it. I think they sold that in stores, just never heard of anyone actually buying it for their room's fragrance. A few pictures of sports vehicles hung on the wall, but other than that, nothing was too out of the ordinary.

I walked over to his desk, trying to mentally rehearse all of the info I had jammed in my brain the day before, pushing my way through the recent memory of my fight with Lewis.

He pulled out a folder from under his bed before sitting down, then opened it. Flipped through a couple pieces of paper.

"So, tell me. If you had to pick one item to be in a grocery store, what would it be?" he asked, still flipping through pages and not making eye contact.

I looked at him for a second, trying to figure out if this was a trick question or if he was just making small talk while he got his things together. He paused and looked up, seeing what my hesitation was about.

"I, uh, I guess I'd be an...uh--" I murmured. "I'd be a flashlight."

He straightened up on his bed, pushing his glasses back up on the bridge of his nose, and squinted with bewilderment. "A flash light? From a grocery store?"

"Well, yeah. They sell flashlights at grocery stores. They even have the little batteries at the front before you check out."

"Hmm...okay. Continue."

"Well light is usually a good thing, especially with the world being so dark. Dark with ignorance, dark with judgment, dark with hopelessness because people can't see a reason to go on. So if nothing else, I'd like be the one who brings the one thing that can combat, if not fix, all of that. I'd bring the light."

He let out a long, "Hmmmmm..." as he rubbed his imaginary beard in deep thought.

He closed his folder and looked at me, his face expressionless. Awkward ensued.

"Nicely done, Shawn. Okay, interview over. I'll help you get down with me and the brothers." he said, putting his folder back under his bed again.

"That's it?"

"Yup."

"Man I did all that studying last night, and you only had one question. One question that had nothing to do with it?"

"Oh, it had everything to do with it, and you nailed it. Good job," he said, starting back towards the door.

I felt like I'd been played.

"So, why that question then?"

"Your answer showed me the way you see the world, which is what I needed to know before we went any further."

Why didn't you say that in the first place, I thought.

He continued, "I think you'll be a great fit, but that's not good enough. Now it's time to convince them," he said, nodding towards the door and the commotion on the other side of it.

"Okay, cool, well how do we do that?"

"We'll talk about that later. I honestly didn't expect you to answer the question that well so I didn't plan for it. Let's just call it a day and I'll send you a text next time we need to discuss anything. No worries, you'll be fine."

He patted me on the back and let his hand rest on my shoulder in reassurance. But the energy I'd gotten from him thus far was everything but reassuring.

I shook my head and let myself out the door, making my way through his frat brothers and their female friends. I was relieved and frustrated at the same time but didn't have time to sweat it.

I was in need of a shower, some sleep, and, with a reminder from my screen saver, a talk with Danielle.

I managed to get my foot in the door but if I didn't hit her up then that door was bound to slam shut without too much time left in the school year to pick the lock. So, I sent her a text.

Me: *Hey Dani. How are you? [7:34 p.m.]*

I knew not to expect a reply any time soon, but figured she might send one through by the time I reached the house.

I started feeling the effects of my little 60 second bout with Lewis. My back was sore and my knuckles were throbbing. I must've missed and hit the ground. Either that or he had a steel enforced chin.

I didn't even like fighting. Swore I'd never be one of those types. I was educated. Civilized. Supposedly beyond the barbaric means of settling disputes. Most of all, I was lucky to get out of there before campus security came lurking for a highlight to their day because that entire situation could've gone left in no time at all.

I pulled in to my apartment and checked my phone. Nothing.

My new addiction to air fresheners and fabric sprays had the house smelling like a fruit orchard. It's how I kept it company-ready, particularly for my clients and partly for the thought of female company. Even though there was no bedroom action going on, I knew there was no better turn-off than for a woman to walk in a place that smelled like old dish rags and possum pussy.

I heard my phone vibrate from the kitchen counter and all

but sprinted. I wasn't going to delay a reply to Danielle for anything. But yet again, it wasn't her.

Chantel: *Hey you. [8:27p.m.]*

It doesn't matter how harmless or kind a text is. If it's not from the person you wanted it to be from, it'll annoy the hell out of you just for getting your hopes up.

I flung my phone on the couch, then walked back in the room, stripping and stepping out of my jeans along the way. Hopped in the shower trying to rinse some of my tension off.

After about thirty minutes and pruned finger tips, I got out with the steam still rising from my shoulders. Thought briefly of the dishes that needed washing then shortly after decided to procrastinate as usual.

I had that problem since I was a little boy. Hated chores paid a hefty price of butt whoopings for it too. But I think the agilities I practiced moving in and out of the furniture when Momma chased me with her belt was partly why I eventually was able to earn my football scholarship. I wonder if my dad would've caught me.

I reached up to the ceiling fan and tugged on the chain to cut the lights out, then flopped back on the bed.

I tried to get comfortable but couldn't shake the feeling I was forgetting something even though I couldn't quite place it.

I knew the stove wasn't on. Pretty sure I locked the door. Don't think I had any homework. I looked over to the wall outlet and saw my phone wasn't on the charger.

Shit.

My phone.

"No, no, no!" I yelled, remembering that I was expecting a text from Danielle.

I hopped up and looked on my dresser. Didn't see it. I grabbed my pants and patted the pockets.

Wasn't there either.

Went back into the living room and tore the couch pillows up. Still couldn't find it.

Okay, so I walked in, I thought out loud, trying to retrace my steps. *Then I came right here, and I turned around and threw my phone to the...*-- I looked on the other side of the couch and saw my phone against the wall.

"Gotcha," I said, triumphantly. I unlocked the phone and saw Danielle's text. My smile wiped away when I saw it was from a half hour ago.

I called her back instead of texting so I could hear her tone in case she was pissed. About the sixth ring, she finally picked up.

"Hello?" she moaned, as if she was awaking out of what was about to be some really good sleep.

"Hey, Danielle. My bad, you weren't asleep, were you?"

"No, I wasn't," she lied. Seemed she still had her old habit of waking up any time I called.

That was a good sign, but I wasn't about to push it. I got straight to the point.

"Look, I need to ask you something."

"Ask me what?"

"That maybe if you weren't busy this weekend, we could hang out?"

She paused for a few seconds, causing me to wish I could go back in time and un-ask the question. I knew I had gotten ahead of myself.

"Hang out where?"

My confidence came back. "At the engineering building. We could make it a study...date. Except, not a date or nothin', but you know. Just some studying."

I really didn't think about the activity before I spoke, but girls like Danielle hated indecisiveness. The whole "I don't know. Whatever you wanna do" would've probably ended in a quick dial tone so I made a decision.

"That's fine. I don't wanna fall asleep on you so just remind me, okay? I'm about to get some rest."

I did the "Michael Jordan after the buzzer beater" fist pump in the air. Moon walked a few steps, even on the carpet.

I was in.

"Okay, cool. Well, then, get some rest. Good night," I said, trying to conceal my excitement.

"Okay, bye," she mumbled. A good night in return would've been nice, but I wasn't tripping. I was in.

Just Go With It

"Why can't you just make my butt a little bigger? Just a little, nobody would notice," Chantel asked as we clicked through the final edits from the photo shoot on my laptop.

"Because I'm a photographer, not a magician. Besides, you don't need any more butt. You've got plenty considering you're a model."

"You think so?" she said, standing up from the couch and turning around so I could see again. She grabbed it playfully with her hand, sending innuendos for me to touch with a maniacal grin.

"Yes, I do," I replied, staring helplessly. It was perfectly shaped, draped underneath black leggings. I could even see the little cuff where my hand could go.

"Go ahead. You can feel if you want."

"I'd better not. Besides, I got some other pictures I gotta get to." I closed the laptop and handed her the USB with her pictures on it.

"Oh yeah, I forgot, *Mr. Professional*," she said, making sarcastic parentheses with her fingers. "One day you're gonna stop being so scary."

"I'm not being scary. I just can't just go groping on all my clients."

The corner of her lip tugged up, "So now I'm just another client?"

"Yes."

"Oh, I see how it is then. Fine." She threw the USB in her purse and grabbed her keys. "Just remember that when I'm all rich and famous."

"No, you remember. You'll be able to actually pay me then."

She ignored me and looked down at my groin area. My semi-erect imprint was showing through my football shorts.

"Yeah. You always say one thing, but *that's* clearly thinking something else. I'll see you around, mister," she smirked, then sashayed out the door.

Damn hormones. They answered to whoever the hell they wanted to, and as much as I didn't want to admit it, they were answering to her.

After a little walk, the blood rushed back to the rest of my body and Danielle came back to mind. I knew her guard was up, as it should be, but I couldn't fight the anticipation of having her in my presence.

I kept up the normal interaction with us so not to press too hard and come off desperate. It also helped that I was preoccupied with fraternity business with Ronnie.

He all-of-a-sudden had these tasks for me to complete just so I could submit my application. Signatures I needed from several different people who never seemed to be in their office during their office hours, transcripts that needed to be mailed, and most importantly, the money.

To even be considered would cost over a thousand dollars with most of it being non-refundable regardless if I was accepted or not.

"Well, it is voluntary," he threw out, looking at me with a

raised eyebrow as I aired out my frustrations with the long drawn-out process.

How did I know this was going to loop back around to how dedicated I was? And honestly, it had even me questioning.

I stood up and put one hand in my pocket to soothe what would be one hell of a blow to it in the near future.

"Look, Ronnie, all I'm saying is that's a bit much to ask, especially of a college student."

"I give you my word that I'll do everything in my power to help ya out, but you gotta trust me."

"Speaking of trust, we don't even know each other yet. I mean, you know what I'm about but I don't know anything about you."

He took a sip from his soda and set it back on the living room table after slowly twisting the cap back on to stall for a moment to think.

"Okay, fine. Ask me anything."

I didn't expect that. But seeing as how I'd eventually be putting a thousand dollars, cash, into his hands, I figured it wouldn't hurt to seize the opportunity to know more about him.

"Where are you from?"

"Birmingham, Alabama."

"Both parents?"

"Yup. Married thirty-five years. Still going strong."

"Siblings?"

"One older brother, no sisters."

"You a Christian?"

"Yup."

"Virgin?"

"Nope."

"What do you wanna be short-term?"

"Happy."

"Long-term?" He hesitated a bit, then looked around before answering. "Anything that'd make my dad proud of me."

He looked down uncomfortably at the floor. Everything about him until this point had been so calculated with somewhat of a superiority complex, but not this time. "It's one of the reasons I joined the frat. Thinking maybe if I followed in his footsteps, he'd finally be proud of me."

"Look man, some people don't even have their dads, at least--"

"--I got one, right?" he finished my sentence for me. "Yeah, that's what everyone says. But it's no point in having one who could've done without you. I'm no athlete like he and my brother was. I'm just a smart kid who enjoyed going to school. Apparently that didn't meet his manly expectations." He looked up at the ceiling and exhaled, "Look, let's change the subject."

I looked at him, wondering if more guys were in his shoes; feeling a sense of inadequacy and trying to fill that void with achievement or groups they thought would help, because men aren't always equipped with proper knowledge on how to articulate emotions, nor are we always the best listeners when someone else is.

"Your dad," I said, "what does he do?"

"He owns his own luxury transportation company."

"Oh, wow. So he drives celebs around and stuff or what?"

"Yeah, pretty much. They're usually high-profiled. Meets a lot of entertainers along the way. He says that's one of the perks. Gets to go to all the really big events. The Grammys, the inauguration, everything. Said he wants me to take over the business once I get out of college."

"That's what's up. You already got a job waitin' on you when you get out."

"But I don't just want a job. I want to have a career, of my own."

"And what's stopping you is...?"

"Look. Enough about me. Are you gonna be able to get the money or not?" he said.

"Yeah, a few trips to the blood and sperm banks and I'll have it covered." We laughed a little, breaking some of the tension from my little questionnaire.

"Well whatever you gotta do, just make sure it's legal. Don't get in any trouble and try to stay low key."

"Most definitely." I said, reaching out for a hand-shake. But instead, he brought it in for a bro-hug.

A bro-hug starts off as a handshake to establish masculinity before the actual hug that ends in a manly pat on the back. Normally it only happens between friends but maybe this was the beginning of just that. A friendship.

*****

Two very long days passed and my study date with Danielle was upon me. I had prepped a binder of reading materials, highlighting a bunch of lines in the textbook that I didn't read. But it looked like I did.

After I finished with that, I flung my books in the car, checked my nostrils in the rearview mirror for uninvited guests, then peeked down at my fuel level. The hand was on E, which meant I had plenty left. That wouldn't be the case with most cars, but mine was different.

We had been through hell and back together, occasionally getting put along side of the road on the way, so I knew exactly how much more fight she had left in her.

I pulled up to the engineering building about an hour early. Picked an empty room on the top floor where I knew no one else would be so we could talk as we pleased with no listening ears or interruption.

A little while later, my phone vibrated.

> **Baby:** *Hey, I'm here but I don't see you. What room???*
> *[9:52 p.m.]*
> **Me:** *428. Fourth floor on the left. [9:52 p.m.]*

It was game time.

I did my hand-in-front-of-the-face breath check then flipped open my books, staring intently at the middle. For good measure, I even slowly drug my finger across the page and mouthed a few words to myself silently. You know, because presentation is everything.

She walked in, natural hair tied back into a poof, her "I'm being mature today" square frames on instead of the contacts she normally wore, and university sweat-suit. Nothing about her said, *I'm trying to look cute for you* and as hard as she wasn't trying, she failed. She was looking damned good.

I played it cool while my heart kicked up and added another count to its usual cadence. "Hey, what's up?"

"Nothing. Mad at you for making me climb up all those steps."

"A few steps ain't never hurt nobody. Might help you tone

44

up those glutes."

She looked at me like I was trying to insult her and had a few seconds to clarify that I wasn't before she snapped.

"Even more," I added, smiling and hoping she would too.

She chuckled. "Yeah, okay. So...what are we studying tonight and why did you need a study partner?"

"Never said I *needed* a partner. I just wanted to hang with you and be constructive in the process."

"So we're hanging now? What's this? Some kind of getting back together 12-step program?"

That's a lot of damn steps, I thought.

"No. Can a brother simply want to see you and decide not to hide it? Why I gotta be up to something? Maybe I just wanted to see you."

Probably because I was up to something and I didn't *just* want to see her. I had plans of this leading to us being in each other's circle a little more closely again. Not necessarily as one, but close.

"Mm-hmm. Okay then, just checking."

She sat down next to me. An elementary school "ooh, you gon' catch the cooties" nervousness crept all over me while she looked completely unbothered.

Over the next two hours I honestly tried to study but to no avail. I was thinking about everything but studying, mostly on whether or not I appeared to be studying.

That plus the fact that I hadn't lost any love for her since the first time I confessed my feelings three years prior when we were parked out by the lake. And even though I knew love alone wasn't enough, love alone is exactly what I had.

But I didn't know what to do with it.

45

"It's getting kinda late," she said,, sighing and sitting back in her chair. "I think I'm going to go ahead and go home. I still gotta cook and the meat isn't even thawed yet."

You cooked? I been hungry as hell, let me get a plate, would've come off needy.

So I just said, "Okay cool, well, let me walk you out."

We went outside with the cool night time air and street lights meeting us. The luminescent moon watched over the parking lot like a protective mother bear.

"Hold on, let me put my books in the car," I said, rushing to my car before we would have to split ways.

On my way, the feeling of missing her trickled back over my chest, again. I wasn't ready to see her go, but wasn't confident I could make her stay. I opened the door and put my books in, trying to think of some kind of excuse to stall a little longer.

I looked at the radio, the same one we used to fight over, but also the same one that used to set the mood for our quality time when we first got together.

"What's taking so long?" she yelled out, her tone irritable from being left standing there holding her books.

"Just one sec, I'm on my way."

Think, Shawn. Think.

I put the key in the ignition and turned the car on. Chris Brown's first album was in the player, one of our favorites to listen to. I skipped to track eleven and turned the volume full blast.

It was almost midnight so no one else was outside. Only a few mosquitoes and occasional police sirens somewhere closer to downtown, but other than that, all you could hear

46

was Chris' sixteen-year-old voice ringing out as he sang his hit single, "Yo(Excuse Me Miss)".

I emerged from the car bobbing my head getting ready to catch the beat. I had watched the music video a million times and memorized the dance routine he and his dancers did, and fortunately, I had enough rhythm to pull it off. In my opinion.

I started mouthing the words, and then I got straight to it.

Kick left, kick right, waterfall fingers in front of the face; I did it all. I thought I was killing it till I caught a glimpse of myself in my car window mid-spin. I looked more like Terry Cruz from *White Chicks* since I was so big, but it was too late to stop now. I was too legit to quit.

Danielle tried to cover her mouth as she politely held back laughter, but I could tell she liked it.

"And I gotta admit that ya got my attention. You makin' me wanna say yoooo," I sang.

I pop-locked my way closer to her with every step, timing it just right as the song was going off. I was sweating, putting my heart into every motion and lyric.

But it was all worth it when I saw her face light up with laughter. "I cannot believe you!"

"What you mean? See, you don't recognize greatness when you see it. I didn't even charge for front
row seats. You should be thanking me."

"Well, thank you, sir. You definitely get an A for effort. I honestly was not expecting that. Did you
rehearse or was that all freestyle?"

"You ain't gotta rehearse it when it's real, girl. You just go with it," I joked, getting a little closer to her now. My body was grooving in a slow rhythm even though the disc was between songs.

The next track was a slower tune. The mood brought about an ultimatum, to kiss or not to kiss. I chose door number two, erring on the side of caution, but couldn't accept the night being over just yet.

"May I have this dance?" I asked, trying to control my breathing enough for it to sound suave.

"Why, yes, I don't see why not." Her brown sugary eyes, melted and mixed with mine.

I grabbed her books from her and set them on the ground. I didn't know if she'd throw a fit since they were like her little bundles of joy, but she didn't. She was just as in the moment as I was.

I placed my right hand on the small of her back and took her right hand in mine. She rested her head trustingly on the planes of my chest, exhaled, and softly chuckled, "Why are you so silly?"

Her closed eyes and smile injected a double entendre so I responded by holding her a little closer, a little tighter, and that seemed to be just fine with her.

A few cars passed by, some slowing down to see what was going on, but we didn't care. We just slow danced. Right there. In the middle of the parking lot.

Nothing else mattered and that alone felt amazing.

I Want You, So I Will Have You

"I don't know, man. She got that look in her eye, that crazy look. The kinda look where you wake up in the morning and see her way across the room, orange juice in one hand and ya dick in the other.

All 'cause she went through your phone and saw something she ain't like," one of the guys said sitting behind me.

"But she still badder than a two-year-old baby." Him and his boys started laughing obnoxiously as the girls across the cafeteria rolled their eyes, flipped their hair, and kept eating.

They were probably freshmen. Hell, everybody looked like freshmen to me; I couldn't tell any difference. That was a sign that I had well overstayed my cafeteria welcome.

My generation belonged off campus, with our soon-to-be wives and children getting ready to go out into the real world. But since I was single, I had to adjust to a different lifestyle--people watching and cafe food. Hell, if they had checkers I'd play those too.

One of the cafe servers, an elderly and always kind woman, had a lot of school spirit since she was born and raised in the city of Tuskegee. She used to give me and my teammates more than the other students for extra motivation to win on Saturday. Even when we wanted to take some to the dorm room, she'd sneak us a plate, like family does at a cook-out. That's why we affectionately called her Auntie.

She was a typical church woman, humming gospel hymns,

short salt-n-pepper wig that was never on straight, glasses just above the tip of her nose, and her school t-shirt always tucked neatly into her long jean skirt that met at the laces of her *Keds* shoes.

She fed students with a smile for decades, like it was more than just a job for her. But as I'd gotten older, I started thinking about the fact that Auntie had a life outside of the cafe. I mean, of course she did, but I didn't really dwell on it until later.

And I don't think any of us ever asked her how her day was without accepting the default, "Good and yours?" that she replied with that surely couldn't have been the case every single time. So I decided to change that.

I finished my food and went over to empty my tray into the trash. I saw her behind the serving counter wiping down and getting ready to put everything up and tried to catch her before she got too busy.

She noticed me walking up and cracked open her usual grin. "Hey, sweetie. You give me just a second. I gotta clean this here mess up and I can go to the back and get you somethin' to take with ya," she said in her deep Southern accent.

I wasn't going to stop her at first because a little extra never hurts.

"Auntie, I'm okay. You don't gotta do that. I just came to see if you was doing all right today," I said with a half smile, trying to make sure I didn't alarm her by being so random.

"Aww, I'm doing just fine, couldn't be better. How you?"

"I'm cool. Full, could use a little rest. Auntie, you don't ever get tired?"

She slowed down her wiping and paused for a minute to

think. "I suppose. I think everybody gets

tired from time to time. But the good Lawd will supply all our needs so no use in worryin'. Ain't gon' make the world spin no slower."

She went back to wiping the counter down. I knew her answer was layered with more than the words she spoke just by the look on her face when I asked.

Sometimes we can be so strong that we fool the world into thinking we're invincible but end up

feeling unimportant because nobody ever checks on us. I've felt like that before.

"You're right. I guess I can let you go ahead and get back to work. Stay up, Auntie, I'll see you later."

"You sure you don't want nothin' to take witcha? There's some mo' food in the back I can get if

you wanna wait over there while I finish up."

"No, ma'am, I'll manage. Thank you though."

She smiled again and with that, I turned and walked away.

*****

Our eyes met.

Her body slow winded almost too slow to see but just fast enough to feel.

My hands gripped tighter by the second as I bit my bottom lip and prepared myself to--

Click

I looked down and checked the back of the Nikon for a preview of the photo. It looked amazing. My three-point lighting really made the contouring of her make-up pop. Even without my retouching, Chantel's creamy vanilla skin seemed to just keep pouring without a single blemish in sight.

"How'd that one look?" she asked anxiously as she came out of her pose. "Let me see."

"In a minute." I waved her off. "Let's try a few more and then we can wrap it up."

It was late, about ten-thirty on a Wednesday night. But I didn't have any morning classes the next day so I hit her up to try for some portfolio shots that I could use to promote to get extra business with. Only thing was, no matter how great they looked, I just couldn't settle on the right one.

"I don't see why you don't just get in front of the camera. You're the one hogging up all the sexy."

I shook my head. "Not now Chan. No time, for experimenting, and besides, that's pretty narcissistic. The photographer who learned photography so he could professionally photograph himself. Imagine that."

"Himself? I'm right here, I can do it. All you do is aim and press this button right here, right?" She reached for my camera and I damned near had a heart attack.

"Actually, no, you do not. And you *will* not."

"I'm just saying, your clientele is mostly female. So, it makes sense to advertise with something females wanna see. What better way than with a guy who's got all these muscles everywhere?"

I looked up at her as we both made eye contact with the understanding she was starting to make sense.

"Shawn, just show me the basics and you can do all the rest later on when you edit. The lighting is already set; all that's left is for you to say cheese." She grinned mischievously.

My hesitation came from the realization that this was either going to be a hit or miss. I'd seen it too many times.

But, if I could pull it off, it could be just the buzz I needed to really catch people's attention. Sex sells, so a little leasing wouldn't hurt.

"Okay, but if you break it, you buy it," I said, putting my Nikon gently in her hands.

I gave her a brief tutorial on how to operate my $1500 investment, all the while trying to rid my imagination of vivid portrayals of a disaster. People crack screens to their iPhones like they lose socks, and here I was handing over my livelihood to a complete amateur.

I walked over and stood by the wall and looked at the camera, then stood in what I felt like was a masculine enough modeling stance. I was trying to look at myself in the mirror beside the camera but was too tall, so it cut off my head.

"Okay, now pose," she barked, like she was the professional.

"I am posing."

"Well, do another pose."

So, I smiled. It was the last trick in the bag. My only secret weapon.

She brought her head from behind the camera and looked at me like she was disappointed. It kinda hurt my feelings. Like my smile wasn't shit.

"How about this? Just take off your shirt."

"I don't know about all that, Chan, I mean--"

"Oh, stop whining and just do it. I've seen a chest before, Shawn."

Trying to be cooperative, I grabbed my shirt from the bottom and began taking it off.

Click. Click. Click. Click.

"What are you doing?" I said through the shirt.

"Don't stop. And don't talk either. Just do as I say and let me work."

I got it all the way off, threw it over on the couch and looked back at her, annoyed that she was bossing me around.

She went on, "Oh yeah, that's it. Give me the pissed-off bad-boy face. I like!"

She kept clicking for a few seconds and then stopped. Walked over to the sink and poured a cup of water.

"Oh, please don't tell me you're exhausted. You've only been back there five minutes and already you need a drink?" I teased.

She walked towards me with the cup. "No, this is for you,"

"But I never said I was thir--"

Before I got my words out she'd already thrown the cup of water, drenching me from my face on down.

She laughed. "Thirsty? Well, these females will be once they see these pics. Now hold what you got right there."

She ran back over to the tripod and started clicking again. My eyes were burning from the unfiltered tap water.

"That's one sexy squint you got there, Shawn. You're a natural."

"I'm not squinting, Chan. I can't even see."

She wasn't listening; she just kept snapping one after another.

"All right, stop," I pleaded, barely able to hear myself over her continuous clicking. "Dammit, I said STOP!!!"

I raised my voice this time so she could hear me, walked over and snatched my camera from her.

"Okay, excuse me, mister," she laughed

Simultaneously, we both looked at the most recent shot's preview and it surprised me. I'd never seen myself shirtless in HD, but my stomach was tight and if I didn't know any better, I'd say I looked pretty damn good.

"See, I told you to let me do it. No fee, this time."

"Yeah, whatever. I mean, they look a'ight, but I can barely tell with this water you threw in my eyes."

"Well, then maybe you'll have to just trust me then. I think I've done enough to earn that from you."

Her voice softened. "I got you, Shawn. I'm in your corner. We all need somebody in our corner. I don't know why you're so afraid of admitting that. You're not a super hero, you're human"

A painful memory of Danielle emerged. The good times when she called me Superman, and to her, I was that super hero. But those days were behind me.

"Look, let's not get into any of that because we both know we're not tryna take it there. This is business and we need to keep it that way."

"Ain't nothin' business about the fact we always find ourselves together. Laughing. Having a good time. You know like I know, this campus is full of pretty ass chicks. And like you said before, I ain't the only one. Yet here I am, and it's because you want me here. You know you can depend on me. You obviously enjoy being around me and you'd be lying if you said you weren't attracted to me. So, what's the hold-up?"

I looked her in her eye, trying to find words to describe exactly what it was but at the same time not sure if she deserved to know. Even if I could explain it, my situation was personal and it needed to stay that way.

"Like I said, let's not get into any of that. Regardless of how many times I see you, we're not tryna take it there. *I'm* not tryna take it there."

I walked over to the kitchen counter and set my camera down, trying to steer clear from sitting on the hot seat any longer.

Despite me missing Danielle like crazy, I couldn't deny that an attempt to fill that void was getting difficult to resist. Chantel was fine as hell.

"Yeah, well, I want you. So I will have you."

"What?"

"I said, I'll be back over later to get the pics," she replied as she walked off, grabbing her purse in stride to the door.

She must not have thought I heard her. But I did. Loud and clear.

She Was Beyoncé, and I Was Just Michelle

Five hundred likes. And counting.

I walked away from my computer for about an hour and came back to over five hundred likes on my pictures with comments not far behind. Far more than I'd ever had or expected or gotten. And as much as people swear that picture likes don't matter, it gave me a rush.

On top of that, my inbox was filled with new admirers, but I wasn't concerned about that. Above all, I needed some paid work and found a few requests for some sprinkled throughout the clutter.

I started booking one photo shoot after another. With two weeks left to get Ronnie the thousand bucks and bills still left to pay, there was no such thing as too many clients. Couples' pics, early graduation pics, maternity pics, everything was thrown at me, and I was catching them left and right.

If that wasn't enough good luck for one day, Danielle texted me right afterwards. First!

Baby: *Watch out Tyson Beckford. lol ;) Nice pics mister.*
[10:21 a.m.]

My chest filled with so much air I could've floated on a puddle. I texted her back.

Me: *I have no idea what you're talking about. Maybe you should*

explain...face to face?? :) [10:23 a.m.]
Baby: *What'd you have in mind? [10:29 a.m.]*
Me: *You. Me. A nice break from studying. Tonight. About 8'oclock. [10:30 a.m.]*
Baby: *Are you asking me on a date? [10:37 a.m.]*
Me: *Are you saying yes? [10:38 a.m.]*
Baby: *Yup. See you at 8. [10:49 a.m.]*

That sealed it.

Just so happened a comedian was on tour and stopping by in a nearby city that night. One more excuse for me to see her again.

We had been talking a little more lately, slowly easing our way back into being comfortable. And although we weren't back together, it was evident that we both missed each other.

I picked her up that night, suited and booted in my Sunday's best. Which wasn't much. Just the clothes I'd been wearing to meet business dress code for class. The one suit that used to be too big but I'd finally begun growing into, but with a lint brush, light iron, and dim lighting of the night, it didn't look half bad.

But when she was walking across the parking lot, it became clear. She was Beyoncé and I was just Michelle.

She had on a fitted little red dress that wrapped around behind her neck leaving an opening atop the split of her breast, just large enough to invite attention but small enough so you didn't get it twisted. Her large pearl earrings dangled from her ears swinging gently into her cheeks that raised into a smile as she got in the car.

"Well, don't you look handsome?" she said, eyeing me up

and down, the street lights dancing on her lip gloss with every word.

"I was going to say the same for you. I mean, you know, not handsome but pretty. Beautiful, even." There was a time when I could charm the socks off any girl, but around this one, my smoothness was rough around the edges...and middle. I think the word for that is smitten. But I went ahead and pulled off so I wouldn't run out the $6.50 I'd put in the gas tank to get us there and possibly back. Yup, I said possibly.

After searching for parking for at least an hour, partly due to conversational distraction and the other part trying to find a big enough space where we could get out without swiping against my dirty car, we finally walked in the packed house that was erupting with laughter.

The comedian had already found a victim on the front row who was going back and forth with him to everyone's delight.

"You got the nerve to call me short?" he said to the little woman in the front. She looked somewhat on the heavier side, judging from the arm she had waving at him as she talked back.

"Yeah, I said it. You short, that's the ONLY reason we laugh at you!" she yelled back at him.

The crowd busted out laughing. Everyone seemed to be on about their third and fourth drinks.

"Well, how tall are you?" he asked her.

"I'm four foot eleven but I'm a woman. I'm fun-sized!"

"Fun-sized? No ma'am, you family-sized!" he yelled, slapping his knee and running around the stage. The crowd erupted into laughter.

I was about to join them, but after examining Danielle's face, I held it in. She wasn't amused.

Danielle was thick. Very thick. So, big girls were like her kindred sisters. I loved big women too, since I had plenty in my family. They could all cook and sing for some reason. But if the joke was on me, they would've laughed without a second thought. But still, I bit my tongue.

He kept going. "You and all yo extra helpings need to stop lying to the mirror. Talking about a *fun* size. Ain't nothing fun about being four foot eleven, 350 pounds. That ain't fun, that's manual labor. Sit yo ass down and let me finish my show!"

The place was going crazy; even the woman was laughing. While they were distracted, I tried to hurry up and find a seat, but it was too late. He spotted me.

"And what do we have here? Ay, man, you think you just gon' walk in all late and I ain't gon' get you too?"

All eyes turned toward me. Danielle and I froze where we stood, me contemplating exactly how far I'd go if he started talking about my baby. He could talk about me, but he'd better leave her out of it.

He came off stage and walked up to us. "Damn, I better not say nothin' to this big muh-fucka here. He already dressing like he going to court."

I laughed, hoping he'd move on to someone else in the audience. Of course, he didn't.

"Yeah, you must really like her." He turned and looked at Danielle. "He good to you?" he asked.

"Yes, he is," she replied.

"Y' all go together?"

She looked at me for an answer. I looked back at her without one.

He turned to the crowd and said, "Oh, she hesitated, y'all. You know what *that* mean. That mean she gon' wait till later on tonight when he tryna get some ass to ask him, 'So what are we doing?' Ladies, y'all love doing that!"

The crowd laughed in agreement, some of the women high-fiving each other.

"Ay, man, I ain't gon' pick on you. Matter of fact, I'm gon' help you out." He came closer to me and reached his arm over my shoulder like he was telling me a secret. "When the waiter come tonight, and he ask you if you want the check together or split separately, you look at ya girl dead in her eye and say, 'You gon' let me get some tonight?' If she don't say yeah, you tell the waiter to split that bitch like the Red Sea!"

Danielle and I, along with the whole crowd broke out into hysteria. On the inside I was relieved; that wasn't so bad at all.

He went back on stage to finish his set, and it was a good one. We laughed, sipped mixed drinks, (mine without the straw for a touch of manliness), and were hand in hand the whole night. That magical twinkle was in our eyes that you used to see in movies back in the day. Or maybe it was the alcohol. Either way, it felt good.

Afterwards, I took her back to my place, hoping she'd come up, get too sleepy to leave, and spend the night with me. Didn't even have to have sex. That first time back with her lying in my arms, going to sleep in our dress clothes, that'd do just fine.

She examined my apartment as she walked in. "Hmm...the place looks nice. You been keeping it up pretty good. Or do you got some chick over here cleaning for you?"

"Nope, I haven't had any girls over here. Just me," I lied. Sorta. Technically, I didn't have any girls over unless they were clients and clients didn't count...at the moment.

She pursed her lips in disbelief but only for a moment before she sat down. I went to the fridge and pulled out my bottle of cheap wine I saw on clearance at the grocery store, then filled her a glass.

"Thank you," she said, receiving the beverage. "So, what have you been up to lately?"

"Besides missing you?"

She rolled her eyes like she'd made lasagna with less cheese than that statement. I probably could've done better. But instead of dwelling, I smiled like I was purposely being corny.

I continued, "Photography. I've been up to that lately as well."

"Yeah, I noticed." She took a few sips and looked at the glass as to try and identify what she was drinking. Cheap had a bitter taste to it, judging by the face she made. "That kinda surprised me."

"Why?"

"I mean, not because I thought you wouldn't be good at it. You were always pretty creative. I guess, for some reason I thought you were going to eventually make something out of your writing."

I sat back in my seat, sipped a few times from my own glass. "Nah, that's not like a real career. That's just what I do when I'm bored."

To me, writing was no different than being really good at building ships out of toothpicks. Nice to admire, but no money in it. Not unless you were telling women to think like men. Since that had already been done, I figured I had better things to do with mine and my family's livelihood than to be another starving artist.

"It's what you love to do. I think you should go for it. You have so many pieces that any book publisher would gawk over."

"You think so?"

"Yeah, go get the one about fallen stars if you still got it. That was one of my favorites."

I set my glass on the table, went into my closet and pulled out my shoe box full of old poems and short story rough drafts. The one she was referring to was one I'd written back in high school but let her read one night out at the lake.

I walked back into the living room, noticing that her glass was almost empty. I handed her the poem and went to go grab the bottle to pour her some more.

While I went and did that, she opened up the folded piece of paper and started reading aloud.

"Your heart's filled with pride and other things you have hard times expressing,

So you lie to yourself but it's no longer effective,

Because the truth that you're not doing so well hurts too much to accept it,

And you don't feel like sitting through another one of your momma's lectures.

Unexpected confessions from exes left you breathless

In deep depression, thinking reckless, even insecure about

features in your reflection.

You always saw the good in people despite their imperfections

Because your Christian values taught you to forgive and forget it,"

She stopped there, looking up from the paper at me.

"Shawn, this is amazing. I can't even finish it because it gets me teary-eyed at the end every time, and with this wine in me, ain't no tellin' how much I'll be crying."

We both laughed while she folded it back up and placed it carefully back into the box. She treated it like it was a precious jewel being placed back into a treasure chest. Little things like that always mattered to me.

I went to give her a refill but she put her hand up, "No, that's enough for me. If I didn't know any better, I'd say you were trying to get me drunk, sir."

"Drunk for what? You was sober for everything else we did. You even let me record it a few times."

She sucked her teeth, "Whatever. Now may be a good time to get some direction about what it is we are actually doing."

My mind went back to the comic from earlier that night. He called this one, eight-ball left corner pocket, and hit it right on the money.

"I don't know. What do you want to be doing and do you think we're ready for it? After everything with--you know..."

"You mean with you cheating on me? I've already forgiven you. I forgave you right after. It's the trust that you lost, not my forgiveness. Now, that might take a while to build again, but if we want it to, it's possible. But it can't just be me; you gotta want it too."

"And I do want it. I just don't want this to keep haunting us, and I don't know if it's been enough time to really have a clean slate. I don't even really know if I'm ready for a relationship. I just know that what I feel for you is real and you always told me that when it's real, it's right."

She looked at me, seemingly trying to decide if whether or not what I just said was acceptable.

"Shawn, I don't do the part-time, let's just go slow and have no accountability situation-ship. Either you want all of me, or you deserve none of me. That's how I've always been."

"I understand," I admitted.

She shifted in her seat and drank the last of her wine. "Quick question. I don't think I ever asked this, but why?"

"Why what?"

"Why did you cheat on me? I'm not tryna badger you about it, but I'm curious as to why? If I'm really what you wanted and still do now, then why did you ever cheat in the first place?"

I paused for a moment, making sure I chose my words carefully. I'd actually tried to explain this to her before, but this was no time to bring that up.

"Honestly, Danielle, it's complicated. I mean the simple answer is that I was too young. Too immature. Needed to get it wrong before I could get it right. And that wouldn't be a lie. But, tonight's a nice night, and if it's okay with you, I'd like to keep it that way. Can we save the long answer for later?"

She shrugged, "Yeah, we can. Like I said, I'm not trying to

throw it in your face. But if you're serious about wanting my trust back, and when you feel like you're ready, I'm willing to give you a chance."

A knocking came at the door. I knew we weren't being loud so it shouldn't have been the police.

They knocked again, a little louder this time.

"Hold on," I said, setting my glass down and going to see who it was.

I opened the door.

Slammed it right back closed. It was Chantel.

She was on the other side and I didn't know why.

"Shawn!" she yelled out, her voice squeezing through the cracks between the door and its frame.

I looked back at Danielle, like an idiot, and of course, her eyes were seething. Not an ounce of love in them. I know she heard Chantel's voice, and no matter what, I was going to have to open that door. So I did, but only slightly.

"Why did you slam the door in my face, Shawn? I just came by to get my pics from you. I saw the ones you posted today."

"The hell you had to come so late for? You couldn't text? Damn, I'm in the middle of something."

"Well, I'm about to head out of town and you wasn't answering your phone so I just came by. Your light was on so I knew you were up. How come you didn't answer my text?"

She really had some nerve. "Like I said, I am in the middle of something. I'll email you the pics tomorrow. You can pick the disc up another time."

"I'm already here. You might as well just go get it for me now."

I didn't want to argue anymore. The longer I took, the longer Danielle was sitting there contemplating how much of what she had just said to me about rebuilding her trust she was going to be taking back.

"Stay *right* here," I told her, articulating myself clearly so there was no mistake. I even waited a second or two for a facial confirmation that she understood before I walked over to the counter to look for the disc with her pictures on them.

A few seconds later, I turned around and saw Chantel already two steps in the house and mid-way through a staring match with Danielle.

"Hello," Chantel said, confrontationally.

"Hi," Danielle replied, not backing down.

I sped walked back, shoving the disc into Chantel's hand and nudging her out.

"Here, take it. Now leave."

I shut the door behind her and turned around to lean on it. Eyes closed, exhaling with *what the fuck?* going through my thoughts.

"No females over, huh? Just you, right?"

"It's not what you think. I swear, she's just a client of mine."

"What kinda client is so comfortable, she just pops up at two in the morning? You know what, don't answer. It's not like we're together or anything. You can do what you want, Shawn. But right now, what I want is for you to take me home, please."

"Danielle, come on, don't be like that. It really isn't what it seems. I promise."

My words fell on deaf ears. She was already standing, purse in hand, and arms folded.

What a night cap.

Stop Resisting

"All right, brosky. The packet looks good, how ya coming along with the money?" Ronnie said, putting down my application for the fraternity and looking back up at me.

"The money is comin'. I'm about three or four photo shoots away from having the full amount and I already have two of those scheduled for later on this week."

"Good. I know it's been stressful, but it'll all be worth it later. Just wait. I know you'll be the tail dog. None of the other aspirants are your size. Just get ready, 'cause this is going to change everything."

"Everything like what?"

"Like the way people see you on campus. The opportunities you have in the real world. Everything. You'll never have to worry about getting the honeys to like you again either."

We still call women honeys?

I rocked back in the chair, sorting through the thoughts of what happened a few nights ago when my date night with Danielle got through into a fiery furnace.

"I can't lie, the professional perk sounds straight, but I ain't really trippin' on having any more honeys. I got cavities as it is."

We both laughed in agreement. He mostly thought I was bragging. That's almost always what brothers do on the subject of women.

I caught a glimpse of a picture on his desk over by his laptop of him and his nearly identical elder.

"So, how's that going?"

"What?" he asked following my eyes to the picture behind him. "Oh, that. I mean, it's not going. I haven't talked to 'im yet. But I will."

"Look, man, don't wait until it's too late. He's your pops. I'm sure he's waiting to hear from you anyway."

"Maybe. I don't know, I'm not that good with words. I don't think it'll come out right, and if it doesn't, it could just make things worse."

"Well, then write it down first. Or just send him a letter."

"I'm not good at that either." He looked down embarrassingly. "Wait, you said something about you used to write. didn't you?" He turned his head back to me, bulbs in his head blinking their way on.

I tried to flip that switch back off. "Yeah, but only poetry. I don't know about anything else. I barely scraped by in my English classes."

"But still, you probably know more than me about how to express stuff like this. Why don't you help me write it. I'll change anything that doesn't fit the way I'm feeling."

"Nah, man, that wouldn't be real. It's gotta come from your heart."

"Well, what would you say to *your* dad in this situation?" he looked at me and asked.

I looked away, a little disturbed by the pressure to actually think about it. I hadn't told Ronnie about me and my pops. I think he assumed we were close because he never asked.

At times I did miss my dad and wondered what kind of

relationship we'd have if he was still in my life.

I began, "I guess, if I was you...I'd just tell my dad that he doesn't know what he's missing, that his son is growing up into someone he'd be proud of if he gave himself the chance to know first-hand. No guarantee, but a chance is better than what some fathers get who are dead or locked up, and since I don't want to take the opportunity for granted, I'm stepping up and letting him know that I miss him, that he's necessary in my life in case he felt otherwise. That his son loves him despite his mistakes but it's time to make it right. Later is no longer good enough. That I need him now."

Silence fell in the room for a few seconds. I was lost in thought as if I really was speaking to my old man.

"Man, that is *perfect*. That's exactly what I'mma say. You might have a gift."

I forced out a smile despite the weight my heart had taken on. If only I could get that message to him in real life.

"Cool, glad I could help. I'm sure if you say that, he'll take it from there. Just be honest with him. That's all you can do."

He pushed his frames up onto the bridge of his nose. "I'm going to take your advice. See, that's why I don't mind helping you. You're a real stand-up guy, Shawn. I could tell when I first met you. I'd be proud to call you my life-long brother and I'll see to it the others agree. I'm going fight for you, man."

We did another bro hug before parting ways. I needed to get to the cafeteria before it closed for the evening.

I walked in to see the last students coming out and all the cafeteria workers cleaning up the tables.

Auntie was over in the corner moving a little slower than

usual, with her eyes dazed as she wiped in one spot over and over.

I forgot about getting food and went over to speak to her first.

"Hey, Auntie. You doing all right?" She parted her lips as if she wanted to say something, but no words came out. "Auntie?"

Her lips started trembling and a tear fell onto the table. "You can talk to me, Auntie. What is it?"

She began weeping silently as she collapsed onto the seat to sit down. I sat down beside her and rubbed her back, hoping it'd provide some kind of comfort.

She quickly composed herself enough to speak. "I won't complain. I won't do it. I won't complain. You got to have faith in the good and the bad. And I won't complain."

"I'm not asking you to complain, I'm just asking you to tell me what's on your mind. That's not a sin, is it?"

"No, I suppose it ain't," she responded. "My grandbaby. He done got himself into some trouble I believe. I done tried my best with him since his mama left 'im but I just don't know what to do no mo'. I was cleaning up the house yesterday and came across a gun stashed under his mattress."

I hated the sound of guns. I promised myself and Danielle after we threw the last one in the lake that it'd be the last time I ever touched one.

"How old is he?"

"He ain't but fifteen years old. Still a baby. Now tell me what a baby doin' with a gun? Nothing besides get himself either killed or in jail," she said, going back into a silent weep with tears refilling the ducts of her eyes.

I hurt for and with her. I didn't know what to do or what to say. But I wanted to do something.

"Maybe I can talk to him since I'm a little younger."

"No, sweetie, you don't needs to be tangled up in no mess with him. You a good boy, and you in school about to get you a good job. I'm just gon' pray and everythang gon' work itself on out. The good Lawd gon' fix it. Yes, he will."

"I'm sure, but maybe he's trying to use me to help fix it. I don't know, but if he's got a gun, there's gotta be a reason. Maybe he's getting bullied or something. Auntie, let me talk to him. I can try to get through, and if not we'll pray some more but faith without works is dead. Ain't that what the Word say?"

I was far from the most religious person in the world. God and I had been on rocky terms once before, mostly just out of my ignorance to the way he worked, but after a while, I started to trust that either he had my back or that if he didn't, there was nothing I could do about it. Might as well keep the faith.

"You shole is right. If you can come tonight that'll be good. I think he planning on going somewhere tomorrow to do something with them lil' boys he hang with. I overheard him talking yesterday. It wouldn't be too much trouble, would it?"

"Not at all, just let me know where to come and I'll be there. We can go for a ride or something and have a man-to-man."

"Okay, sweetie. I live over on Franklin Street, the first house right there on the corner, the blue one. You can't miss it." She wiped her eyes and sniffled. "Thank you so much, young man. God bless you."

"Ain't no problem, Auntie. I'mma see you later on tonight."

I got up, shook.

I was a little nervous about the whole thing. I was a country boy, and while I knew a few guys from the hood, I was no gangster. Not even close.

Don't get me wrong, I had heart, but I couldn't possibly imagine what I had to offer to someone who was really about that life. I just know I needed to tell him something, something my dad would tell me.

I arrived that night about nine o'clock, curious if anyone was home because there was no car in the driveway and the lights were all off. Her house was small, a torn-up screen door in the front, patchy grass that needed to be cut, and an old Buick in the front that look like it'd been through every hurricane, tornado, and tsunami.

I had to have waited at least five minutes before her grandson came out.

He was about average height, very dark skinned with dreads and a full beard. This fifteen-year-old looked like he could be my uncle with the exception that he dressed like a teenager. His pants sagged off his behind and he was wearing a shirt that was at minimum, four sizes too big, plain black like the rest of his outfit.

He opened the passenger side door, then got in and closed it without saying a word, looking straight forward.

"What's good, man? I'm Shawn," I said breaking the silence and leaving my hand out for him to shake it.

He didn't even look my way. I almost kicked him out my

damned car for his rudeness and the fact he reeked of marijuana, but I remembered telling Auntie I would try, so I bit
my tongue and pulled out the driveway.

I didn't have a destination, but I did have enough gas for
at least a thirty-minute ride.

About twenty went by with neither of us saying anything
before I got fed up with the silence.

"Look, I ain't here to beg you. I ain't here to be your best
friend. Your grandmother told me you might be getting into
some heavy stuff so I just wanted to talk to you about it."

"For what? What's that gon' do?" he said, speaking for the
first time.

His voice had a little too much base in it for my taste, but
again, I kept cool and went ahead talking to him.

"I don't know but it's a start. You can at least tell me your
name."

"I ain't telling you nothin'. You and everybody else already
got an opinion of me. My name ain't gon' make no difference."

"Fine then, you won't have a name in here. What's the deal
with you carrying a gun around the crib?"

He looked at me and shook his head. "I knew she was
gon' find it."

"Well?"

"Well, what?"

"What you doing with a gun?"

"You don't know what guns are for? You a school boy,
surely they done taught you what guns do even if you only
seen 'em on TV."

That was it. Didn't know or care who he was at this point.

Enough was enough. "You got one more time to talk to me like you crazy. I'm on your side. I'm tryna help you."

"Help me how? You gon' put food on the table? Huh? You gon' go get the lights cut back on?" He raised his voice louder. "You gon' raise my grandmama's pay after forty years working the same fuckin' job with nothing to show for it?"

I could hear pain in his voice. "Look, my bad, I didn't mean it like that--"

"You gon' finally get her a car so she can stop walking to that job every day? Six miles there, six miles back. Every day for forty years. You gon' make my mama come back and give a damn about me enough to stop gettin' high on dope 'bout every day?" His voice was cracking now, on the verge of tears. "No. You not. So sit there and drive us back to my house. I'll tell Grandma you did a good job so she can keep giving you more food than you know you supposed to get. That's all you use her for anyway."

"First off, I don't use your grandmother for anything. She comes to work, she does her job, and sometimes, yes, she does give more than she has to. That's just because what kind of lady she is. That's why it bothers me you stressing her out even more. No, I don't know you but I do know that much."

"I'm stressing her out but I'm the only reason we still got a place to stay. They doubled the rent on us three years ago. Electric bill damn near did the same thing. You think she been paying that? No. I'm paying that. And it just so happens, I need a lil' protection to make sure I can continue. Stress is better than homeless."

"No, it's not."

"Yeah, like you know."

"Actually I do. I got kicked out the house a while back. My parents, they didn't want anything to do with me so I had to leave."

He looked at me disarmingly. "So you know yo mama, and she *still* did that?"

We came up on a red light out on the outskirts, so I was able to stop long enough to look him in the eye. "Yeah. She did. But people make mistakes, and that doesn't have to be the way the story ends. Same with you. I know you got some stuff going on, but you're also young with plenty time to get yourself together."

"I don't know, bruh. Sometimes, I wonder if it's even worth it. I ain't never been no school boy. Them teachers don't care 'bout us either. Not me anyway."

"It ain't about them. If you sell drugs then you gotta be able to count. Division, multiplication, even algebra would come easy to you. Why not use that to go into engineering or something instead? Make some legit paper. Ain't no future in this street life, dude. It's called the trap for a reason. Because all it does is trap people like you into thinking that the cheese can be yours without getting caught up."

"Well, life is too short, and I think I like it that way. I don't know why anybody in my shoes would want a future in the first place."

"Because your grandmother walks every day to a job that won't pay her enough so she can finally rest. That's why. Get something that you can do long-term so that she can finally relax the way she deserves to." I looked at him, making eye contact again. I was finally getting through to him.

I continued, "Guns around the house, not speaking up to tell her what's on your mind, staying out in the streets all night. You gotta chill out with that."

"I can't help the staying out part. My stomach empty, my pockets empty, and I'm sleepy; that's two against one. Sleep loses. We gotta eat. You can't pay for food with eight hours of rest. It just don't work like that, bruh."

Blue flashing lights came on behind us.

I checked my speed. It was on cruise control going just two miles over the speed limit. I looked down at both of our seatbelts and they were on securely and visibly. I didn't know why I was getting pulled over.

I slowed down and veered off to the curb, assuming it was some kind of mistake.

I turned and looked at him. "You got anything on you?"

"Nah, I left that at the crib."

"You sure?"

"Yeah, I'm sure."

"Okay, cool. Don't say anything, you hear me? Let me do the talking."

I looked in my side mirror and saw a cop getting out the car walking cautiously up to the car, another one on the other side.

He motioned for me to roll down my window.

"Where you boys headed tonight?" the officer asked, flashing his light into my eyes and then into the back seat.

"Officer, what's your reason for stopping me?"

"I asked you a question, son. Where you two headed?"

"Officer, I don't have to answer that." I said affirmatively. I was no expert, but I knew the basics to my rights when

78

getting pulled over.

"Oh, okay, I see what you're tryna do here. Well, looks like your tail light was out so I'm gonna need to see a license, proof of insurance, and registration there."

I reached for the glove compartment and the officer standing on the passenger side reached for his gun. I froze. Completely still. My heart pounding now.

This was a hostile situation.

"Oh, don't worry, he's just bein' cautious. Don't tell me ya scared now?" the officer laughed. He had an old western type of accent, and his voice was as cold as ice.

Auntie's grandson was sitting in his seat, motionless and staring forward as I'd told him to do with his hands visible.

I went on slowly to get the insurance out of the glove compartment as the officers shined their lights on it to peek inside.

"Here you go. I had no idea my headlight was out. I can get that fixed no problem--"

"Uh, not so fast. I'm gon' need licenses from both of ya. That includes your little buddy."

I looked over at him. "You got ID?"

"Nah, I don't. I'm only fifteen,"

I turned and looked at the officer. "He's only fifteen, he doesn't have a license."

"Fifteen huh? Don't look fifteen to me, the officer said directing his flashlight at him now. "As a matter of fact, he looks quite familiar." He directed the light into his eyes until he started squinting. "I've seen you before. Lamarcus. Lamarcus Wright. That you?"

He kept quiet, not making eye contact with the officer.

"Yeah, that's you. I locked your mama up many a times, I wouldn't forget that face anywhere. I'm gon' need you two to step out of the car."

"For what reason?"

"Now, you're obstructing justice. I said, step out of the car and do it slowly with your hands in plain sight."

Lamarcus and I followed instruction. A few cars passed by, and I could feel the wind from them as I opened the door.

The first officer yelled out to the other, "You take care of these two. I'm gonna see what we find in here."

We walked over towards the flashing police lights of the first cruiser. "Put your hands against the hood of the car and spread your legs," the second officer said.

I looked back at the first policeman who was tearing everything out of my car and tossing it on the ground. My CDs, my books, my water bottles. Everything.

After an overly thorough patting down, the first officer came back over to us.

"What'd you find, Rick?" he asked his partner.

"They're clean."

I exhaled, relieved Lamarcus wasn't lying after all.

"Wait, I don't know about this one." The cop walked back over to Lamarcus and started patting him again.

Lamarcus looked at me confused, and I looked back at him the same way.

The policeman skipped the normal pat-down and went straight for his groin area.

"Yo, chill, man! That's my balls you grabbing--"

"Shut up! I didn't tell you to open your damn mouth."

The second officer began looking uncomfortable.

"Come on, Danny. I just checked his pockets. The kid is clean."

"Well, I don't think I like his attitude. Probably best he have some time in jail to think about it." He slammed his head into the hood of the car pushing the palm of his hand into Lamarcus' cheeks.

I moved to help him and the other second officer drew his gun and pointed it at me.

I stopped without even taking a step. "Officer, what you're doing is wrong." My voice trembling was trembling. I was officially scared and I felt helpless.

Lamarcus yelled, "Ay man, don't let them do this to me! Tell them to let me go!"

"Stop resisting arrest you little piece of--"

"Please," I pleaded this time. "He's just a kid."

"Don't make me fear for my safety," he said as he ignored me, pulling his gun from his holster and putting it to LaMarcus' temple. "Because you know what comes after that--"

"All right, that's enough Danny. Knock it off. Let's get them to the station. Ain't got all night. Martha's gonna be bitching if I miss dinner again."

The policeman smiled with a devilish squint in his eye as he let off of Lamarcus' face and put hand cuffs on him before proceeding to me. The cuffs were so tight they cut off my circulation, but I knew better than to say anything about it. It was only going to make things worse.

The ride down to the station was surreal. I was in the back of a cop car for the first time in my life, with no real reason as to why. I'd only seen things like this in movies, heard about them happening during the 60's, but couldn't believe it was really happening to me.

I didn't know how I was going to explain this to Auntie. How this would affect me graduating? How'd I prepare myself to tell Danielle? I was feeling overwhelmed with fear and anxiety at the thought.

We pulled up to the police station, then went through the booking process. Finger-prints, mug shots, recorded interview.

The charges, according to the police report, were on suspicion of marijuana, obstruction of justice, resisting arrest, and yelling obscenities at an officer. None of it too serious but enough to keep us in a holding cell until someone came and posted bond that was set at $500 for Lamarcus since he was a minor, and $1000 for me.

I could barely look Lamarcus in the eye, knowing I'd gotten him into this mess. How could I preach about walking a straight line, meanwhile getting him arrested? Some mentor I was.

"You get one phone call. Make it count," the officer said, shoving the phone into my chest.

I didn't have many choices. Momma was hours away and would probably use up most of the time trying to get a grasp on how I got there as opposed to actually coming to get me. Ronnie and I were cool, but until I got this figured out, he didn't need to know about me being in trouble with the law.

Danielle was my best shot. Our last encounter was a bit rough, and since then, her guard had been back up pretty high. She didn't carry on small talk very long and was making it clear that if I was going to get back into good graces with her, it was going to take some work. Which was cool. I've always worked for what I wanted, and I wanted her more than anything. But I needed her, and she'd always come through for me before.

I began dialing her number, getting increasingly nervous as to whether or not she was going to pick up.

One ring and a half later, I got my answer. It cut short to voicemail, which meant she was ignoring me. On purpose.

"Hey, Danielle. It's me, Shawn. I'm guessing you're ignoring because this is a strange number but I'm down at the police station. I got in some trouble but I need you to come get me. My bond is at $1000. I got most of that in my apartment. I can pay you back when we get there but just come get me, please."

I hung up the phone, looking at the desk clerk smacking her gum and shaking her head as if to confirm that my words were in vain. Like she'd heard that voice message a million times before and I was just another.

I went back to the holding cell, followed by Lamarcus. We sat there for a few minutes in dead silence. Me, trying to make sense of everything and I assumed he just had nothing to say to me. I didn't blame him.

"Thanks, bruh," Lamarcus mumbled.

"Look, I had no idea--"

"Nah, I ain't tryna be funny. I mean it. I 'preciate you." He looked up at me so I could see the seriousness in his eyes. "Not too many folks care about us out here. But you do."

"Don't thank me. I didn't do nothin' but get us in trouble."

"I done been in trouble befo'. Ain't the end of the world."

"It's not the world I'm worried about."

"Well, Grandma always told me, 'What God bless, no man can curse.' I don't always know where her faith come from, but if it's any truth to it, we gon' be straight, bruh. Just wait."

I looked at him, seeing for the first time a hopeful look on his face. It confused me because this was arguably one of the worst nights of my life, but here he was speaking to me about faith. Either he knew something I didn't or I really underestimated a normal day for him.

Auntie came about ten minutes later to pick him up. I didn't get to see or speak to her since she was outside, but I was hoping Lamarcus would be somewhat tactful in his recount of the night's events to allow me a chance to be heard out later on.

I tried to get comfortable on the concrete slab they called a bed, wondering if Danielle was coming that night or in the morning, or at all. It wasn't like her to ignore my call, no matter what she was doing.

I knew I was in the dog-house, but damn. This was an emergency.

I sat there, back against the wall with my eyes growing increasingly sore from being open so long. Somehow I managed to fall asleep despite the blaring light that never turned off.

"Hey, wake up. Fletcher. Someone's here to get you," an officer said, nudging me on the shoulder with his baton.

I woke up, forgetting I'd been in the cell altogether, more so feeling like it was just one really bad dream.

Danielle finally got my message. Better late than never I suppose. I walked out of the cell to grab my things and put my shoes back on that they'd made me take off.

Walking outside, I was looking for Danielle's car and didn't see it anywhere. Just a silver Infinity, out waiting by the curb, still with the engine on. The windows were tinted so I couldn't see inside and wasn't about to walk up to a strange car. Maybe Danielle had to circle around and was about to come back.

Next thing I know, the passenger side window rolled down and Chantel was leaning over and smiling at me.

"You gonna hop in, or would you rather go back to your suite?"

This Tea, Though...

"**O**h, don't look so happy to see me. You're only getting out of jail," she said cynically on the drive back."

"It's not even like that. I told you I appreciate this, but I'm curious on how you knew I was there."

"Well, I thought I drove past you earlier getting pulled over, but there was another guy that didn't look like anyone you'd be with so I just figured it wasn't you. But when I drove by afterwards, I was able to see your car more closely. I called. You didn't answer your phone, like always, but I figured that this time you might actually be in some trouble. Went down to the station, and yup. They said you were in there."

"So you fronted a stack. For me? Just like that? Man... that's deep. Thanks again for it. I'll pay you back as soon as we get to the apartment."

"I spend that much on makeup. I can definitely spare that to get your freedom back. What happened in there anyway?"

She had this look on her face, like she just knew her cool points were piling on top of each other. I wasn't going to ruin her flow, but at the moment I was having mixed feelings. Glad to be out of that hell hole, but unable to escape the curiosity of what had Danielle so tied up that she couldn't come get me. Surely she got my message.

"I really don't wanna talk about it. Let's just get home so I can finally get some rest."

I leaned back in the seat ready to get home. It was almost three o'clock in the morning. Fortunately, it was a Saturday so there were no classes, but it didn't matter what day it was. After a night like that, the next day was going to be Saturday for me regardless.

Chantel followed me up to my door. It didn't hit me until I'd already started twisting my key to get in that maybe she was tired. Maybe she needed a place to crash. Damn sure couldn't tell her no. A part of me didn't want to.

"You want something to drink? Orange juice? Bottled water? Almond milk?" I asked her after shutting the door behind us.

"I'll take a water. Dasani, right?"

"Of course."

"Good. So, what happened with your little date you had the other night? I didn't mean to disturb that by the way. Don't want you to think I was tryna block," she said, looking around for feminine evidence to cross reference with my answer.

"Well, you did block," I saw her smirk as if she accomplished something. "But, the date was cool. We had fun before you showed up."

"You like her?"

"I don't think that's any of your business."

She put her hands up innocently. "Excuse me. My bad. A little sensitive. I understand, you've had a rough night."

I handed her the bottle of water and sat down on the couch beside her. My eyes were burning, my eyelids opening and closing almost manually with the effort it took to keep up small talk.

"I think I'm about to go to sleep, Chan. You tryna crash here or what?"

"Well, I wasn't going to invite myself but sure, if you're okay with that. I'd like to stay over."

"All right, I'll bring you out a cover and some--"

"But I will not be sleeping on this couch. I don't do couches."

That woke me up. Chantel was back at it, again.

"Okay, I'll take the couch. You can grab the bed."

"I think it's better if we both just take the bed. Shawn, look me in my eye and tell me you're not attracted to me."

I looked away, trying to get my lie together. "Chantel, it's too late for this."

"You're single, aren't you?" she moved her head in the path of my sight to force eye contact.

My first thought was Danielle. How I was single, but not really. How I was spoken for emotionally but physically, alone as any other single man. But then again, I was tired of being alone. And I was, both physically and emotionally. And I was definitely tired of lying to myself trying to be convinced I wasn't.

"Yes, I am single."

"And I know you're an adult. So let's be adults and get in the bed, together. I can help you relax. You know you need it, and a part of you wants it too. Don't you?" She reached up and lightly massaged the tops of my shoulders.

My lying machine was out of service for the night. "Yeah. I do."

She smiled. We got up with her grabbing my hand, leading me into the bedroom.

I turned on the shower, taking off my clothes to give the water time to heat up. She came in and joined me.

She began wiggling out of her jeans as they scrunched down to her ankles and she stepped out of them. I kept undressing, not willing to miss any part of her show either.

My shower wasn't very large but allowed enough room for us both to fit with standing room only. The water poured over me, hitting my back. She grabbed a sponge from my drawer, almost already knowing exactly where to look for it, and began softly rubbing. I felt the suds dripping down my body and her off-hand holding me steady at my waist.

She used that hand to slide down to my dick to feel for a progress report, but not much was going on.

As if it was a challenge, she reached down between my thighs, massaging me gently, her perky breasts pressing against my back. It all felt amazing--her up against me and me shifting around in the palm of her hand. I kept scrubbing my body, not caring to stay in the shower much longer. If we were going to have sex, I didn't care for it to be in there. The water, the suds--too dangerous. Maybe it'd work in a movie or in some romance novel, but not in real life.

By the time I stepped out, I was no longer sleepy, but rather trying to decide exactly what to do with my newfound energy. I had a pretty good idea, but wasn't sure if I was up for the challenge. Only one way to find out.

I handed Chantel a towel and grabbed one for myself. Normally, air drying was my thing, but I wasn't going to be able to sprawl out as usual for my normal breeze so a towel would have to suffice.

I grabbed a pair of boxers from the top drawer, just to

be on the safe side in case we happened to fall asleep. She looked at me as if she was offended when I did.

"What are you doing with those?"

"Well, I was about to put them on, but never mind I guess." I put them back in and hopped in the bed, reaching for my just-in-case condom stash I had in my jewelry box on the night-stand. I still wasn't hard yet, but hoping things would change soon. Music would help set the mood and get things right.

I reached over to my phone and found my Pandora app. It'd been a while since I'd had sex and the last time I did was with Danielle. We'd always had a playlist ready in the stereo but in an effort to let go of the memories, I'd deleted it months ago.

So I clicked on the first name that came to mind, R. Kelly. Definitely a safe bet for baby-making practice. So I thought.

Chantel slipped under the covers, head first like she was deep sea diving on her way to my penis. She felt around for a moment then began kissing and sucking me back to life.

As much as I was trying to stay focused on the moment, I couldn't. I had a horrible run-in with the police and still didn't have answers as to what it was Danielle was doing that was more important than checking her voicemail and coming to get me.

It was too much in one day.

I grabbed on to Chantel's ass. It was small but soft. Danielle's was much bigger and rounder to my taste. But this would do.

When I finally reached full erection, I tried to slide the condom on under the covers, something I'd never been good at before but this time it worked.

I kept my erection all of five seconds once it was on. Not only was the condom foreign to me after three years of relationship sex, but Pandora and its trusty playlist of associated songs somehow went from R. Kelly's slow jams to Donnie McClurkin with *We Fall Down.* (No pun intended.) But no way was I about to have sex to a gospel song.

She emerged from under the cover, looking at me frustrated. "Are you tired?"

"Not really, at least, I don't think so. Maybe. I don't know." I took off the condom as I spoke, admitting defeat for the first time. Optimus Prime had always been dependable, but these circumstances were too much for even he to transform under. My poor penis.

"You want me to just suck it for you?"

"Nah, you don't have to do that. The sun'll be up any minute now. Let's just try to get some rest before it rises. We can try again later."

She sucked her teeth. "All right, Shawn. Have it your way."

I reached over and turned my phone off. All the way off. I needed something to blame for the way that ended, and it was the scapegoat of choice.

****

Woke up the next morning, unconsciously flinging my hand over beside me to feel for Chantel. Nothing was there.

As my senses came to, I noticed the muffled sounds from a radio blasting from the kitchen. The same radio I had tucked away in my closet once my new neighbors moved in about two months before because they kept calling the apartment security on me for having my music too loud. My last warning came with a 100 dollar fine. My next one would come with an eviction slip.

I hopped out of bed, speed walking to the kitchen where breakfast was already in progress. Chantel was standing near the stove, switching her hips from side to side and bobbing her head to Queen Bey's new single on the radio. Completely naked, a sight every man deserves to see at least once in his lifetime.

She did a half spin and caught me out of the corner of her eye, then paused for a moment to smile.

"Well, good morning sleepyhead," she said, proudly being caught in the act of preparing breakfast in her birthday suit, a skillfully tailored suit at that. Her pale skin contrasted well with her nipples. I'd seen them the night before but with the full portrait in front of me in broad daylight, I was able to actually appreciate it.

I peeked over at the microwave and looked at the time. It was only seven in the morning.

"Good morning," I mumbled, trying to match her alertness and failing miserably. "Why you got the music so loud? You gon' wake my neighbors."

"They'll live. I closed the door so I wouldn't wake you up, though. But I like to have a little music when I cook. Oh, and you need to go shopping. You're almost out of sausage." She looked down at my boxers and walked up to me. "Speaking of sausage. . ."

"Chill, Chan. We need to turn this music down before my neighbors get upset and call the--"

As I said that, two knocks came at the door.

We both looked to where the sound came from, and then two more knocks came again, even louder.

"Dammit!" I yelled, going to hit the volume on the radio.

She looked at me with the "My bad" expression, and it only made me more frustrated for not pulling the plug earlier.

"Go in the room and get some clothes on while I talk to these folks. Hurry," I said with a hard tone.

Tried to think of excuses I could give to talk the security guard down. He was usually pretty cool but never appreciated having to come up the steps to my apartment for the same complaint every time. He was also very adamant about doing what he had to do, even if that meant I'd be out of a place to stay.

I walked over to the door, clearing my throat so I could speak clearly, and inhaled.

"Hi, Mr. Dae-Hoe."

Thank God, I thought. It wasn't security. Instead it was my little Korean neighbor who stood in front of me with his broom in his hand upside down like a weapon.

"You play rap music loud and wake wife!"

It wasn't rap music. But in his mind, any music black people played must've been rap music.

"I apologize for that. Please tell her I apologize. Won't happen again, my bad."

"Your bad now. Your ass next time! Turn rap music down or I call police!"

I closed the door in his face. Not only did I not want to hear anymore, his breath was being dramatic. Bad was an understatement. His was so bad it was sad and it was so sad, it could bring tears to your eyes. That's why it was dramatic and I didn't enjoy that drama all coming in my house.

He knocked again, and I opened the door.

"I said a'ight, Mr.--Umm...hey, Danielle."

"Hey, I got your message last night. You all right? I came as soon as I could. What happened? How'd you get out? Why'd you go in?"

I was stuck.

"Hello? Talk to me," she said, scanning me up and down for evidence of some criminal activity that'd lead me into going to jail.

"Hey. I mean, yeah, I did call you last night. What happened to you?" I said, trying to switch the subject momentarily while I figured out what exactly to do to keep her on that side of the door.

Stepping outside to meet her there would have been too obvious and I didn't have my key, so I would've been locked out in my underwear until I knocked for Chantel to open the door.

She beat me to a decision and pushed her way through me, dropping her keys on the kitchen counter as she walked in. "You have no idea. I was in my room and I could have sworn..."

She stopped. So did my heart.

"You cooking breakfast now?" She sniffed a few times, following her nose to the kitchen. "Since when you get up this early to start cooking? I never remember you getting up this early to cook. Why are you acting so strange, Shawn?"

I figured it was best I go ahead and let her know Chantel was there while I had to chance. With any luck she'd get pissed off and leave.

"So last night, I went to jail. I thought it was you coming to pick me up, but it wasn't. It was--"

"Hey," Chantel said, standing in the hallway opening and looking at us. "What's going on?"

Danielle slowly turned around to see who was talking as I silently whispered a few cuss words to myself. My luck had to be the worst.

Danielle turned and looked back at me. "Is that?"

I already could see the memories from the previous visit after our date playing across her forehead.

I nodded, yes.

"With the shirt on that *I* got you?"

I looked past her to Chantel to verify, then sighed in defeat. Out of all the shirts she could've chosen.

Damn.

"Look, Danielle it's not what it looks like. I mean it kinda is, but just listen."

"You know it's rude to whisper, guys," Chantel cut in with her arms folding. Danielle and I both turned and looked at her. "Danielle, is it? How about you join us for breakfast? We'd love to have you. I'm sure you've worked up an appetite. You look really....*really* tired." She grinned.

Shoot. I walked towards her to try and get her to the room, "Chantel, this ain't none of--"

"I accept," Danielle snapped. "I'd love to join the two of you."

Please...Put the Knife Down

The eggs. Bitter.

The sausage. Stale.

The grits. Pasty.

At least that's how it tasted through my struggle to act like the clinging of forks hitting the plates was more than just the calm before the storm.

I tried multiple times to evacuate before it hit. "Danielle, look, there's a better way to go about thi--"

"So Chantel. How did you guys meet?" she said, ignoring me.

I put my head down and kept force feeding myself. I didn't have a snowball's chance in the Sahara to get out of this one.

"Short version or the long version?" she asked cynically.

"Hmm...so there's a *long* version? Well, that's nice, but I'll pass. The short one will do."

"Well, a mutual friend linked us together after finding out I modeled."

"So you were a referral?" Danielle asked.

"I guess....wait, what is a referral to you?"

"A referral. Like a recommendation. You know, *passed to the homies*. If this is what you call modeling, then you were definitely that. Just a referral. For lack of a better, and maybe a more fitting term."

"Oh, then- I'd say I'm more like a promotion. Whoever had the position before clearly wasn't getting the job done."

Danielle lowered her eyes while her tongue swiped over the top row of her teeth. I didn't notice at the time, but my mouth was wide open and so were my eyes. I scanned the table for anything heavy and possibly projectile-like that could be used as a weapon, but Danielle caught it first.

She grabbed her plate and slung it like a Frisbee towards Chantel's neck. Despite the precision, Chantel moved out of the way, but not before it nicked her jaw and ricocheted into the wall.

"All right, that's enough!" I protested. "Danielle, you know better than this."

She scooted her chair back from the table. "I don't want to hear it, Shawn! I'm tired of you playing me like a fool."

"You? Tired of me?" I said, my voice raising with the heat of the moment. "So when I needed you most, you were nowhere to be found. But you're tired of me?!"

"I came as soon as I could. I went to the police station the moment I got your voicemail this morning and they said you'd already found your way home so I came straight here."

"You just so happened to not have your phone on you? Every other time you do but not this time? What were you doing last night that was so important? Huh?"

"You got the nerve to be asking while your little slut that, by the way, you told me was just your client is over here eating breakfast with no underwear."

Chantel snapped back, "Who are you calling--"

"Watch your mouth or get slapped in it," Danielle gnarled at her.

"Both of you, chill," I said, stretching my hands out between the two of them now that Danielle's fists were clenched and Chantel had stood up.

I repeated myself. "Danielle, answer the question. What were you doing last night?"

"Who are you? You're not my daddy. You're not my husband or my boyfriend."

That stung.

"Title or no title, we're supposed to take care of each other. Remember that?"

She deflated a bit and looked around as if she was coming out of her emotions. I was still knee-deep in mine.

"If this is what you call taking care of me," she said, cutting her eyes at Chantel, "then keep it. Y'all have fun."

She walked out the door. She didn't slam it, but instead closed it gently as if in those few steps she'd composed herself enough to make a decision she'd stick with this time.

I followed over to the door, making sure it was closed.

"So, you're just gonna let her throw things and then call me out of my name?"

"What do you mean, *let*? You was standing here just like I was."

"That bitch wouldn't even pick up her phone for you and you act like it's all good that she just dogged me out."

"I didn't let her do anything and I'm not going to let you disrespect her either."

"Fuck her!"

"Chantel, that's the last time. I mean it."

"You so defensive about her but she's clearly not tripping over you. I can see why," she said, looking down at my boxers again.

I took that as a jab that I didn't stay hard the night before.

"So we're going there now?"

She let out a *hmph* as to say, *Yeah so what you gon' do about it?*

"You know what, this is childish. You need to get your shit and go."

She sighed, "Wait, okay... I'm sorry. I didn't mean that. Let's just start over, okay?"

"Actually, let's not."

She walked over to me and drug her finger down the middle of my chest. "I promise, I can make it up to you."

I reckon she figured it'd take a bit more convincing once I didn't respond, because she dropped down to her knees and licked her lips, staring at my pelvis.

She repeated herself again, this time in a softer and more sensual tone, "Like I said, let's just start--"

"What part of no don't you understand?" I gnarled. "OUCH!" A pain shot through my stomach. I looked down and saw she had my scrotum clenched mercilessly in her hands. I pulled away and she grabbed tighter.

"Oh, Shawn," she moaned, slowly. "Why must you tease me so?"

"You cannot be serious right now."

"Oh, but I am,"

I don't know if she was trying to rape me or if she thought I was into the whole kinky, pain-is-pleasure thing, but I felt my fists clenching the more I ached. "Chantel, I swear to God. If you don't let me go, I'mma--"

"What? Hit me? You're going to hit me?" she looked up daringly and biting her bottom lip.

"I left my..." Danielle flung the door open and focused on Chantel. "Keys."

Fuck. I forgot to lock the door.

I closed my eyes, trying to just disappear from the moment. Pretending this day wasn't happening. Hoping that when I opened them again, I'd be waking up from a bad dream. Didn't work.

Danielle continued over to the kitchen counter where she'd set them down.

Chantel loosened her grip, without moving. We both just stared silently at Danielle, studying her every move.

She grabbed her keys, and on her way back to the door, paused by the kitchen and looked over near the sink. Then she walked over and reached and grabbed a meat cleaver out of the drainer.

"Danielle, please," I pleaded. "Put the knife down."

"I'm afraid I can't do that," she responded as she walked out of the kitchen. Her eyes focused again on Chantel who had not moved from the floor on her knees. "I was looking for this knife. Seems I left it here when I moved out. I'll take it back now. Have a good day." And she walked out.

I exhaled, as the door shut. Grateful that didn't take the turn it could have.

"Look, just go. Now," I said to Chantel.

"Fine," she puffed out as she stood back to her feet. "But first, where's my money?"

I walked back to the room and dug into the left-hand corner of my dresser where the money I'd saved up to join the fraternity was at. I grabbed the full wad. Her shoes and clothes were in a pile by the foot of the bed so I grabbed those, too, while I was at it.

"Here. Anything else, I'll give it to you later. Just go," I said, shoving the money and her things into her hands.

She walked out two steps onto the porch before she turned around and said, "Do you know how many guys try me every single day? Plenty. And here you are telling me to leave as I stand here, unfucked. You must be gay."

"You know how many people go to a mall and flock to the clearance rack? Plenty. Doesn't say much about the quality of the goods, though, now does it?"

I shut the door before she could answer then went back to the table to finish my breakfast.

*****

The next few days were a blur.

With no conversation from Danielle, Chantel, or Ronnie, I had all three of their voices playing in my head over and over.

I came up with a million *what-I-should've-said-was* responses for Danielle and Chantel. They always seem to come to you when it's too little, too late.

I thought back to Ronnie, too, and what he'd probably say once he found out we went through all that work to get me into the fraternity just for me to come up with no money.

There was less than two weeks left until the submission deadlines for my application, but it wouldn't even be viewed without either the money or one hell of a voucher from Ronnie. I tried calling him a few times only to get his voice-mail, something I didn't care to leave messages with at the moment.

Outside of fraternity business, it would've done me some good to just sit down and talk with another brother. There was no better time than now to get an outside perspective, and that's what your boys are supposed to be for.

I needed a break from ruining relationships with bad news and failed explanations, so I'd been avoiding going to the cafe to see Auntie in the meantime.

I stepped out early one morning to clear my head, just my Nikon and water bottle somewhere in the middle of the woods. I didn't do a lot of nature photography but being from the country, I always felt a connection with the wildlife of southeastern Alabama.

They were like the stepchildren of Mother Nature. Most of the animals there ended up as road kill. Never made it to the zoos to be admired by kindergarten classes or on any brochures for forest parks. Just possums, wild rabbits, and mosquitoes with an occasional deer that nobody cared about unless it was hunting season.

And me, I was karma's middle child, forgotten for everything good I'd done, but the moment I stepped out of line she was right there. She popped up every time like I owed her five dollars.

A vibration went off in my pocket and I realized I'd forgotten to leave my phone in the car. It was no later than six in the morning so I knew it could only be one person calling me.

Momma.

She didn't care one bit about the possibility of me still being asleep, as she never did in the past when she used to wake me up every morning. Sometimes she called just to ask me why I hadn't called her first, something mothers do.

"Hello?" I said, trying to steady my feet on the uneven dirt between thorny vines and trees lined with ants.

"Hey, why you up so early?" she asked.

"How did you know I was up?"

"I can hear it in your voice. You outside? I hear birds or something."

"Yes, ma'am. Just out taking some pictures."

"It's that bad, huh?"

"What's that bad?"

"Your legal trouble."

"Wait, who told you--"

"I got a letter in the mail yesterday. Something about you needing to appear in court here in a few weeks, but it didn't say what for. Figured I'd call and let you know since I knew you wasn't gon' call me."

Damn. I knew I should've changed my address on my license when I had the chance.

"Momma, it's kind of a long story--"

"Pray."

"Ma'am?"

"I said pray. You too busy trying to tell me what's going on so I understand. You ever thought about telling God so he'd understand?"

"God gave me these problems. Why would I--"

"Because he's trying to get you to talk to him. So talk to him. Not me. Love you. Bye."

"Hello? Momma? Hello?"

She'd already hung up.

She made sense. I'd always viewed faith as something that needed to be a last resort. Like it should only be an option once you'd done your due diligence in getting on the right path, but the more I did, the worse things had gotten. Maybe a prayer wasn't a bad idea.

I put my camera back in my book bag and found a clean place to kneel and close my eyes. I never understood why or if kneeling and closed eyes were necessary, but I saw no reason to take chances now.

"Dear God, thank you. Thank you for this day and thank you for this meal--ah, damn,"

A cussword slipped out after I went into auto pilot saying grace over food I wasn't eating so I opened my eyes.

God had heard me curse before. I wasn't fooling him with any political correctness now. Maybe being real with him instead of pretending he wasn't around 24/7 to know how I really talked was a better angle anyway.

I started over.

"Dear Lord, I'm sorry for cursing. But, I've been through a lot. I know it's nothing compared to what kids in Africa are going through and people in the military and so on, but it's a lot for me. It's more than I understand and probably will be more than I can handle here in the near future. Please, if you're listening, help me. I have nothing to bargain with. No good deeds that make me deserving, no promises to you I can keep. I just need help and I don't know how I'mma make it without you. Amen."

I opened my eyes and saw what had to be the Godzilla of spiders less than two feet away crawling towards me. It was about the size of the palm of my hand, the same palm I used to throw the nearest stick at it. I don't think I've ever made a dumber decision in my life.

It jumped, and I sprinted. Every ounce of athleticism came rushing back through my body as I tore through the hanging limbs, stepping over emerged roots covered in leaves, and maneuvering in and out of the trees like I'd been training for this all my life. If I left anything behind, it now belonged to Spidey Godzilla.

I got to my car winded and sweating, fully awake if I wasn't before and looking up at the sky figuratively at God thinking, *What was that for?* Must've been my slap on the wrist for cursing.

I drove back to my apartment, scared to even hear another curse word, and noticed a familiar face standing on the street corner.

It was Lamarcus.

An ice cold feeling flushed across my chest. I wanted better for him. Auntie did too. But we'd done the best we could do. I guess it was God's turn now.

I pulled up to the light and made sure to make eye contact with him before I pulled off. When I did, he smiled and ran over to my car, motioning for me to roll down the window.

"What's good, bruh?!" he beamed, as if we were long-lost family members.

I was still a little cautious. "I don't know. What's good with you?"

"Chillin', man."

Seeing as how he was going to beat around the bush and I was about to be holding up traffic, I stopped wasting time.

"Why are you out here? After all that we went through this past weekend, you still haven't learned yet?"

"What you mean?"

"You know what I mean. You out here on the block again, slinging. You just don't know when to quit, do you?"

He looked at me confused then shook his head before busting out laughing. "Man, I ain't out here selling no drugs. I'm waiting for the bus. I'm going to school."

He reached under his shirt and pulled out a notebook that was wedged under his belt.

"Yeah, ain't have no book bag so I had to improvise a lil' bit. But hey, at least I got it. I'm done with the street life."

I laughed at my stupidity and exhaled at the fact he actually appeared to be telling the truth.

"That's what's up, and my bad for assuming. I wasn't tryna play you. Hop in, I'll give you a ride."

He opened the door and got in. I inhaled, expecting traces of marijuana to be in the air. But there were none.

"So, you back in school now?" I asked.

"Yeah, I wasn't out that long or nothin'. Just skipped when I knew I had to but I'm not missing no more days. Talked to my teacher and made a deal with her. She said if I came for the rest of the year she wouldn't hold me back."

"That's good. How'd Auntie take the news about us getting locked up?"

"How you think? She damn near fainted. Not for me, but for you."

"For me?"

"Yeah, you. I get in trouble all the time. She thought I got you caught up. That was until I told her 'bout my phone."

"Wait, what about your phone?"

"Oh, she ain't told you? My recording saved before it went dead. I got every single word those cops said because while you was talking, I set up my voice recorder to use in court."

"You better not be playing with me, Lamarcus. I swear

I'll turn this car around if you're tryna be funny!" I said, my heart pounding with excitement now.

"Nah, I put that on everything. Ain't my first time getting caught up with twelve. I knew it was worth a shot, and when I played it back, realized they never read us our rights. We gon' be straight, bruh. I told you."

I pulled up to the front of his school and stopped the car. He reached his hand for a congratulatory dap, but I reached and grabbed his neck for a hug. A weight was ascending from my shoulders for every split second I held on.

But of course, we both parted, awkwardly.

"I can't thank you enough. I didn't know what I was going to do. Man this is huge."

"Nah, I should be thanking you. We still ain't got a lot of money, but seeing you doing your thing and taking time to talk to me; it really meant a lot, bruh. For real. I'mma gon' head and get to class so I can get on this schoolwork. Tell Grandma I love her."

"I got you," I returned, this time for a dap and finger snap.

After he got out, I looked up through the windshield and into the clouds again, realizing my prayers were heard.

Me, Myself, and I

"Hey, what's good, Ronnie? It's Shawn. I tried calling you a few times. Not sure what's up with your phone or whatever. But hit me back when you get a chance. Peace."

This was the second voice-mail following at least five unanswered texts to Ronnie over the last week. I wasn't sure if this was some kind of test to see how persistent I could be, or if something had happened to him, but I'd much rather him just pick up the damn phone. Popping up at his house wouldn't be my style, but it was about to come to that with the deadline for the application submission approaching and me still not having a chance to tell him I wasn't going to have the money.

But whatever. If he wasn't stressing it, neither was I.

With Chantel out of the picture, I didn't have many shoots to do or pictures to edit so it freed up some time to get back focused on my studies. I was approaching the final stretch of college and I needed to finish strong and get the hell out of there.

What I was going to do next was the only question.

My photography was on point, but the income was almost seasonal. Great during graduation season but during the summer, nothing. I hated doing family portraits because the kids would never sit still and the wives of the family never liked how they looked in the camera and blamed it on both me and my camera. Then the husband, although he didn't want to take the pictures in the first place, had to display some level of dissatisfaction to make sure his wife knew he was in her corner.

I could do without those.

Weddings too. They paid the most, but the moment you arrived, you were officially working for every family member of the bride. If the mother told you to sit, you'd damned well better sit. If she told you to hold her dollar store disposable camera so she could get her own pictures, you'd better do that too. If she asked you to take a picture with her 2005 original Motorola Razor flip phone that she felt so hipped for still having in working order seven years later and the picture came out blurry, it was your fault.

Between that and trying to aim the camera over the flood of friends and family who also wanted their own photos to put on Facebook during the most priceless moments of the wedding, just for you to get blamed for ruining memories of a lifetime, no amount of money was worth it.

I only wanted to do model shoots and occasional senior portraits, but more than anything, I needed to keep some money in my pocket so I could keep my gas light off.

But as for a career, I needed something more stable. More secure, and with a good starting salary.

There was a career fair coming up and that would be my best shot. The worst that could happen was being told no. But best case scenario, I'd update my resumé, put on my best tie and smile and get lucky enough to interview with a male recruiter who loved sports or a female recruiter who loved guys who loved sports.

So I finished my last class for the day, still with no word from Ronnie, and headed over to the library to print out my resumé.

I walked across the ave that connected the yard to the library, looking both ways a few times since my headphones were in. I started listening to music more often to keep people from wanting to start conversations, and it helped occupy my mind from thinking about Danielle.

A part of me missed her; a bigger part of me missed what we had. She had an effect on me I wasn't used to, one I didn't want to part with. We could laugh and chill; we could make passionate love, or we could not say a thing to one another and I'd still be happy just to have her there with me. And her support, that seemed to glue everything I was trying to accomplish together. Without that glue, my goals were defunct.

It was gloomy outside, assumedly getting ready to rain. As I walked through the gates, getting closer to the door, I looked through the top window and saw what looked like her, but was hard to tell from three floors down. I usually could spot her with no doubt, but when you miss someone, everyone seems to be them at first glance. So, I wasn't sure.

Wouldn't hurt to find out though.

I continued through the door, trying to think of what I'd say when I saw her. If I saw her. If it was her at all.

Don't think she quite had enough time to cool off, and even if she did, did it even matter anymore? I felt like crap after getting caught with Chantel over at the crib, and it was my guess that Danielle couldn't care less.

I walked by the work study librarian student who hadn't

noticed that the couple in the room beside her was probably having hand sex. His closed eyes, jacket on his lap covering his girl's hand, and her death stare at me when I walked by gave them away. I politely smiled and continued walking.

Instead of the elevator, I took the stairs up all three flights, skipping every other step to get there faster. My heart was beating and I was getting nervous. Figured maybe I'd just keep it cool when I saw her. No need to make a scene. I'd just speak briefly, hopefully pick up on some good vibes, and take it from there.

I finally made it to the door of the computer lab and got my confirmation. It was her. This time standing by the printer getting her papers from it.

"Hey, Danielle," I mumbled. Just in case she ignored me, I could just pretend I was talking to myself.

She looked up, and at the sight of me, her expression changed to less than excited.

"Hi, Shawn." She grabbed the last of her printouts and went to staple them.

"You know, it's good to see--"

"You ready to go?" A guy cut me off mid-sentence. I looked up and saw he was talking to Danielle with her books in his hand. He was tall, probably mixed with black and white, a lot of tattoos on his forearm with a somewhat familiar face but I couldn't quite place where I'd seen him before.

I knew the books belonged to her because she never changed her notebook since her freshman year, and it was the same notebook I set on the ground the night we slow danced in the parking lot.

She looked at him and replied, "Yeah. I'm done now." Then back at me with a brief smile, somewhat out of pity before walking off with him.

I can't lie, I felt stuck. Like, I couldn't say anything or do anything; I just stood there in the same place for a few seconds picking up my face.

This didn't look like any casual study buddy or person she was tutoring. There was a non-platonic energy, just in the way he was carrying her books and cut me off to ask if she was ready to go. And she was ready to leave. With him. Away from me.

I snapped out of it and went over to the window to see what I wish I hadn't. They left out into the parking lot, one of his hands hanging over her opposite shoulder before he went and opened the passenger side door to his car for her to get in.

I'd never seen her with another guy. Not in pictures, not mentally or even in my worst nightmare.

Jealousy. Anger. Confusion. Pick one. I felt them all at the thought of how easy it was for her to move on so quickly.

Trust me, I know I had no right to be mad, but the decision wasn't voluntary. I just was. I did what a lot of guys do; I put her in this light, on somewhat of a pedestal that there was never going to be another guy for her besides me. Unrealistic for sure. But she was never realistic to begin with. She was my dream girl.

I did an about-face to head back downstairs to my car. I wasn't going to follow them despite the curiosity of where they were going next. Because no matter where they went, it wasn't going to make it easier on me.

I just needed to get away.

Jazmin was gone and that made me miss her absence like crazy. I needed her tough love and comforting laughter more than anything right now, but I screwed that up. Ronnie would've been clutch but he still hadn't called or texted back. I needed somebody, but didn't have anybody. Mostly the fault of my own. Again.

I went home this time, trying to gather my thoughts and establish exactly the way I needed to feel and proceed from there.

Was this the point where I deleted her number and blocked her from everything online? Did I need to approach her no matter where she was and let her know how I felt? Write a letter? Break down? Deal with it?

Deal with it.

That's what I chose. I was tired of breaking down. As a man, you make your bed and you sleep in it. If you toss and turn all night, your fault. Should've thought about that before you chose the sheets.

*****

I woke up the next morning, missing my first class so I could have some time to my thoughts. I think we all need that from time to time. Without that occasional catching up, the changes we go through can make us a stranger to ourselves.

My disposition of being in the wrong and getting exactly what I deserved felt foreign although surely I had been there before. The difference this time was that I was no longer taking the moral escape route of "Only God can judge me," but instead, just accepting the fact that I'm...ordinary.

I messed up. I did wrong. Intentions didn't matter once the damage was done so there was nothing left but to take what was coming. That just so happened to be the best thing to happen to me walking away and being justified in every single step.

I did end up making a return to the library, which went a lot smoother this time. No sign of Danielle and her new guy, no drama at all, so I was able to print out my résumés as planned.

I drove from the library, taking a detour by Ronnie's apartment complex to see if his car was outside. The curiosity had gotten the best of me, but I wasn't going to go knock on his door. At least if I knew his car was there, I could cross out the possibility of something being wrong with him.

And it turned out, he was good. Car parked, light in his living room window on.

I pulled off a few seconds later, ready to charge it all to the game, when in my review mirror I saw him coming out of his apartment with some of his fraternity brothers. Impulse guided my hands to turn the car around although I wasn't sure if it was a good idea.

Correction, I was absolutely positive that it wasn't a good idea.

"Hey, what's good, Ronnie?" I said, walking up to him.

He looked at me, then at his brothers who were all looking at him with the "You know him?" face. His hesitation made me defensive and confirmed I'd made a horrible decision.

"Umm...'tsup, Shawn? I'm going to have to meet with you another time. I'm on my way somewhere right now."

"Look, man, it's cool. I don't know what your deal is, but I don't do the whole hint sending and catching thing with other grown men. I wouldn't even be pressing you if it wasn't for the deadline coming up but--"

"Oh, so this is the dude you were talking about?" one of his brothers laughed, cutting me off. "The little jail bird, right?"

I looked at him then back at Ronnie. "What?"

His frat brothers busted out laughing. I caught on to what they were talking about. Not sure how they got wind about me getting arrested, but apparently it had already been a topic of conversation.

"Look, Shawn. I told you it's not a good time."

"Honestly, I don't know what I was thinking anyway. This whole thing never sat right with me from the beginning, but I thought a little more of you than this."

"More of me? You mean, you're running around breaking the law and still expect to get down with the brothers of Alpha Kap--"

"No. I expected the brother who needed help communicating with his father to realize that I been down. Regardless of his fraternity."

His frat brother chimed in, "It's more than just a fraternity, it's a lifelong bond of--"

"I wasn't talkin' to you."

He looked at me as if I'd crossed the line. As far as I was concerned, the line was long gone.

I got back in my car, halfway feeling stupid and the other half glad I didn't give them a dime of my money after all. The fraternity thing may have had its perks, but I could do without filling out applications and paying for people to

claim me as a friend. My social circle would be a dot consisting of me, myself, and I before I went that route again.
Ever.

The Thot-osphere

The recruiter continued looking over my résumé before asking me another obvious ass question I was going to have to answer with responses I'd memorized instead of what I really wanted to say.

"Okay, so Mr. Fletcher, tell me. Why do you want this job?"

My thoughts: *Because I don't want to be broke the rest of my life. Broke people stay hungry because food costs money. Money requires a job. The job requires me to be in here with this suit I'll never wear again pretending I've actually been a great student so you'll believe I can be a great employee. But even that's questionable.*

I answered, "Well, I felt like the mission of the company aligned well with my strengths and the values posed the kind of potential for professional and personal development I'm seeking over the long-term, sir."

"I see. That's not a bad reason to want a job at all." He smiled as if he was impressed. I was nervous since the beginning of the interview, but holding together well. He continued, "Well, I'm curious. How did you hear about us?"

My thoughts: *Last-minute Google search once I found out you had an empty slot for interviews.*

I responded, "Well, your company is second to none when it comes to a long-standing tradition of excellence in sales leadership. You're practically a household name amongst the students here. I figured everyone knew who you were, but

I was anxious for the opportunity to talk to someone like yourself within the company and find out more from your experience in which I'm sure you have plenty of insight to offer, sir."

He took off his glasses and smiled, "Well, I'm glad you asked. I've been with the company for 14 years now, and I've always loved..." so on and so forth about how the company saved his life.

It was a tire manufacturing company. I didn't know or care anything about a tire, but they had a job willing to pay 70k to anybody that could impress the Uncle Phil-looking guy in front of me who had sweated out the armpits of his shirt trying to pretend he was comfortable squeezing in his chair.

While I was considerate enough to pretend I was listening intently, I was partly distracted by my thoughts of all that had gone on in the last month, so I didn't know how the interview was going in his eyes.

My little life game of *Who's Next to Go* had already gotten old, and so was I. Well, not exactly old, but I was growing up without my priorities. Here I was less than a month away from graduation with no job, and my biggest concern was who was going to be my friend.

This interview, or some interview was going to have to work.

"Well, Mr. Fletcher. I must say that I'm thoroughly impressed with you and what you've been able to do. I can't give you an answer right now until I've at least seen the other candidates, but from where I'm sitting, your chances look pretty darn good." He stood, reaching his hand out.

"I'm honored, sir, and regardless of the outcome, this has

truly been a privilege. I look forward to hearing from you." I met his hand and forced out a Colgate smile until I was out the door and completely out of sight.

Other students were outside, a nervous wreck, last-minute prepping for their interviews, and all I could hope was that he hated them. All of them.

I loosened up my tie on the way to the parking lot, rolled the window down once I got inside the car, and made my way to the cafe. I'd not been in a while, hoping to let things cool off before seeing Auntie. With things working out for the better on the legal end, now was as good a time as any.

She was cordial through the line as usual. Nothing was out of the ordinary with exception to what I saw when I got back to my seat.

"Well, hey there, stranger. " Chantel crossed her long legs, slightly leaning to one side to reveal her thigh showing between the black mini skirt and knee-high leather boots she had on.

I exhaled uncomfortably, "What's going on?"

"Nothing much. You just gon' act like you didn't see me in here, huh?"

"Act like what? I really didn't--You know what, I'm just trying to eat my food. I didn't come here for all--"

"Calm down. I'm not here to stir you up. Just figured I could speak. It ain't like you to smash and dash, ya know? I think you're changing."

"I'm changing? You didn't know me to begin with."

"Well, what I do know is that I'm a week late, and if I don't start my cycle in the next few days, we'll both be getting to know each other really well over the next 18 years."

I almost swallowed my fork. "Late? Late to where? I know you're not talking about your period."

"That's exactly what I'm talking about."

"Chantel, we didn't even have sex. I never even got to--"

"Damn, Mr. Bunched Panties, take a joke. I was just playing. You really are stressed out, aren't you?"

I looked at her for a moment, refusing to return her smile. "Nah, I'm not stressed out. Well, maybe a little. I just haven't figured out this whole on-again, off-again blister."

"What blister? I didn't see a blister."

"Doctor said it's probably nothing and who knows? It might not be nothing. It comes and goes. And it hurts."

"Wait, so you have blisters, and you let me suck your dick?!" she yelled, her pitch becoming frenzied.

The surrounding tables began side-eyeing the both of us, me being the only one who noticed or cared for that matter.

"Chan, chill. I was just kidding. Can't you take a joke?"

She threw one of my napkins at me. "Shawn, that's not funny!"

"Yes, it was. Clearly I'm laughing," I chuckled.

Her voice went back to soft and sweet, "Okay, but seriously, so when do I get to see you again or are you still mad about last time?"

"Not mad. But I am done. Not trying to start nothing back up. Let's just leave it where we left off."

She rolled her eyes. "Still hung up on ol' girl, huh?"

"That's none of your business, Chan."

"Well, what you need to make your business is the fact she's running around here with another guy. I was hoping that would have brought you to your senses by now, but I guess not."

"What she does ain't my concern either."

She cocked her head to one side and squinted. "You mean, you're a swinger?"

"No, I mean I'm not with her. She's not with me. She's grown."

"Well, at least that makes one of you."

I stood up from the table, "It was nice seeing you, Chantel."

"Wait, wait. Sit back down. I didn't mean it like that." she said, grabbing my arm to stop me from leaving.

I didn't care to finish my meal, at least not with her there. But was patient enough to allow her a few more words before I pulled away.

"So you really not gon' finish eating? Cool. Then I'll go. You stay and finish your food. I just wanted to speak," she said, defeated.

She walked off, twisting her hips with every step as if she were on the catwalk, seemingly reconstructing her pride along the way.

By this time the cafeteria had begun clearing out and Auntie was no longer behind the serving counter. That meant she was prepping to wipe down tables.

I went ahead and scarfed down the rest of my food, and like clockwork, five minutes later she was heading towards my table before any other. She must've had something to say to me too.

"How you doin', baby?" her voice rang out with that thick country accent leading the way. She had a lot more energy than usual.

"I'm doing good, Auntie. How you?"

"I'm blessed. Aw'ways blessed by the Lawd."

"You know, I apologize for everything that happened. I didn't mean to--"

"I already know what you's 'bout to say, and far as I'm concerned, the Lawd told me to be done with it. So I'm done with it and I advise you to do the same."

"Lamarcus told you?"

"Yeah, he did. Before he told me, the Lawd told me so I wasn't worried about that no way."

I decided to change the subject. There was no going back and forth with religious people. Any objection or question you had became a test to their faith that they got more determined to pass the longer you talked.

"Well, that's good. Other than that, you been all right?"

"Don't worry 'bout me. What's botherin' you? That young lady I saw you sitting with, is that yo' girlfriend?"

"No, ma'am. Just an, um...associate."

"Well, where is yo' girlfriend? I know a handsome young man like you ain't runnin' round here alone."

"I guess you could say that's kinda what's bothering me, Auntie. I don't have one...anymore. She's gone."

"Gone? How so?"

"She said it."

"With what?"

"Her mouth."

"But what did her heart say?"

"I don't know, Auntie. All I have to go on is seeing her leave, and now she's with another guy. I don't know. I didn't mean to bring my problems all on you or nothin'. I'm just having a hard time tryna--"

"Do the same thing you been doing that still ain't workin'?" she asked.

I shook my head, "Yeah, I guess so."

"Well, there's one problem right there. Baby, you can't keep following the same path and expect to end up at a different place. Life don't work like that. You got to try something new."

"Like what?"

"I have a feeling you can figure that out," she said as she smiled. "Until then, I think I best gon' head and get back to work. You take care of yaself, okay?"

"Yes, ma'am."

I sat there a few minutes, elbows propped on my knees, my head hanging and staring at my shoes. The cafe was empty and so was my box of answers. I hated moments like these, but I knew sound advice when I heard it. It was definitely time to try something new.

It was Friday evening and the night was young. I could use a break from the house and I needed a drink. Scratch that, I needed ten drinks, but since I was my designated driver, one was going to have to do.

I could take a rain check on Auntie's life advice but my stress wasn't interested in waiting. I had to deal with that immediately.

I hadn't been to a club since my freshman year. Cost too much money, not enough return on the investment. But now that I was nearing the close of my college tenure and I had a few dollars to my name, why not?

I foraged around my drawer for a grey V-neck I got from

the mall. It was plain, but the fabric stretched to fit (either that or it was a size too small), hugging my biceps and revealing the cuts in the top of my chest. Same trick girls used with their cleavage except mine never got me out of any speeding tickets.

I took my time getting out of the house, being that I wasn't meeting anyone there nor did I feel like being the first one in the club. For some reason, that always just seemed like a sad position to be in.

But I chose the wrong night to be fashionably late. It was free before eleven, and packed both inside and outside. Cars were lined up down the road at least a half mile away from everyone trying to get their party on for the last time before summer break.

Made me wonder if more young people would read books with a *Free Before eleven* advertisement on the front of a bookstore.

So, I paid the unreasonably high cover to get in, then realized absolutely nothing had changed about the club scene since I last stepped foot in one.

Plain Janes I'd seen walking around at school were transformed into half naked(I say *half* loosely) eye candies.

There was the somebody's-grandaddy-aged man sitting at the bar in his baggy suit he got forty years ago when he first became a deacon.

There was the timid girl, clutching her purse over by the bathroom who'd been scared straight by friends telling her if she didn't get out more, she'd grow up to be an old lady with a house of cats.

There were the wanna-be cool brothers who let one of

their friends cut their hair. I could tell because they had a fade that didn't fade; it just came to an abrupt stop.

And of course, there was still the guy who got there super early, already drenched in sweat and break dancing his heart out like he was on *America's Got Talent.*

And all of it was just fine with me. I went and ordered a vodka and cranberry, then sat back and enjoyed the show. As I sipped and the alcohol set in, my thoughts drifted to my conversation with Auntie.

You can't follow the same path and expect to end up at a different place, I thought. What did she mean by that?

"Eh-hem," I heard someone clear their throat beside me. Then they coughed a little louder.

I tried not to look since, you know, staring is rude. But they kept going. I looked to my right and saw a girl cutting eyes at me almost to see if I'd noticed she was pretending to be choking.

"You all right?" I asked.

Her throat magically cleared up, "Yes, I think I'll be all right."

"Yeah, maybe you should get something to drink."

"I know, right?" she responded before waiting for me to go on. I turned my head back forward to continue my drink, so she continued, "I would but I left my wallet in the car."

"Damn, don't you hate when that happens?" I yelled back.

She looked less than pleased with my answer. I realized I was being a bit inconsiderate and decided to do the gentleman thing and get her a drink.

I wailed, "Bartender!" trying to overpower the boom of the club music. "Can I have a water please? For the lady." I nodded to the girl beside me as she rolled her eyes and got out of the chair, heading back to the dance floor.

Ungrateful.

But then it dawned on me. The *something new* I needed to try was another fish in the sea. It was full that night and my net had been empty due to the seemingly gaping holes I could never mend to keep the one I really wanted.

I put a hand in front of my face to check my breath real quick, making sure it didn't smell too strongly of the liquor or the turkey burger I'd eaten a little earlier that day, then slid my tip on the counter, wedging it beneath my glass.

I walked to the dance floor, peering through the artificial fog and towering over everyone, feeling awkward.

When most guys go out, they first look for a few lesser-attractive fish, to get their feet wet before they aim for the big ones. A rookie mistake. Fine sisters noticed everything, and whether successful or not, if you went for someone they didn't consider to be up to par, you were black-listed. Even if she didn't actually see you, her friends would hip her to the game the moment you walked off and you'd be getting the *who this?* reply to your first text.

It may have been a while since I'd gone, but I knew better. I understood the environment, the layers of the atmosphere.

The Snooty-sphere Layer was against the wall where girls that were dressed to kill, resurrect, and then kill again grooved within their own circle. They dared any brother to come close before they publicly (and proudly) shamed him, migrating away in some fashion that called the attention of those nearby.

The Flake-osphere, consisting of those girls who were

a little intoxicated but still being ladylike were a little off the wall, still on the outskirts of the dance floor. They were grooving on each other, doing the fake-gay thing that'd become all the new rage; that's where they earned their name. Every now and then they'd dance with a brother, but he'd have to be either extremely good-looking in the dark or familiar to them. I wasn't completely sure I was either, but this was more my speed.

Beyond them was the Forget-usphere. These were the girls who wanted to dance but didn't have anyone to dance with. While they may have all had wonderful personalities, rarely does anyone go to the club looking for a soul-mate. So unless a girl was extremely attractive or visually selling sex, there'd likely be no customers waiting in her line, which may be a good thing.

But their layer ran adjacent with the Thirst-osphere Layer of guys who were waiting for their turn with the girls in the Thot-osphere.

This was the nucleus, where the life of the party really stemmed from. These were the three-point-stance, no shame in their game, cheap leggings and dollar store flip-flop-wearing, eight-month-pregnant, dropping-into-a-split-from-hand-stand girls. No Thot-osphere; no party. This layer was critical.

Occasionally girls from the outer layers would dip in once they got the nerve or enough alcohol in their system. Seen a lot of relationships end that way. Good girls, proudly claimed as wifey by their man, getting liquor poured down their throat. And every man knows that once another man pours liquor down your girl's throat, she's no longer your girl.

I walked on to the dance floor bobbing my head with the music, trying to establish some rhythm and mesh with the scene. I saw some cute chicks eyeing me a few people over to my right. I edged my way over as *Racks on Racks* by YC had just come on. That was the biggest track of the year so the club was going crazy.

On my way, I accidentally bumped into a girl from the Forget-usphere Layer. She took what she thought was a hint and started dancing on me. Since I didn't initiate the encounter, it wouldn't count against me so I went ahead and started dancing. She so happened to be about a foot shorter, so I had to stoop down low so as not to lose a knee cap when she started thrusting her ass against it. I gained a new appreciation for the work girls put in when they bent down and danced. My quads were on fire.

Once that workout was over and the DJ switched to Rihanna's *Birthday Cake* track, it calmed down enough for me to get closer to the girls I was originally aiming for.

I made it over to the Flake-osphere and there were two young ladies looking my way. But experience taught me there was an 88% chance that one of them was off limits. The one who was off limits looked anyway to further complicate my decision-making for absolutely no reason at all, but if I was to choose wrongly, I'd be on the first thing smoking towards the blacklist.

To hell with it.

This was a night out on the town, not *Jeopardy*.

The closest one to me slowly maneuvered her back against my pelvis, and once her friends gave her the nod of approval, it was on.

Even in the dim lights, my hormones had night vision. This sister was decked out from head to toe, a *freakum* dress she'd been waiting for the right night to wear showing her curves that ran every stop-light between her knees and shoulders.

In her heels, she was a good 5'10 to my 6'6 with Timbs on, just right and a lot more comfortable than my last dance. And she didn't twerk, but she didn't have to.

Once the melodies of *Lotus Flower Bomb* by Wale filled the room, her eyes closed, her head leaned back on my chest, and her right hand pulled my hand around her waist so I wouldn't leave while her left hand reached behind us to the back of my neck. She was either feeling me, the song, or both.

My penis was stiffening the more she wound her body against it. Not too much, not too little.

Very seductive.

I mentally vacationed to a secluded room with just her and me, the music playing from the sounds we made.

Naked. Without so much as exchanging first names. Just her moans as the ad-libs to the lyrics and my breathing as the cadence.

I wondered what it'd feel like to explore her inside before her out. Guessing her every hot spot and getting it just right on the first try uninhibited by the rules of social correctness and letting nature take over.

From her hip movement, I pieced together a visual of her on top of me, reaching back to grip my testicles and using the other hand to massage her nipple. Me being too selfish to allow her to steal the show, moving my hips deeper into her on every descent of her vagina.

The longer I fantasized, the harder I got and the more her body language told me that she was fantasizing right along with me.

"Oh, HELL no!" a female's voice rang out.

It Was a One-Night Extravaganza

We both looked up and saw Chantel barreling through the crowd, yanking the girl by her wrist off of me like a protective mother bear.

I stood there, my imprint protruding through my jeans since I didn't have the girl there to shield me, pissed that out of all people coming to rudely awake me from my fantasy, it was Chantel.

The girl I was dancing with looked at the two of us, confused as to what was going on.

"What's your problem?!" I yelled over the music.

"You think you just gon' be up in here grinding up on my home girl like it's all good? You don't want to talk to me after you done fucked me, but you want my friend. Don't you?" In an instant, every girl in their circle had convicted me as the bad guy. No trial. No jury. They were the judge. Chantel, the executioner.

"How was I supposed to know--"

She reached up to try and slap me but my reflexes yanked my head back just in time. Despite me only dodging her attack, you would think I'd balled my fist up and hit her by the crowd's reaction. Everybody tensed up, preparing to defend her. Not me. Her. Yes, the attacker. They wanted to keep the attacker safe.

"Look, Chan, it was just a dance. I don't even know her, and as for me and you, that's a different story, but this ain't the time nor place."

The girl I'd just danced with, chimed in, "You don't talk to her like that!"

As the seconds went by, the attention on us was spreading like malaria around the club. I felt like such a lame, arguing with a group of girls, knowing good and well there was no way for me to win. To outsiders, it just looked like a situation where I'd been rejected and couldn't handle it. Regardless of what the truth was, perception was both reality and damned good entertainment.

I threw my hands up in defeat, then made my way through the crowd trying to get away as fast as I could, looking back and gladly seeing that I wasn't being followed.

Chantel's manic penchant to ruin anything good in my life was becoming a nuisance.

I got in my car--sweaty, horny, frustrated, embarrassed, horny, confused, horny. That was my chance to do something, someone different, and it went up in flames. Speaking of flames, I could really go for a burger.

I didn't too much care for fast food, but McDonald's was the only thing open so it would have to do.

The drive-through line was wrapped around the building, but the lobby wasn't too packed so I pulled in the parking lot and went inside.

The sweat and steam had loosened my shirt off my body, and the stench of weed and Black & Milds still lingered on my clothes. I needed to get my ass home.

I stared at the menu for a few minutes, trying to use process of elimination to choose my order since everything suddenly looked so delicious. I stepped up to the counter. The cashier looked me up and down like I was inconveniencing her, rolled her neck harder than Shanaynay from *Martin*.

"What'chu want?" she murmured.

Talk about customer service.

"Let me get a...umm...the number two with no mayo, with a large Coke to drink," I said, still finalizing my choices. Out of the corner of my eye, I noticed a few girls over to my left who were waiting for their food had started looking at me.

"You know what, make that fry a large too."

Their observation became a bit more obvious at the sound of my upgrade. I figured they must've been hungry, but I had no intention of sharing.

"Is that all you want?" the cashier retorted, trying to shut me up so she could go back to her misery in peace.

I didn't oblige. "Actually, no. With that, go ahead and add a ten-piece nugget. Not the combo, just the nuggets. Honey mustard on that one."

The cashier exhaled obnoxiously while the girls beside me were now blatantly looking to get my attention. I glanced over to get a better look. They were both younger, maybe eighteen or nineteen. From their attire it seemed they'd just left the Thot-osphere Layer to get something to eat too.

"So that's a number two, a large fry and large coke. Right?"

"Yes."

The girls giggled, batting their eye lashes.

"And then after dat you want a ten piece, just the nuggets with honey mustard sauce, right?"

"That is correct."

"Yo total is elem-fifty nine," she said, reaching her hand out and scratching her wig with the other.

I handed her a twenty. The Thot-osphere Layer girls eyes widened as I stretched my hand out to the cashier. One of them nudged the other and said, "You better go talk to him, girl," just loud enough where I could hear even though I pretended not to.

The cashier snatched the money from me, took my change out, and threw it in my hand before turning to go and gather the orders. With attitude, of course.

Instead of continuing to glance, I just turned and looked at the young girls. The one who was getting peer pressured to come talk to me was short with a nice shape, but her tattoo choices took away from it. She had a few names in script across her chest and a snake going up the length of her leg wrapping around to her cookie. It was supposed to be realistic, but it looked a lot like the kind you saw in coloring books except the tattoo artist had colored outside the lines. Another tattoo was done in fifth grade handwriting on her forearm, probably by a family member when she was too young to see a professional.

Her weave was freshly done but her roots weren't, albeit not too obvious. I just had a keen eye for that since Danielle pointed it out every chance she could so I would appreciate her natural do more.

"What's up?" I said, putting my change back in my pocket and nodding to the girls. I didn't have anything better to do while I waited for my food so small talk wouldn't hurt.

"Mmm, nothin'. What's up witchu?" the one who was supposed to come talk to me responded, with an *it's-your-move* grin. Her fake eyelashes batted over blue-colored contacts. She had a squeaky voice to match her small frame.

"Coolin'," I said, nonchalantly. "Just tryna get somethin' to eat to kill these munchies."

"Oh, so you burn?"

"Nah, I don't smoke, it's just late. Drank a little, but that's about it."

"Yeah, I can see. You must be real healthy and stuff. Yo arms' so big. You can probably pick me up, huh?"

Her girlfriend snickered. She bit her bottom lip, waited for me to respond.

The thought crossed my mind to laugh it off, get my food, and take my ass home. But Auntie told me to try something new. I was down for some fun and struck out at the club earlier so this was better than nothing. Possibly a sign. Besides, she was laying it on thick and I didn't have room to be too choosy.

"Depends if you're old enough."

"I'm nineteen."

"Okay, then it'd depend on the reason."

"What if I just asked you to?"

"I doubt you'd have to ask."

The cashier interrupted, "I saaaaid, order number 259! Yo food is ready."

She nodded over to her home girl to go get their bags so she could finish her little word sparring with me.

"Well, life too short to be waitin' on everybody else. Who knows, I might not never see you again," she said, suggestively.

"Then see me tonight. Tell ya girl, I got you."

She smiled with victory and went back to her friend to discuss it. I looked over at the cashier who was now waiting on me to pick up my food like I wasn't worth wasting her breath to call out my order.

"Yeah, girl, I'mma call you da-morra," she said to her friend as she walked off.

"You know, I don't remember you telling me your name," I said.

"Daneisha-Shantell, but my friends call me Ju-Ju."

I tried sounding out the syllables in her name to see what that was short for. She saw my struggle.

"Oh, it ain't short for nun, that's just what they call me," she said proudly with a smile.

"Um...okay, cool. Ju-ju. If you ready to roll, we can go ahead and go now."

We walked back to my 99 Grand Am. It was rough-looking, barely working, and not working at all in some of its features. But with the extent I'd just dropped my standards, I didn't feel so concerned.

"Oooh, that's my jay-um! Turn it up."

I turned the volume as high as it would go. The radio was still playing club hits, this one, *Bands A Make Her Dance* and she began popping in the seat like Juicy J was serenading her.

While she popped, she opened up her bag and pulled out her McDouble then reached down into her purse. She rummaged around a few seconds then out came a travel-sized bottle of ranch. I didn't even know they made those.

"Wait, what is that?"

"Oh, my bad. I ain't mean to be rude. You want some?" She reached the bottle out towards me.

"Nah, I'm cool. Is that ranch dressing or am I trippin'?"

"Nah, it's ranch. I keep mine on deck 'cause you neeeeva

know. I had some hot sauce, too, but I ran out earlier when I was at the Chipotle."

I turned my head back towards the road without responding and refused to look again. This was about to be a long ass night.

She polished off the burger before we got in my driveway and threw her trash out in the grass. I was about to tell her to pick it up before we got a fine, but at three in the morning, even my own give-a-damn had clocked out.

"Oooh, this is nice. You must got money."

I let her continue in the house while she took herself on a tour.

"Um...not really. But go ahead and make yourself at home. Got drinks in the fridge if you're thirsty."

She continued walking through. "Ooh, you got shower curtains and everything. I used to have shower curtains before Rodney started hanging on them."

"Rodney who? You gotta boyfriend?"

"El oh el." She sounded out the acronym instead of just laughing out loud. "No. Rodney ain't nothin' but six."

She held up her phone with a picture of a kid in a kindergarten graduation robe.

"Oh, okay, How many siblings you got?"

"How many whet?"

"I said, how many siblings. Like your brothers and sisters. You know, siblings."

"Oh, I ain't neva heard it been called that befo'. I got three older brothers."

"That's what's up. Rodney, he's the youngest?"

"Oh nah, Rodney is my son, silly," she chuckled.

I took a hard gulp and sat on the couch.

"Your son? And he's how old?"

"Six. I know, I know. I started young, but it's a'ight. He with his lil' brother at my mama 'nem house right now. Probably bein' bad."

Thinking to myself how afraid I was to ask just how many children she had at nineteen and whether or not I felt like knowing the truth or just shutting up and eating my food, I chose the latter.

I was officially dealing with a real-life hood rat. Like the kind Craig dated in the movie *Friday*. The positive was that she was easily impressed. Actually, she was just plain easy. She still didn't know my first name and there she was, in my house.

On the other hand, she was a little too easy. Somewhat suspiciously. She didn't give off any bad vibes outside of having absolutely no class, but I'd have to keep an eye on her. She was a little too cognizant of my things.

And sex was now out of the question. Not only was she fertile as hell, but if I slipped up and got her pregnant, my life would practically be over. I could see it now, her getting the child support check and going straight to the grocery store to restock on travel-sized bottles of hot sauce and ranch to go with her fast food. Hell no.

I finished eating my feast of delicious carbs, fat, and sodium then went into the room to settle down. She took her shower, then came back with her weave detached from her head.

Nothing was surprising me anymore, though.

We settled in bed and I purposely played sleep until my

play became the real deal.

The next morning, I heard loud claps coming from the living room.

"I swear to GOD!!" *clap* "If a bitch," *clap* "ever fuck my baby daddy," *clap* "while my kid's in da house, she gon' have to see ME!!!" *clap*

I walked out into the living room to check on the ruckus. "You all right in here?"

She looked pissed and then disarmed upon eye contact, "My bad. Yeah, I'm a'ight. I had to come watch my stories this morning and these ho's just be making me so mad. Oh em geee!!"

I didn't know soap operas aired on the weekend so I stepped over to the couch to see what she was watching.

Should've known. Maury.

On this episode, best friends were confessing to sleeping with their friend's boyfriends and getting pregnant. Nothing new.

I needed to get her out of the house, and quick.

A faint smell had hit me when I walked over to the couch. I looked over to the kitchen and didn't see anything on the stove although it smelled like it.

"You cooking somethin'?"

"Oh nah, that's just my hair."

"I don't see nothing in your hair," I said, examining her scalp.

"No, my other hair. It's in the oven. When it's real dry, it curl better, long as you moisturize it right after. My suh-stah do hair and taught me dat a long time ago."

"Wait, you have hair in my oven?!" I ran over to the oven,

yanked it open, and smoke billowed out filled with Dax hair grease and cocoa butter.

"Whet?! You act like you got a better way to do it."

"That's a damn fire hazard, Daneisha. I mean JuJu. I mean whatever your name is."

She sucked her teeth, "First off, it's Daneisha-Shantell. If you gon' say it, say it right. Second off, you doin' too much. It's...jest...hair." She rolled her neck as she stressed the last three words then rolled her eyes to top it all off.

I'd had enough.

"Maybe it's time we go ahead and wrap this up," I said walking to the room.

She had already overstayed her welcome before she even got there but I tried. I really did.

We got in the car so I could drop her off, pretending to ignore her as she called her friend to open up the door on the way back to her house. I think it was her house. Actually, I didn't even care. I just wanted her gone.

Maybe I was getting to be a little high-maintenance. Maybe I was just irritable from all the stress I'd had lately. Or maybe something new just wasn't for me.

Maybe I needed that old thing back.

Yo Ho Don't Want You No Mo'

"Okay, Momma, you ready?"

"Yes, son. You starting to worry me. Go on, now. Say it."

"I GOT THE JOB!" I yelled into the phone at the top of my lungs.

I was standing on the balcony of my apartment in my boxers after waking up to an email from the recruiter I'd interviewed with a few weeks prior. I guess I did enough to impress him after all.

"Boy, stop yelling in my ear. I'm already old. You want this to be my last announcement I ever get, huh?" she said jokingly.

"Momma, you're not old. Fifty-something-year-olds run marathons and having babies these days."

"Well this fifty-something-year old ain't running and my baby days are over till you and that nice girl of yours give me some grandbabies. How is she doin' anyway?"

Momma met Danielle at a few of my football games. Just my luck, they hit it off well. Really well. And she hadn't let go of their connection any more than I had.

"Come on, Momma. Why you gotta bring her up right now? I just told you I got a job offer. They paying me 70k starting out, benefits, free company car and gas card, the whole nine. You talking about grandbabies?"

"Well, you're the one who brought it up, I'm just sayin'.

But that's good, Bud. God is really smiling on you. Graduation coming up and you already got yaself a job. That's real good, I'm proud. Never doubted you for one second."

"Thank you. That's all I needed to hear."

"Now the real question is, did you thank God?"

I quickly said a quick thank you in my head to God.

"Yes, ma'am. I sure did."

"Good. It don't matter what happen. Don't you ever forget who it is that's really helping you through. You're not in control of all this."

"I got it, Momma, and I agree. So, how's things down there in good ole' Enterprise? I wanna come home to visit soon. Just gotta get through these finals."

"Yeah, you know, ain't a whole lot going on this way. Letting these collards soak in the sink right now. I suppose I can cook me some with a lil' tilapia later this evening."

I felt my stomach cry out for her cooking through rumbling and tears unseen. Ain't nothing like my momma's home cooking.

"That sounds too good right about now. I would be treating myself out but I'm still trying to budget so I'm stuck on this cafe food. Matter of fact, I'm about to head over there now. They stop serving breakfast at nine so I'mma have to call you back later on when--"

"Before you go," she interrupted, "promise me one thing."

"Yes, ma'am? What is it?"

"Promise me you gon' pray a real prayer and thank the Lord. I know you ain't think twice about thanking him before I said somethin' so you need to get to praying as soon as we get off this phone. You act ungrateful, and he can take them blessings as easy as he gave 'em to you."

"Got it. Will do."

"All right. I'll talk to you later, baby. You be safe, ya hear?"

"Yes ma'am. Love you."

"Love you too."

It seemed like over the years, Momma had gotten a lot more spiritual than she used to be. That wasn't a bad thing, but it definitely had shown up in our conversations.

I still had my hang-ups about religion. These days, it was hard to know what to believe or who was in control, and if they were in control, why they let so many bad things happen.

Every other story was about another preacher doing something wild and if we're supposed to be following their lead then where would that land us?

Not having a definite answer to that question kept me away from the church but never separated me from my personal relationship with God. That was one thing nobody could take from me no matter how much I sinned or how many of his ways I didn't understand. If he was mad at me for that, he had a funny way of showing it.

As I promised, I took about ten minutes and had my heart to heart with the Lord. It was genuine and passionate. I started reflecting on everything I'd been through, all the people I'd lost and what I was supposed to learn from it.

Jazmin taught me a lot about the side effects of both loyalty and lies. Danielle taught me about how good girls have their limits just like anyone else. No matter how strong their love is, eventually it'll run out if it's not returned in the same amount.

Ronnie taught me about forcing friendships and how that was never a good idea. Speaking of Ronnie, I wondered how his dad situation went. That made me think of my dad. I didn't know what I was supposed to learn from losing him. But I guess I couldn't learn if I never talked to him. With me finishing school, that might be something worth digging into. Tracking him down, getting real answers. Deciding whether it was closure or a rebuilding of our relationship that was next.

Lunch time came around and I was back headed to the cafe again, still floating on the good news I'd gotten from what would be my new job post-graduation. But the one person I wanted to share it with most besides my mom wasn't even speaking to me.

As time went on, it sure seemed like Danielle was as done as she said she would be. Didn't know how to accept that or if I wanted to.

I walked in the cafe and got my plate. The guy I'd been seeing Danielle with just so happened to walk in, then came and sat one table behind me, him and another group of guys with a seat saved on his left.

I got nervous. How awkward it was going to be if Danielle was coming to meet him there, to have lunch with him. With me, right there and exposed to whatever conversation they'd be having. His face looked so damn familiar, but I just couldn't put my finger on it.

I was in a good mood and had been keeping myself composed rather well. I didn't need this to come wrecking it, so I tried to hurry and finish my food, damn near choking in the process.

Five minutes later, I was chewing my last mouthful and getting up to go dump my plate, but the moment I turned my head, I saw the very person I least expected.

Lewis.

He stopped short a few feet, cautiously. That was until his other homeboys stood up when they noticed the temperament of the situation.

"You again," he mumbled.

"Look, I'm not here for no trouble. Was just leaving matter of fact."

The guy behind me that Danielle had been with turned around to look. Right then it hit me.

That was the same guy I'd seen before standing on the side of the building with Lewis when we got in the fight. He was Lewis' homeboy. That's where I knew him from.

He spoke up, "Nah, he ain't gon' do nothin' now. Ain't got nobody to protect no more."

Lewis chimed in, "Oh, yeah. That's right. You was doing all that fighting tryna be super-save-a-ho while he was out here fuckin' yo bitch."

The whole table of friends starting laughing, including his homeboy. I was more alert for action than I was actually entertaining his comments. A part of me felt embarrassed because with how things played out, it could be true. But again, it was no time to decide that.

"Bruh, just let it go. Yo ho don't want you no mo'. She mine and soon enough she'll be somebody else's," his homeboy said.

"Like I said, I'm not here for no trouble." My temperature was rising. If I swung, I wanted to hit Lewis' homeboy first, then Lewis. I could take them both for sure. Not sure about what'd happen when the others jumped in.

Neither his tone nor his stance leaned toward civil. "Yeah, you not here for trouble, a'ight. But I don't think we finished that little talk we had before. I might have a few words to say."

"Well, don't bite your tongue. Say what's on your mind," I said out of reflex, stepping toward him. His boys all moved as I did like they were actually ready to jump in this time.

"What's going on here?" a voice said behind Lewis.

Everyone looked around and saw Danielle standing behind him, looking confused.

"Shawn?" she asked.

I answered, "Danielle," sobering out of my anger, but only temporarily.

Lewis' homeboy flashed a proprietary smile, "Hey, babe, ain't nothing wrong. We just was talking."

"Nah, we wasn't just talking," Lewis puffed out. "We was about to settle a lil' score from the last time we threw hands. That's what was about to happen."

"Shawn, you're fighting now?"

"It was a while back, Danielle. I'm not tryna fight, I'm just tryna leave."

"Lewis, let him out. Y'all need to stop acting all crazy." she said sternly.

Lewis let off a slight grin as he turned sideways to allow me walking room out from between the tables.

The rest of the cafe was staring, watching the show.

I eased out, fully alert for what could be Lewis' next move. He tried to scare me when I got close enough and yelled,

"Boo!"

I seized the opportunity and grabbed him in a choke hold. His knees buckled, but I kept him from falling with his neck wedged within the fold of my arm.

His boys came forward and I gripped tighter until Lewis put his hands up for them to stop.

"Y'all, I said cut it out!" Danielle barked.

I waited a few seconds then let him go. He yanked away, rubbing his neck.

I looked back at Danielle. Somewhere in those eyes was the girl I'd fallen in love with. Being that close again just reawakened my desire even with the current situation on scratching at that fresh wound of her leaving me.

I went ahead and walked out of the cafe, glad to be making it out of there without getting in any real trouble, but pissed at the fact I was once getting the short hand of the stick.

I got home and did pushups till I dropped, losing count after about 400.

All of the ways I wanted to cause severe bodily harm to both Lewis and his homeboy.

It wasn't like me to be so violent. So I thought. But when you're in love, you don't have the same control you used to. People lose their minds amidst heartbreaks all the time. I think that's what was happening to me. My ego had been involved in the breaking and that never helped.

After about an hour of push-ups and too-loud music, my body dripping sweat and my arms limp from the workout, I flopped against the wall and slid down to the floor to gather my thoughts.

My next move was going to have to be drastic, one way or the other.

Either get things off my chest, starting with kicking Lewis' and his boy's ass. Or find a way to get Danielle to listen to me one last time. If I could just get her to listen, despite the result, I think I could have some kind of closure.

Closure or handing out ass whoopings. Handing out ass whoopings or closure.

Momma's voice rang in my head, *"Maybe you should ask God."*

Her voice was right. So I did. I sat and prayed myself to sleep but not before getting my answer.

God would never tell somebody to hand out an ass whooping so that confirmed it for me; I needed to try one more time at getting that closure. It was either all or nothing.

I Hope He Buys You Flowers

I woke up from my slumber and forced myself into the shower to rinse some of my filth off. I'd only been to asleep a few hours, a decent nap in the middle of the day that'd certainly keep me up later that night.

When I logged on to Facebook, I saw that Danielle had blocked me from everything. She only did that when she was really pissed. I should've known I'd end up being the bad guy.

Her new little boyfriend really had gotten in my head.

I started getting curious if he was just talking or if he and Danielle really had sex. She wasn't that type of girl. At least not with me.

I chose to trust our experience over the words of some dude I really didn't know, but if given the chance, I know I'd ask.

But he did call her "Babe". And she didn't stop him either. That meant something. It had to. And that sucked if it did.

When a guy moves on from a girl, it's only physically and most times temporarily. But when a girl moves on, she takes her heart and soul with her. She's the full package when she's in love and out of it. That's why brothers are always the ones to run back after our little physical vacation is over with and we still want a home to come to.

After I got out of the shower, I opened up my laptop to try and distract myself for a while. At the top of my Face-

book newsfeed was a life quote, as usual, but this one read:
***"If you love something, let it go. If it never comes back,
then it was never yours to begin with."***

I sat against the headboard of my bed, analyzing it over
and over again in my head. What if you don't let it go, but
instead you push it away? Does it still have the obligation of
coming back or does it then become your responsibility to
go get it?

Of course, the person who posted it didn't have the answer, but with a little digging I went on a search to see what
the experts had to say.

Relationship gurus were all the new rage. Steve Harvey had
opened the door, and right behind him came your every-day
unemployed opportunist knocking the wall down with some
recycled lines from *The Notebook* and a pretty profile picture.
I loved good words, but I was always weary of those types.

I clicked around on YouTube sifting through them for
about an hour. The "A real man_____" (fill in the
blank with something women would love to hear)-type gurus made up the majority. Then there were the "I know this
isn't in the Bible, but God told me to tell you_____" (fill
in the blank with something God never said) types. I'm sure
some of them were legit, but it's hard to take anyone serious
when they all sound the same.

After a little exhaustion and a lot of disappointment, I
decided to give it one more try and refine my search from
Relationship Advice to Relationship Advice for Men. After scrolling to the very bottom, past all of the previously
viewed videos, there was a video titled, "Stop Being a Lil'

Bitch and Get Yo Gal Back 101".

I had to click it.

He started off the video with, "Relationship issues are like cockroaches. You may not see 'em, but they gon' follow you everywhere you go if you ignore 'em."

From then on I was hooked. Finally, somebody who wasn't regurgitating the same ole same.

He wasn't in a suit and tie like the others, and he didn't have a freshly trimmed goatee nor any book tours he was promoting. He was a regular guy, mid to late thirties with a few tats that suggested he may or may not have been to prison before. Well...that and the du-rag, khakis(no belt), and a cigarette hanging on for dear life off of his bottom lip all suggested that actually. His teeth were a little crooked, even the ones with the gold caps, but other than that, he seemed fine. Definitely didn't come off as some politically correct puppet of marketability, so it was a breath of fresh air.

"If you wanna get yo gal back, this is how you do it, homie. I'mma tell you straight up so you ain't out here mo-pin' 'round in Starbucks, looking like somebody done kill't yo pet catfish and wipin yo punk ass tears with the pages of some relationship book full of Marilyn Monroe's life advice. This that real, homie."

Of course, I turned up the volume. I knew whatever he was going to suggest had to be good.

"First thang you got to do, is send her a picture of that weed-whacka and I ain't talmbout the murda weapon, um..I mean ain't talmbout the gardenin' tool.

"Now you might be saying to yoself, 'Right, that way she can remember what she had, get horny, and come knockin' on my door by sun up' but you'd be mistaken, lil' homie. If you was doin' it right the first time, she wouldn't have forgotten yo hard-to-remember sex-having ass as it is.

"Nah, you sendin' a flick of that sausage roll in hopes of her new man seein' it.

"Now, hol' up, wait, I know what you thankin'. But this ain't on no fruity loops shit, mane. I ain't hatin' though, if boys is yo choice of toys, do yo thang. But this video is for lovin' up on these gals, you can turn to *Lifetime* for all that other riff-raff."

This guy was like a ghetto Confucius. I could see him being the appointed counselor for his cell mates in prison, everyone pulling up their buckets to sit and listen to his hood-inspirational-isms.

"But like I was sayin', you need to spark that insecurity in her new man, because surely she got herself one. Just cuz you stopped hittin' it don't mean she stopped gettin' hit.

"You gotta get that new man to start questionin' his manhood. Bring out some of them insecurities. From that insecurity gon' come the arguin', the pointin' fingers, and what-not, then BAM! You roll up on eem one day, make sure that chest hair coming up out the top of dat button-up real strong like Richard Pryor used to have it, get you some of that *BOD* spray from the dollar store so you can smell good, or you can just do what I do and mix up a teaspoon of gasoline and a cup of Listerine with a touch of lemon 'cause that makes for a manly fragrance as well; then swoop in and let her know that her new man's a square. Tell her she need 'em out her circle so y'all can get back right and get it in from every angle, feel me?

"Do it just like that, I promise you it's gon' work like a charm."

Yeah, he was definitely cut from a different cloth, all right. His theme music was NWA's *Straight Out of Compton* and just before the video went off, he gave one last disclaimer.

"For all you little trick-or-treat-sized, premature baby dick-havin' ass suckas out there, you need to Photoshop the dick from a real nigga and put it on yours or don't send the pic at all. Her new man see yo lil' Gerber dick, he gone get even mo' confidence and then he gon' American Pie yo gal betta than befo'. They'll be married within a week. Don't say I ain't warn you, homie. God bless."

Interesting.

I don't think his videos were to be taken literally, but they always say to every joke, there's a silver lining of truth.

I began to wonder if sending her a naked picture actually would help. Maybe it was risqué but women liked risqué. Taking chances was sexy and everyone loved sexy.

I headed to the bathroom to assess my lighting. A professional picture from my Nikon would be too much, but a camera phone pic would come from the heart. A lot more genuine.

I tidied up around the sink and cleaned the mirror because everyone knows there's nothing worse than a good-looking person in a struggling bathroom.

Once it was clean, and I'd gotten Optimus full of steam and ready to pose, I took a couple shots then graded myself.

First one was blurry and the second one looked forced. Plus, it sorta looked liked I didn't work my legs because of the angle so I stood on the tub and tried again.

This set was a little better with the exception of my knees now showing just how ashy they were. I ran into the room, fully erect, and threw on some lotion and then I tried again.

Along the way, I realized just how ridiculous I looked trying to use nudes to get back with Danielle. I could never be physically appealing enough to win back a woman I lost with emotional mishandling. The hell was I thinking?

I went through and deleted my little mini-porn star reel then hopped in the bed, laptop and lights off.

For the first time, it dawned on me how it was taking all of this thought to try and fix a problem I caused by not thinking at all.

****

"Simple. Lie to her."

"What?"

"Life is too short, bruh. You need to lie."

I looked at Lamarcus like he'd lost his damned mind. I should've known better than to let him into my personal business, but it came out anyway while I was proofreading his fast food job applications. He was transitioning from the street life, and in return for helping him, I charged him a listening ear. Felt like it wasn't too much to ask and besides, my friend-tank was on E. Couldn't fill up at the moment, but this five dollars might hold me till the next stop.

"Did you hear anything I just said? I got in this mess by lying. How in the hell you figure that's a solution?"

"Look, mane, they say the truth will set you free. But if that truth comes after you been lying a long time, it's gon' get you fucked up.

"Watch your mouth."

"My bad. Messed up. Point is, it's time for you to lie. Again."

"Okay, lie," I said, trying to figure out where he was going with this. Appalled at the initial thought but still intrigued at his audacity to believe the words coming out of his own mouth, I wanted to know more. "I'm listening."

He sipped on one of the protein shakes I'd made for us as he interlocked his fingers and looked at me like he was my magistrate. Kid had seen one too many courtrooms in his day. "Okay, maybe you don't have to exactly *lie*. That's such a dirty word. How about...deceive? Trick. Conspire." As if any of those were better. "You gotta be creative. You said ol' boy and her dating now, right? And you need to talk to her, right? But she won't talk to you? Well, I bet you money she'll talk to him."

"So you telling me to ask him to negotiate for me? You're trippin', 'Marcus."

"Nah. I'm sayin' you need to *conspire*...to be him, Use ya head, Shawn. Write her a note, but don't tell her it's from you. You know what I'm sayin'? What's that word for it, like it's ano-mano--"

"Anonymous."

"Yeah, anonymous. Write the note, act like it's from him and then when she goes to talk to him, you show up."

"What happens when she sees me?"

"You think she still loves you?"

"Of course she does."

"She'll stay. Long as you 'on't say no stupid shit, she'll stay."

"Watch ya mouth," I threw out. I was trying to get him to stop cursing so he could at least get through his job interview without doing it.

He cleared his throat, "My bad. Stupid things. But put it like this; just say you got two cocaine bricks on you, all white and sealed tight, but you can't do nun wit' em till you go to the plug and check in first." He was good for a drug dealing analogy to make his points, but since it was all he knew, I tolerated it. "Now you know why you going to see the plug, right? Because if you don't, the plug gon' feel disrespected and kill you. Danielle, she's the plug and if you don't find a way to talk to her, that's gon' kill you and y'all relationship as far as she concerned.

"But since you have two all-white bricks, or in your case, a heart of gold and intentions on making thangs right, it's on you to find a way to go see her. Don't matter what you do to see her. Once she see dem all-white bricks, she gon' be willing to listen. That don't mean she gon' let you sell it on her block, but it's 'bout the only chance you got to make it out of that alive. Either that, or get up out the country and make sure she never see you again. That's on you."

I didn't want to admit it, but the young brother was starting to make sense. And the last time he came up with a plan, it saved both our asses from what would've been nasty legal troubles. So maybe he was on to something.

So I said, "My bricks. If she sees the bricks, but tells me to go sell my bricks on somebody else's block because she's done with my sorry ass bricks, then what?"

"It's my guess that if you honestly could see yo-self sellin' on somebody else's block, you would've been there by now

158

getting money, climbing up the ranks to be that new kingpin. But seein' as how you not, look to me like you need to either try to convince her to let you back in her hood or get out the dope game altogether, ya dig?"

He basically was telling me to go back, try again, and if it didn't work then quit. It was all eloquently laid out in street logic.

He continued, "Or you can sit there and let these other hustlas run her block while you over here contemplatin' and what-not."

"All right, all right," I interrupted the thoughts while he calmly kept sipping on his drink. "I'll try it. If this backfires, you're going right back to waiting on the bus. Deal?"

"Deal. Just know, the clock is ticking. Don't wait too long to do what you feel, might not get another chance. But anyway, you gotta belt I can borrow?"

"Yeah, I do. Since when you started wearing belts?" I asked, getting up from the table.

"Since my wardrobe came wit' a death sentence."

I stopped walking and turned around. He had a look of uneasiness in his eyes.

"What you mean by that, Lamarcus?"

His heart seemed heavy, and his voice, wounded. "Exactly what I said. My teacher said if I don't stop looking I'mma get killed. Said ain't no protection for dudes like me. Law only apply to us when it's to lock us up or justify killin' us."

"It's not what you look like that's the problem," I said. "It's what people see when they look at you. A belt can't fix that."

"Yeah, you say that as yo shirt is neatly tucked in."

"My shirt is tucked in because I'm comfortable this way and I think sagging is tacky, but it's not a measure of character. If the other boys at your school can wear gothic trench coats, black lipstick, and spiked Mohawks, then what you wear shouldn't be a problem so long as you're not exposing private parts."

"Nah, I ain't doin' none of that. But I ain't stupid. We come out the womb violating America's dress code. Ain't never seen no flicks of Martin Luther King with his shirt untucked and they capped him so it probably won't even make no difference." he said, shaking his head.

I went into my room to fetch a spare belt and gave it to him, anyway. That conversation was going to be a bit too much to unpack in one sitting.

After dropping him off at school, I got back home and went to draw up the letter he'd suggested. I started off a few times, but didn't get very far.

~~Dear, Danielle,~~

~~Hey what's good,~~

~~Yo Danielle,~~

~~To: Danielle, From: Me~~

My luck, I didn't know anything about her boyfriend other than him being Lewis' friend to effectively impersonate him. Not sure if I wanted to impersonate him at all.

So I didn't. I hadn't written her any letters outside of my short stories and poetry because we'd communicated otherwise, so hopefully it wouldn't be too obvious. I just needed to keep it short and simple; the rest would be on her.

Danielle,

Sorry about the little misunderstanding in the cafeteria the other day. Just got caught up in the moment and didn't like the idea of somebody disrespecting you so I lost my temper. Regardless, that ain't how your man should be conducting himself so let me make that up to you. Meet me at the same location you find this letter. Tonight at 8 o'clock. I got something special for you.

Sincerely

—Me.

P.S. Don't bring it up until then because I'll act like I don't know what you're talking about and cancel the surprise altogether. ;)

Inconspicuous enough. And technically, I didn't even lie.

I drove around campus looking for her car. It wasn't hard to spot, no one else on campus had anything even close. Electric blue 2000 Subaru that her uncle had passed down to her when she graduated high school. It looked like one of those cars on Fast & Furious with the work under the hood to match.

I found it, sitting in one of the business building parking lots close to the rear. Her parking spots didn't change much because she always tried to get far away from other cars so nobody else could scratch hers.

I went and slipped the note under her windshield wiper as quickly as I could then got back into my car. I felt like a mad man. Like a damned stalker. But like Lamarcus said, one more drop, and I was going to be out of the game for good.

One way or the other.

After leaving, I thought back to myself about what'd happen if someone else got the note. What if she got it and still mentioned it to her boyfriend? Would he tell her it wasn't from him and then they both narrow it down to me?

I kept driving, went home, and flopped on the bed. Pulled out my blue Superman watch from the drawer, put in a new battery, and watched the minutes go by. This was going to be one hell of a day.

****

I strolled over about an hour early. Her car was gone. She had to have gotten it.

I thought back to what Momma always told me, *"If you're going to pray, then don't worry. If you're going to worry, then don't pray."*

I'd been praying more lately. Not for things, but just for peace, a place to go when I didn't have it all in control. I'd prayed many times over my relationship with Danielle, and if there was ever a time that things weren't in my control, it was then. I squeezed my eyes, tried to block thoughts of her bringing my letter to me as a bag of confetti, burning it to a crisp with her friends watching and recording for social media laughs, or worse, her just not showing up at all.

Seven-fifty five rolled around. I was sitting outside in another parking lot across from the location I'd told her to meet me at.

I was losing my fight to not worry and already prepping myself to handle the worst. Hoped that seeing it mentally would help lessen the sting when it actually happened. The lights that illuminated the parking lot rained down memories of Danielle and me the last time we met in a parking lot, when we were on the very cusp of *us* again, dancing like no one else existed and embracing each other. Letting go of all the strength we'd used to stay away from one another. Being vulnerable. Letting love live again. What a feeling.

I reached to roll my windows down for a little air and heard her muffler coming up the road behind me. I ducked in the car so I wasn't visible.

Once I heard her engine go off, I popped back up and looked. She didn't get out at first. I was too far away to see if she'd come alone or had someone with her so I gave her a few minutes, hoping she'd get out of the car and show her face.

She did. Letter in hand, and resting against the hood.

She was beautiful, even from a distance. Her ponytail was pulled back into a poof once again, the kind you spray water on to help get the strands on the side to lay down a little better. Her tank top and blue jean pants told me she had been busy all day, but made time to see what the surprise was about.

I got out of the car and walked from where I was. My heart pounding. I was digging deep for the confidence a man was supposed to have under any circumstance. Deep breaths. Controlled exhales.

Just wasn't working this time.

She looked my way last minute, her expression unchanged when she saw me.

"What's up, Danielle?"

"So it *was* you, huh?" she said, folding her arms.

I looked down at the ground then back at her, "Yeah. Sorry to disappoint."

"Figured. Seemed like your speed. Just saying you wanted to talk would've been too normal. Had to be a surprise."

We both let off a slight chuckle, easing the tension.

"Would you have come?"

She looked away for a moment, "I don't know. Guess it depends. Wasn't quite sure I was going to come tonight. Was running some errands and figured why not?" she said

That casual. Like it was no big deal. But I saw through her mask. She never did anything unless it mattered.

"Cool, well, I'm glad you did. Just kinda seems weird, ya know?"

"What seems weird?"

"This," I said, motioning to the space between us. "Me. You. We're not this. We may not be what we were, but I know for a fact we're not this. Not after everything we've been through. And I'm tired of pretending I'm something I'm not."

"Well, maybe you're not who you thought you were."

That stung. "Okay, I guess I walked into that one."

"I'm not tryna kick you while you're down, Shawn. I don't even like that you're down. Maybe you and I were supposed to be something else and everything that happened was just another step closer to that."

"I don't want to be closer to that; I want to be closer to you, Danielle."

"Shawn, please," she said, rolling her eyes. Pain was seeping through her body language. Pain she had already buried that I was exhuming.

164

"I'm serious. I wouldn't be here if I wasn't." She looked unconvinced. "Look at me and tell me you don't love me."

She hesitated, then parted her lips to speak before exhaling as if the words wouldn't come out.

I responded, "Exactly."

"But you know what they say. Love will get you killed." She smiled.

"We all gotta die sometime," I threw back.

"You been watching them movies again? I feel like that's some Scarface type of stuff you just pulled on me."

"But it was smooth, though, wasn't it?"

She laughed again, her body language less crude, "Yeah, whatever. I see you ain't changed too much." She looked down at my socks.

Both of them were white tube socks but from different companies so the ribs were different. It was one of her pet peeves when we lived together so she used to put them in separate drawers to try and break me of the habit.

"Well, one thing that hasn't changed is the fact that I miss you."

"Shawn--" she said, looking at me disappointedly that I was still steering the conversation that route.

"Look, being dishonest is where I went wrong before. I won't make that same mistake now. Let me be honest with you. I'm--"

"Shawn--"

"Please, let me finish. Please?" I asked.

She pursed her lips in silence, allowing me to continue.

"I'm not here to waste your time. I've done enough of that. I just want to put this in proper perspective.

"We're still young. We started this thing when we were really young, only teenagers. We were in love but neither of us knew what we were doing. We just knew we needed to make it work and to make anything work, you have to learn how it works. Some of the things we learned together hurt, but we learned them. Just like those couples who last together for decades and get to see their grandkids have kids. That's what they did to make it that far. They learned and used what they learned to make it work."

She looked at me, tears forming in her eyes, inviting my own. The part of her that believed in me before, it was alive. It was still believing in me.

"Your trust, I broke it," I continued, "and that was wrong of me. But if there's even an ounce left, I promise and will prove to you that I can take that ounce, protect, and build it again. Stronger than it was before. I was careless, but I was never out to do you wrong. Every year we've invested into each other has to count for something. I'm not expecting for this to be easy, just tell me it's possible. Just tell me that enough of you is willing to fight for us and I will fight with you."

"Shawn," she mumbled.

"I'll fight for our family. I just got a good job so I'll be able to provide for us and our future children and we can get--"

"Shawn," she said, louder this time. Her tears had flown down her deep cinnamon brown cheeks dropping onto her tank. "This is probably the last conversation we'll ever have."

I thought my ears had deceived me. "Say what?"

"I've been dating someone else, and quite frankly, he treats me like a queen. I'm finally happy and I think I deserve

166

that." she forced out, looking at the ground with uncertainty.

"*Finally* happy? Um...wow."

"I came here to tell you that, I just got side tracked, but it's best I go ahead and stop you while you're ahead and let you know. I didn't want to...." her words drowned out in the noise of hearing my heart fall to its knees. It went to the twelfth round, and it lost by a knockout.

I stood there, possibly looking like I was listening. I'm not sure.

Her previous statement was still sinking in. Or rather, melting through. It burned like the fire it was meant to be, and I couldn't do anything but stay there and take it.

Whatever she was saying to try and provide some explanation had come to a pause, and that's when I said, "I understand. That's cool. I'm happy for you."

And then I watched my baby, my dream girl, walk away and take my dreams with her.

To Be My Sunshine After the Rain

I skipped breakfast the next morning and went to the weight room instead. Had a final exam to take later on that day, but if I didn't purge the energy I was using to over-think, I likely wouldn't even be able to finish.

The clinging and ringing all came from the weights at first, then next it was my throbbing headache. Lifting heavy on an empty stomach is never a good idea, but that 400 pounds I was pushing off my chest felt like a feather compared to the weight that was really on it. I just didn't want to dwell on what happened the night before with Danielle. Even though a piece of me expected the outcome, the rest of me still needed to find a way to get my mind off of it.

I texted Lamarcus. Figured I'd spare him the results of my attempt at implementing his theory and instead just inquired about how his application submittals had been going. Hope-fully put some good news back in my life.

I'd given him all the tools to win. Taught him how to get through a paragraph without cursing, gave him a belt, and I even gave him a shirt a few X's smaller than the 4XLs he'd been wearing. So long as he tucked it in, smiled, and didn't go in there making drug analogies to explain his availability to work, he should've been fine.

Then I realized, it was school hours; probably wasn't go-ing to text back anytime soon. Might as well just go by the cafe, grab an early lunch, and see if Auntie could tell me how it'd been going.

Just my luck, she wasn't there. But Chantel was.

She made eye contact long enough to roll her eyes and continued talking to her girls I'd seen with her in the club the other night. I was relieved by her attitude; meant she wasn't going to come and bother me.

Ronnie and his frat brothers were doing their strolls, or what us outsiders would identify with as line dances. The more I watched them, the more I realized how unlike me it would've been to join.

I'm too much of a loner. I only trust a few people, and for those I don't, I'm horrible at pretending I do. I can't smile and shake hands with someone that doesn't really have my back, and I damn sure can't call them my brother. While I'm sure they aren't all the same, I wonder why those who were legit never spoke up about the flakes among them. But either way, that was no longer my battle.

Midway through the day, I still hadn't gotten a text back from Lamarcus. I called once and got his voicemail, which he'd also changed to be a little more professional. It was no longer, "Ay, I ain't here." *Beep.* Now it was the standard, "Sorry I can't get to my phone," spiel. A little more appropriate for hiring managers to call back to. That change didn't come from me; he did it on his own. The boy was making progress.

I swung by Auntie's place to try and get a hold of him. Cars were lined up down the street, people in their yard talking to one another and very cognizant of whoever drove by. As is normal in most black neighborhoods. Figured it was a barbeque, but I didn't smell any grills going when I pulled up.

I found an empty space to park about a block down, and walked back up to the house. An older guy met me by the mail box with salt-and-peppered gray hair and an off-white linen short set.

He asked, "Who are you?"

I looked at him for a moment, ready to disrespect him for his rude greeting. I decided not to in case he was related to Auntie somehow. "Shawn," I said, reaching out my hand.

He left my hand hanging. "And who is Shawn?"

"Umm...Lamarcus' friend. Just stoppin' by to see if he was available. Sir, I'm sorry but I didn't catch your name?"

His face lit up with anger the moment I asked, "You son of a bitch."

"What?!" I said, preparing myself for a confrontation. It seemed like I couldn't avoid them these days.

He shuffled around some spare change in his pocket for a few seconds then pulled out a blade, "If you know what's good for you, you'd gon' get yo-self from 'round here. Young punk."

He waved the knife around as he talked and when I didn't move he came closer to me.

I gritted my teeth, trying to decide if I'd hit him or begin backing up. I had too much respect for Auntie's home to bring drama to it, but at the same time, backing down was never my style either. If he had respectfully asked me to leave, fine. But this complete stranger had crossed the line. Not me.

"Hey!" a voice rang out from the house. A slim brother about my age came running through the yard. "Pops, what's going on? What's the problem?"

"One of Marc-Marc's little *homies* came to visit," he said cynically.

The younger guy looked at me, scanned me up and down and said, "What's ya name, man?"

"Shawn. But I didn't come here for any trouble. Just tell Lamarcus I came--"

"Oh, Shawn? You go to the university right?"

"Yeah, that's me."

He looked back at the older man who still had his blade out and by his side. "Come on, Dad, it's all good. Let me handle this. Go on back inside and wait for me in there."

Grudgingly, the man walked away, eyeing me one last time before folding his knife back into his pocket.

"Sorry about that, bruh. My name's Xavier. I'm Lamarcus' cousin. My dad is just on edge right now 'cause Grandma's so upset." He reached out his hand to shake mine.

I did and asked, "What's the matter with her?"

"Oh, you don't know?"

"Know what?"

He looked back at the house then back at me, lowering his tone, "Marc-Marc got killed this morning."

"Wait. What?!"

Everyone in the yard looked at us. Xavier looked uncomfortable.

"Yeah, man. It happened after he got off the school bus. They stabbed and shot him."

My heart bled out a little as I fought back tears. *Why didn't he just call me?* was my first irrational thought.

"They, who?"

172

"Well, we don't know for sure, but the police say the way he was killed was supposed to be a message. Some gang type of stuff they do when one of 'em leaves the others hanging. Like a punishment for traitors, which is basically anybody that wants out. Grandma told me he was finally comin' around. That you'd been helping him out and everything. But with his ties to the gang...you know."

My knees felt weak, and I got short of breath. I continued to war with my watering eyes, trying to deny the inevitable guilt that this was my fault. I had no idea it was that serious.

He saw my face and rested a hand on my shoulder in comfort, "I know, man. Everybody's real broken up about it. We from Mississippi but Dad was telling me about how he was doing his thing now. I just wish his momma could've seen what he was doing with his life first."

I forced out, "Where is she?"

"Aunt Jenna still ain't came. Probably don't know her son is dead either. But her phone off so chances are, she's out in these streets somewhere. Dad and her ain't talked in years. He tried to get her to go to rehab a while back, but she wouldn't have it. So they lost touch."

"I'm sorry man, I didn't know. I just...I'm sorry. I'm so sorry." My voice was cracking with the news still setting in on me.

"Don't be, man. It's not your fault. If it wasn't for you, he wouldn't have had a chance at all. Hopefully we find out who did it, and that'll at least bring some kind of peace. Right now, everybody just tryna be strong for Grandma. You can come inside and speak if you want."

"Nah, I'll let y'all have y'all time together as a family.

I'mma go ahead and get going. Thanks for letting me know, though," I said, rushing off.

I wanted to see Auntie, but I couldn't imagine what I'd say. Or if I was in any shape to say it.

Once my car door was shut, I balled like a baby. I had been holding it together long enough, but I needed a moment to completely break down. I wanted my momma near me, somebody who could help me and convince me everything would be okay.

He was so young and had just begun seeing the potential in himself I'd seen in him since we'd met. But that potential was gone. Rather, it was murdered.

****

Two weeks had passed, and I passed every day without smiling once, even for my graduation.

The depression I'd fought months before had come back, but I'd committed to getting through it this time. Determined that after all of my hard work, I'd know the feeling of being a college graduate.

But memories of Lamarcus still had me shook. I had gone to his funeral service, sitting at the back so as not to be noticed and left early as well. It was too much to bear knowing he was in that casket while I listened to the family speak of his childhood stories.

How he used to make such good grades in elementary school and was a momma's boy. Just like me. While no one actually said it, it seemed that all that stopped when his mother left. I could only imagine what that felt like, but I thought it selfish of me to let my emotions show in front of those who knew and loved him most.

But now that it was finally my big day, I needed to get my facial hair and apartment together. They were both a mess, and if Momma saw it like that she'd have a fit. Every time we saw each other she did a quick scan for any signs of neglect.

"And why has this robe not been ironed?" she said, marching through the door, barely even making eye contact with me.

"Momma, it's not supposed to be ironed. Ain't nobody else ironing theirs."

"I thought I taught you better than that, but I guess not. You tryna walk 'cross that stage looking like a tall bag of chitterlin's. I don't think so. Take it off, right now," she ordered.

So of course, I did. She went into my room, and plugged up the iron. Then I saw her snatch off my bed sheet, put it on top of the graduation gown for protection, and ironed every wrinkle and fold from it.

She came back ready to help me get my arms through the sleeves before stepping back to look at me again. "You been eating?" she asked, as she poked at my shoulders.

"Yes, ma'am. Not as much because of my finals, but those are over now."

"Look like you done lost a couple pounds, that's all. You shoulda sent me this suit. I could've tried to take in a bit for you."

"It's not even gonna show. I could wear a tank top and swimming trunks underneath, and I'd be just fine."

She smiled, relieved at my humor. "Well, Bud. Before we leave and ya sisters get here, I just need to let you know something."

"What's that?" I got worried. Usually, I'm the last to know anything and she only has something to tell me when it's bad.

"That I'm sorry."

"Sorry?"

"Yes, baby." She took my hand in hers. "I understand, I ain't always been the easiest to deal with. Since the divorce, I had a lot of time to think about what happened the day you left the house. A lot. And it just dawned on me that I never really took time to let you know that I'm proud of you. You make me so proud."

"Thank you, Momma. I mean, I think you've said that at some point or another. You don't have to apologize for anything."

"What I mean is that I look around to some of these boys out here, tryna become men on they own. The same thing you had to do in a lot of ways. And they don't fare well. Not in this world, they don't. I don't know if it's peer pressure, pain, or what, but whatever it is, you didn't let it send you down the same path. God protected you and led you, but I know he can't lead what ain't willing to follow. And I just want to let you know that I'm proud of you, baby."

Tears filled the ducts of her eyes, and while I hated seeing her cry, this was the therapy I needed. I felt a sense of purpose, being validated in the eyes of the woman that meant the world to me.

We embraced for a while, understanding that as much as this was about me, she needed to do that for her own good as well. Women can sometimes get so good at being strong, they forget that they owe it to themselves to be human too.

We released, and in her hand was an envelope. "Here, take this." she said.

I smiled and opened it gently. It was a little thick and heavy to be a card. "Momma, no. I can't." I said handing it back to her.

It was a wad of twenties. I didn't count it but it was probably somewhere around 1500 or so.

"Yes, baby. I want you to have it. I told you I'd get around to paying you back for all that rent you helped me with, and I'm a woman of my word. It's time I make right on that promise to you. It's okay, take it." She pushed it back in to me.

I was about to give it back again, but figured this was something she'd been wanting to do for a while. Humbly, I thanked her, kissed her on the forehead and accepted my gift.

Once we got to the gymnasium, she split to go find my sisters before they took their seats while I went into the back room with the rest of the seniors who were waiting for the processional to begin.

Danielle was in the front laughing with some of her friends. Maybe they were associates. Not really sure. I'd lost track of who she dealt with over the past few months. But her hair was straightened under her cap, her skin glowing, and she seemed to be having a good time.

Everyone else was taking selfies with their best friends, laughing, and reminiscing. Some of the weed heads who slipped through the cracks throughout the years rightfully couldn't believe they'd made it. Hell, I was even surprised at some of them.

A few of my classmates were getting pulled outside in the hallways because they were sadly mistaken about their graduation status. Glad I wasn't them.

As we walked to our seats and the pianist played, families cheered and beckoned for their graduating senior's attention, I scanned the crowd looking for my own clan.

But I might as well have been looking for a needle in a haystack. Way too many people.

I sat down, suffered through the commencement speech about life and everything that was sure to come. After putting us through years of lectures and tens of thousands of dollars in tuition, the polite thing would've been to send the speaker's speech in an email and spend the money it took to book him on a Tupac hologram concert; but that would've been too much to ask, huh?

Finally it was over, and it was time to grab my degree from the president who was about to smile in my face like we were best friends. I was ready to smile right back because I didn't have to grease his palms anymore.

But when I walked off-stage, I noticed Auntie being helped down the bleachers onto the floor by some of my old teammates.

It's not rare for school employees to be at functions like this one, but I didn't expect to see her nor know why she was walking out into the floor because no one was allowed to.

She turned and headed towards me, piercingly looking me in the eye with sadness in hers underlined by a smile. I returned one as we met together and embraced.

Everyone walking behind me seamlessly just went around

us, and even the school security stayed back.

She kissed my cheek as she let go. "Ya done good, baby. Ya done real good."

I reached for her face and wiped the tears from them, "Thank you, Auntie. For everything. I won't forget it."

"Just doing my job."

"And a fine one at that." I hesitated before speaking again, even though I knew what was on both of our minds, but I had to let it out. "He was fortunate to have you in his life. I know he's up there watching me right now."

She gave me an assuring smile. "Yes and he's just as proud of you as I am. Talked about you all the time. I thank the Lawd for putting y'all two together. It was good for 'im."

I thought back to my first conversation with Lamarcus and how his priority, more than anything was taking care of Auntie. How he took on the role as the man of the house, financially securing the both of them. Even though it was illegal, he put survival first, just like anybody else would've done. Just like I would've done.

I unzipped my robe and reached into my suit for the envelope I'd gotten from Momma.

"Take this," I said.

She felt the envelope and recognized what was in it before looking at me again. Her expression was asking me if it was okay, so I nodded in confirmation.

She hugged me again and thought out loud, "Lawd will supply all our needs." It seemed she had been praying for help for her own situation by the relief in her voice. "Thank you, baby. God bless you. Come back to see me sometime, all right?"

I nodded and went on back to my seat.

After everything was over and all of the caps and gowns had been thrown, I caught a glimpse of Danielle staring at me. She seemed to be with her mother. Her hateful ass mother, and a few more cousins I hadn't met.

Her mother never quite bought the idea of me being in Danielle's life, most likely because of the conversations Danielle had with her in our low points. I was never there to hear them, but chances are they went something like, "And Mom, you won't believe what he said," Then out would come only the bad, that was also meant to be private. As usual. And that would form her mother's opinion of me from that point on.

I saw Danielle making her way through the sea of people towards me. Couldn't possibly imagine what she had to say. According to her we'd already had our last conversation.

She just walked up to me but didn't say anything. She looked at me, I looked at her. Then she reached up and hugged me, but only briefly because I didn't hug her back. I left my hands by my side, eyes open, and forward.

She let go, looked at me with a concerned face. "You okay?"

No, I thought.

But I didn't say anything. I didn't nod. I just looked at her, waiting for her to get mad and storm away.

She seemed to have noticed a difference in me, beyond my lack of response to her embrace. She usually could, and it was in her ability that I found comfort. But I wasn't about to fool myself anymore. She was gone. And I needed to be okay with that.

"Danielle, honey. Come here, we have to get some pictures so we can beat the traffic. Come now," her mother called out.

Reluctantly, she walked away, looking back again before getting lost in the mix of everyone. And I haven't seen her since.

PART TWO

Lucky Charm

D r. Holley waited a few seconds, staring at me as I lay back on the couch replaying those moments for her. It seemed like it all had just happened yesterday.

"Wait, is that it?" she asked.

"What do you mean, *is that it*? Yeah, that's it. Basically."

"No, Mr. Fletcher, I mean what else happened? Did you date again? Did you successfully let go this time?"

"Well, I went my way, she went hers. I don't know where she's at now and it doesn't really matter. I got my job in corporate America. Stayed on my poetry and short stories before the publishing agency called me up and we inked the deal for a few books. Now I'm writing full-time, trying to bring my love life up to speed."

"But you didn't answer my question. Did you date again? Did you finally let her go?"

"Had a fling here and there, nothing major. I haven't really figured out how to take anyone serious, including myself. The part of me that loved, I think it's pretty much out of service. That's why I'm here."

"Well, it's not. The things you write about, that comes

from somewhere."

"Memory. I write from memory."

"So you do still remember what it feels like then."

"Yes, I remember. But I'd like to experience it again, not just remember."

"What is it that's stopping you?"

"That's why I've been spending all day on this couch for you to figure out. So with all due respect, can you give me a damn answer already?"

I felt my frustrations flaring and checked myself.

"Fine, Mr. Fletcher. I'll tell you this. Unless you're completely sure, and I mean 100% sure that Danielle is no longer in love with you, you may just have made the biggest mistake of your life."

I paused for a moment, confused. "Did you not hear anything I just said? I did my part. I went back and tried to win her over. I even wrote a note. Prayed, meditated, you name it. None of it worked. It's time for me to move on while I still have a chance. I'm young, decent-looking, and I have my money right. I should be an easy client for you. Just help me get back on the right track, not on the old, rusty, and broken track."

"I heard you say she wasn't quite sure. And I also heard you detail a chemistry and connection like few people ever experience in their lifetimes that led up to that."

"Which is over now. Don't forget, you heard that part too."

"If it was really over, you would've moved on by now. Have you ever considered that maybe, just maybe she's out fighting the same emotional war you are? Trying to force something to stop that was never meant to once it started up?"

"You know what, Jessica? I mean Dr. Holley. I'm done. This session is done. Keep the money. You just wasted my time."

I got up and headed for the door, sliding on my shoes on the way out.

"When you lose something, it's inconvenient for a while, but eventually you get it back or something else that pretty much functions in the same way. But when you lose someone, someone that never wanted to go in the first place nor that you ever planned on letting go, it changes you. It lessens you. It slowly kills you day by day until there's nothing left but memories of every moment you had with them that you never knew would be your last."

Her voice was trembling now, as if she was crying. I stopped short at the door and turned around to see she wasn't looking at me but at the space where the framed picture of her and the guy was on her desk before she snatched it off. The one she'd caught me looking at when I first came in.

"I told him to stay away from me. March 1, 2007. He was only twenty years old."

I walked back towards Jessica, dropping my keys on the way hoping to console her. She was really starting to break down now, and it came out of nowhere.

"He always told me that tomorrow was never promised. But he was wrong. Today isn't even promised. He forgot our second anniversary, and I thought I could punish him by telling him how he didn't deserve me. Telling him to go away."

A cold feeling hit me in the pit of my stomach. That's why she'd gotten so angry when I was snooping around her desk. And that'd also explain why the candles were lit around the photo. "Jessica, I'm sorry. I had no idea when I first saw the picture, I promise," I said.

"But he didn't listen. Even when the storms came. I was in class and he was at work. He got off early to come and keep me safe. But the tornado had touched down earlier than expected and sent a tree on top of his car, with him inside. He died instantly."

"Jessica, I don't know what to say. I apologize for not respecting your privacy earlier. It was inconsiderate and wrong, and I'm sorry."

"No, Mr. Fletcher. I'm telling you that there was once a man who loved me so much, he was willing to give his life to never give up on me. I have to live with that every day."

"I'm not the one who gave up on her, Jessica. She gave up on me."

"No, you're not understanding. Men work differently than women, and historically, that's always been the case. Men keep trying by coming back, women keep trying by never leaving.

So the time you cheated, the times you lied, and the time you made her look like a fool while she never left; that was her not giving up on you. But after a while, you want to make sure someone would be willing to do the same for you. Through thick and thin. Willing to never give up on you. It's human nature to need that reciprocity, especially if your heart only knows two speeds--all or nothing.

So unless you're completely sure beyond a shadow of a

doubt that she's done with you, I strongly advise that you not give up on her. Because the regret of realizing you were the one that let go of a good thing you can't get back...I wouldn't wish that on my worst enemy."

I stood while she sat for a few moments. I really couldn't believe my ears. How anyone in their right minds could possibly think that after everything I'd already done to make amends, the solution was to do more. And honestly, I wasn't all the way sure she was in her right mind. While it'd be understandably so, she sounded like she was speaking from trauma, not just experience.

"Dr. Holley, thanks for caring. I feel like you really put your heart into your work, and for me, that means a lot. You've given me a lot to think about. I can't say for sure what I'm going to do other than that. I'll think about it."

I walked out, she didn't stop me. Her checks were already deposited before the day started anyway so she had no reason to.

I hopped in Daisy Duke and drove back home, texting my assistant Stacy to drop off something for dinner later on when she brought my notes for tomorrow's Women Empowerment Seminar I was headlining. I usually handled both on my own but I'd been looking forward to my meeting with Dr. Holley, I couldn't focus and now that it was over, I still couldn't focus.

Then I remembered that I needed to go stop by Pete's for a minute, get his opinion on things which would cut into the time I would otherwise use to cook, anyway. As much as he tripped me out, something about his theories usually made sense. Even when they didn't, I knew I could count on him to check me when I was tripping.

I pulled up to his house. Well, Shonda's house. Pete was hitting some hard times so he hadn't had a place to stay and refused to take the guest room at my spot. I don't blame him. Much rather be laid up with a woman than rooming with a homeboy any day.

I walked up on the porch and raised my hand to knock before I heard yelling behind the door. They seemed to be arguing.

Shonda's voice rang out, "I told you once, and I'mma tell you again! If you put that thing there one more time, I'mma break it!"

He yelled back, "You act like it's frickin' taboo! Porn stars do it! And God made porn stars! So you're telling me you're better than God?!"

"Look, boy! If you want you some asshole, you go right on ahead in them Yellow Pages and find you some in the area. But if you go the wrong way down this one way, there will be no citation. You will be shot on sight. I said NO!"

Knock! Knock! Knock!

I'd already heard enough. Enough, as in too much.

They started whispering. Pete said, "Why I gotta answer it? This is your house."

She whispered back, "You just remember that when it's time to pay rent."

"Fine, I'll get it. Damn."

He opened the door. I was standing off the porch a few steps.

"Oh, what's good bro?" He turned around and yelled towards the kitchen. "Hey, babe, it's Shawn."

"Heeeeey, Shawn!" she yelled out.

A shirtless Pete, holding onto his pants with no under-wear, clenching at the zipper asked, "What brings you this way?"

"Just needed to holla at you. But first...go wash your hands. And remind me not to eat another thing out this house."

"Oh, come on, man, washing hands is so yesterday. We sanitize now." He reached by the door and pressed a few times to what seemed to be an installed sanitizer dispenser.

"Quick question. Why do you have a four-leaf clover tat-tooed around your belly button?"

He looked down, as if he'd forgotten about the artwork stained beneath his rat trail stomach hair.

"Oh this? It's my street basketball name. Lucky Charm. Could hit from half court with my eyes closed."

"Interesting. How many shots a game?"

"Nah, just did it once. That's why I gave myself the name, Lucky Charm."

"So you named yoursel--nevermind. Let's just...drop it."

He smiled proudly and walked out to the porch, sitting down on the front step. "So what's on your mind, bro?"

I went into my whole spiel about the rest of my college love saga and how the session went with Jessica. I briefly gave him a shorter version of the story then summarized her last sentiments she expressed before I left.

He pulled some pecans out of the pocket of his pants, un-beknownst to me as to where they came from or how long they'd been there. "So that's what she said, huh?"

"Yup. What you think?"

"Depends. How long did she say it'd take to get your refund again?"

"I didn't get a refund. I told her she could keep it. But I think I reminded her of somebody she knew...or something. I don't know, man. I just had to make sure it wasn't me."

"No, it was you. You spent all day and too much money to hear an emotionally damaged therapist totally make your own emotional damage all about her."

"Really, P.? Really."

"Well, I'm just sayin'. But don't feel bad, man. We've all got our shit. Some people flush it and keep it moving while others need a plunger. And I got just the plunger for you."

I looked around trying to put his analogy together. He noticed my confusion.

"Her name's Dominique," he continued. "You'll love her man. Ya know, if I wasn't dating Rashonda, I'd definitely try to be with her. She's got a nice rack."

"Okay, so who is she?"

"Rashonda's best friend."

"Sure you need to be saying that while your lady's on the other side of those walls?"

"Oh, no worries, dude. These doors. They're practically sound-proof. She can't hear a thing."

He smiled at me triumphantly. Little did he know. But whatever.

I said, "You know, I've been trying to wait to start dating until I got this little thing figured out but maybe I will give it a try. When you guys trying to go out?"

"Who said *we* were going out?"

"Well, this is your people and I don't do blind dates alone. Not after that time I went out with Terri."

"Oh yeah, I remember her. You should've known something was up when you saw all of her ex's pictures duct taped to her bumper," Pete said.

I laughed, "Talkin' bout it's 'cause she's put them behind her now."

"Right. I mean, who uses duct tape? It's so tacky. Double-sided and she would've been a keeper."

I stared at Pete for a few seconds to see if he would laugh, but no. He was serious.

I was getting a little paranoid with the way people coming into the complex would slow down as they passed by my car. While I could appreciate the admiration, I knew the hood well. Admiration was the warm-up to a plot. I didn't feel like being there a whole lot longer.

"Okay, so this Dominique woman. I'll trust you on this only because it's Shonda's girl. Let's go out tomorrow after I get back from my seminar. It should be over around six. I'll come scoop you guys up, we can carpool so it's real casual."

"What are we? Middle school kids? No, I can drive and you can drive."

"Well, excuse me then, Mr. Adult. Do your thing. Just tryna save on ga--"

"You mind if I hold a few bucks for gas though? You know, kinda strapped right now but I'm good for it. I'll pay you back. Swear."

I shook my head, laughing on the inside because I should've seen it coming. Just pretended I didn't even hear him say that. "So tomorrow at six o'clock. I'll just meet you at whatever restaurant. You can choose."

I walked off. He started calling my name, but I knew he

was only trying to ask me for gas money again. He wasn't trying to use me. He just didn't feel like getting cursed out by Rashonda. She stayed checking his ass and occasionally would put him on nookie time-out for even having the nerve to ask her for money.

I got home and saw that Stacy had hooked me up with a few turkey sandwiches from the deli and my notes for the seminar were prepared too. It was more of a Q&A than a lecture. Had a love-hate relationship with these.

The dialogue was great but it could easily go left if a few scorned women or defensive brothers were in the crowd trying to make it all about them. Too many pinned-up emotions and not enough communication skills and I'd easily become their scapegoat for everything wrong that ever happened in their love life.

But, that only happened once.

And don't get me started on the "feminazis". Unlike real feminists who wanted equality, these extremists wanted me to answer questions like, "So, why do I have to change my name when we get married instead of him changing his?" and my favorite, "Why is a king sized bed bigger than a queen-sized?" Like I had the rules of society in my pocket and could just rewrite them at will.

So, I finished my sandwiches and all of the note studying I was going to do for one night. My bed needed me and I needed it. My feet ached and my eyes were burning from the long day but the last walk to my mattress felt like my bed and I were running through a field of flowers and met in the middle with one big embrace and a symphony harmonizing in the background.

Just before the credits rolled, my phone buzzed.

It was my second missed call from Pete. I called him back.

"Yeah, what's up?"

He sounded wide awake. "Hey, bro, I got an idea."

I sighed, "What now?"

"No, you're going to love this one. Okay so you know how we talked earlier, right? What I said, it was pretty much on some Osho type of knowledge. Like mental super-saiyan slash Gandhi right?"

"Get to the point, P., I gotta get up early for my seminar."

"I'm glad you brought that up. How about you let me join you. Like, as a co-host. We can both give love advice to the ladies...together."

I Thought You'd Never Ask

"Yes, ma'am."

"And you put on extra deodorant, didn't ya?"

"Momma. Come on now, you act like I'm ten years old or something. Of course, I'm good on deodorant too."

"Nawl, I'm acting like I already know, don't no woman like no musty-smellin' man. You get to wavin' ya arms 'round too much and sweating everywhere and you ain't got nothing on them armpits; you gon' have every seat in there empty or filled with women that done fainted. And not for the right reasons neither."

"I got it, Momma. My nails are clean; my clothes are ironed; and I promise, if I start getting musty I'll cut it short and go home."

"You know, I wouldn't have to ask all this if you just went and got you one of them nice girls up there to settle down with. I need me some more grandbabies, ya sisters 'bout dried up I think."

We both started laughing. I couldn't get enough of her pep talks before my events. It was her way of telling me she missed me and I missed her just as much. But I had work to do. She sacrificed so much to see me get to this point, I knew I couldn't drop the ball now.

"Well, don't hold your breath. I might dry up myself by the time I find the one," I said.

"Don't start talkin' like that now. You just need to keep on praying and every--"

"Thing will be all right," we finished her sentence together. "I know, Momma. We go through this all the time and you're right. I'm just being patient, I guess. Extra patient. But hey, I gotta go ahead and get out this house. I love you. I'mma catch up with you later to let you know how it went."

"All right, baby, go do yo thang today, ya hear?"

"I'm on it. Love you."

"Love you too, Bud."

We hung up. I took another ten minutes making the life decision of tie or no tie before throwing the tie in the garbage for making my life so difficult then headed out the house.

I got to the conference center and saw the line wrapped all the way around the side of the building. I've had big crowds before, but this one, it was different. It was women of all shades, shapes, and sizes, most of them well put together and neatly dressed and a few brothers who tagged along to make sure their woman wasn't getting brainwashed.

I texted Stacy to touch bases, making sure she was somewhere near to help me get in through a back entrance.

"Hey, Shawn!" Pete yelled out coming towards my car. A few heads turned from the crowd, but luckily, my windows were tinted so not too many were deterred from their own conversations.

I unlocked the door for him to get in. "See, you're already starting off wrong. I told you when you got here, call my phone and I would come meet you in the parking lot. Do you know what you almost did just now?"

"So you're worried about a mob of women stampeding

towards your car? Poor you," he said sarcastically. I whipped the car away from the front and parked on the side where Stacy and the event coordinator were waiting for me.

"Who's this?" Stacy asked when Pete got out of the car.

"That's my...um, my special guest."

"We didn't discuss this in the budget, Mr. Fletcher," the coordinator chimed in.

"Added bonus. He's doing this pro-bono. Just this once."

I looked at Pete and his chest filled up with air as he grinned. For whatever reason, it gave me a really bad feeling for what was about to happen.

I pointed toward the third row to the woman with her hand up. "Yes, ma'am. What's your question?"

She grabbed the microphone and stood to her feet. "Hi, first let me say that I am a huge fan of yours. But I wonder, why is it that guys like yourself that have it all together seem so hard to find?"

"Well, first, thank you very much. Secondly--"

"He does NOT have it all together," Pete laughed. I looked over at him like he had one more time before I called security to throw him out as if we were complete strangers. He interpreted correctly and fell back.

I continued, "As my co-host stated, I really don't have it all together. None of us do. But I think what you mean is why do I appear to have enough to work with?" She nodded her head in agreement.

"Well, to women with mature priorities, that's exactly what it means to have it all. Because you know all you need is that, and you can work with a man to get everything else he's capable of. That's why brothers often don't see success until after they've encountered a good woman. As for other brothers not having that, it's a matter of where you're looking. Sometimes we get caught up trying to fish in the desert and blaming our empty buckets on the bait. Get around like-minded people, change up the environment, and you'll find that good brothers not only aren't so hard to find, but will flock to you."

She smiled and sat down. Other hands went up.

"What do you think about giving a man husband privileges before the ring? Sex in particular?"

Another woman from the audience chimed in before I could speak, "Why buy the cow if you gettin' the milk for free, honey?"

The rest of the ladies added a few "Mm-hmms" and "I know that's right" cosigns.

I knew I was treading deep water, so I thought for a moment before I spoke. "A man won't buy the cow if he's getting the milk for free...only if he's a broke ass man. Even if a broke ass man does buy the cow, he's still going to be out taste-testing anybody else that's offering free milk after his purchase, so the focus should be choosing a man who's in it for more than just your milk before you give him any of yours in the first place."

I scanned the faces of the ladies in the room. They were sitting still for a moment so I got nervous. Like all of my logic got caught in the filter of "Fuck that." But fortunately, I noticed a few smiles that assured me they received my message.

Left corner, in the back a woman stood and broke the silence, "Okay, I need to know how to catch a man cheating.

I know, I'm supposed to trust and all that, but please, just let me know how I can catch my man cheating because I know he is. But without proof he just gon' blame it on my insecurities and trust issues like always."

The rest of the crowd looked at her like she was crazy at first but then turned to me like it was a good question deserving of a real answer.

Pete looked at me for the okay to take this one. I let him.

"Okay, so as a guy who's gotten caught more times than I can count, I think it's best I answer this. I'm pretty much an expert at getting caught cheating, except I can't stop getting caught.

"Anyway, the last time I got caught cheating, my girl did the sneezing technique. Is anyone in here familiar with the sneezing technique?" he asked the room.

No one raised their hands, but everyone was all ears, including me.

"You simply wait till he gets a suspicious call, possibly from his side chick. Before he can leave and go in the bathroom with his phone, you sneeze. Now, he has to make a decision. He either says 'Bless you', in which you will say 'Thank you' loud enough for his mistress to hear your voice or he won't say a thing in which you can then go off.

"Me, I chose door number two and didn't say anything. As you can imagine, my phone made it to the toilet before I did. So that's one way."

All around the room, women began pulling out pieces of paper and asking to borrow pens from each other. Pete looked at me like he didn't know what to do next, and I looked at him like he needed to keep going.

"Um...okay, another way is to text the girl in question. Pretend to be him by saying you have a new number." I noticed his eyes getting glossy as he stared off. "She'll keep up an entire conversation with you and won't get suspicious or think to just double check with him by calling in case he has a psychotic girlfriend who's going to break his car windows once she finds out I'm cheating. Even though I'm only cheating for a little while, I was going to be faithful again sooner or later, I swear!"

The room became hushed, and everyone was side eying each other like, "What in the hell just happened?"

"P...P!" I whispered over to him.

I looked to the event coordinator who was looking at me for a signal. She then said, "Ladies and gents, let's take a ten-minute break. Restrooms and refreshments are out front. Thank you."

"Pete. You good, man?"

"Yeah, dude. Just haven't quite learned to let go yet."

"I know how it is. Losing a good woman will do that to you."

He looked up at me. "To hell with the woman. I'm talking about my car. She knew I loved that damn car."

*****

"Okay....so, how do I look?"

"You look fine, Shawn," Stacy said as she adjusted my collar one more time and smoothed out the back of my shirt.

"Not too dressy is it?"

"No such thing. She's going to love your outfit. Dressing up on a first date shows respect. At least she'll know that you cared enough to try and make a decent impression."

I smiled, grateful for a woman's opinion. Stacy was a first-year grad student looking to earn a few extra dollars and get her feet wet in the writing industry herself. We were close in age so we understood each other and had gotten close as a result ever since I'd hired her last year to be my assistant.

"Well, good. Maybe this one will go a lot better than the last."

She looked up at the ceiling, repeating me silently to herself as if she was trying to remember who I was talking about. "Oh yeah, Terri. Wall-of-shame bumper stickers-Terri."

"Yup. That's her."

"Lighter fluid pouring on your front lawn until the neighbors came outside-Terri."

"Wait what? When did that happen?"

My door bell rang. Stacy went to go see who it was without answering me.

My driver was parked outside in the rental for the night. I would've taken Daisy Duke, but I kept her tucked away for the very reason Stacy and I had just discussed. Those kinds of things--cars, clothes, job--can be seen as collateral by a woman who didn't like hearing the word, no.

"Okay, Shawn. You're all set. I'll catch up with you tomorrow to update you on the rest of your bookings, but tonight, promise me you'll give her a chance and just try to relax."

"Got it, Stace. I owe it to myself. I need this to go well."

The address Pete sent me led us to a Red Lobster downtown. He must've been trying to propose tonight because this was five-star dining for him. If it didn't have a drive-through, you pretty much wouldn't catch him there.

201

"P., what's good brother?" I said, as I walked up to him and embraced before leaning in to Rashonda for a hug.

Pete had on a Hawaiian print button-up he'd likely gotten at a thrift shop that was "pretty much brand new". Some plain khakis and penny loafers. His hair was slicked back in a smooth pony tail; that part was his girlfriend's touch.

"Hello, Shonda. Nice seeing you. Lookin' lovely as always."

"Thank you very much." She smiled, quickly glancing at Pete as if he'd forgotten to compliment her before they came out. "Dom' said she's on her way. She should be here any minute now."

Pete walked up to me and patted me on the shoulder and whispered, "Let me talk to you for a sec, bro." He walked me away from the front where 'Shonda waited for us yelling back, "Be right back, babe."

"What's good?" I asked him once we got to a safe distance.

His face looked sketchy, unsure of something. Nervous almost. "Okay, so I just want to say that Dominique--oh crap, there she is."

A black Range Rover pulled up into the parking lot. Brand new, fresh off the lot.

"Hurry up and tell me. What's up with her?" I said.

He looked down at the ground, dubiously. "It's kinda hard to say."

"Dammit, P., you pick a fine time. Tell me before she comes."

"Okay," he said as she got out of her car. We began walking back so as not to be rude. "She may...or may not have an

Adam's apple. Just thought you should know."

"The fu--"

"Peter, y'all hurry up. You know it ain't polite to keep us waitin'," Rashonda threw out.

We were now within hearing distance so I sealed my lips while staring Pete down for setting me up. This dude here, I tell you.

"See her heart, not her past, bro," Pete said.

"What?" Rashonda responded for me.

"Dominique, meet Shawn. Shawn--Dominique," Pete avoided.

I forced a smile and finally laid eyes on Dominique with a quick glance to her throat. That part was clear.

Her eyes were soft and her cheek-bone structure was strong but not masculine. She clearly put a lot of work in on her body too, particularly her legs. She looked like she could've been older than me, but not by much. The maturity looked good on her. Hopefully she was a her.

She reached out and said, "Pleasure to meet you, sir."

I met her hand and gently shook it, assuming she was from a corporate culture of some sort. That would explain the car, the Tiffany diamonds around her wrist, and her Red Bottom heels. She had very expensive taste and probably an income to support the habit.

"Pleasure's mine," I responded.

"Now that we got that out the way, let's go eat!" Pete said, punctuating through the awkwardness of both Dominique and me trying to gather as much information from the first impression as possible.

He and Rashonda led the way in as Dominique didn't wait

for me to walk beside her.

A woman with that much money put into her appearance, attractive, and going on a blind date; either she had little to no time to go out on dates, little to no tolerance for nonsense, or both. But the sister certainly wasn't just any old girl from the block.

The cheddar biscuits came out and Pete's eyes lit up like a kid on Christmas.

After a few bites, he said, "So Dominique, you know Shawn writes poetry and stuff? He's deep."

"And Shawn, you know Dominique is a certified personal trainer? I'm sure you can tell," Rashonda added.

Dominique and I both looked at each other and laughed. We'd barely gotten a word in since Pete and Rashonda talked so much.

I chimed in,. "Well, I know now. But we're sitting right here. We can talk to each other."

"I know, bro, just sayin'. And Dominique, Shawn's like a really big deal but he doesn't like to talk about it so don't bring it up."

"Well, Dominique is too. Voted as one of the top twenty-five celebrity fitness trainers by *Essence*," Rashonda retorted.

They were in a contest of who had the better friend like two kids arguing over whose dad could beat the other kid's dad's ass.

"Alright alright," Pete blurted out. "Let's cut to the chase and get down to what everyone's really been waiting for. A little game of Truth or Dare."

Everyone looked at each other awkwardly before looking

back at Pete.

Dominique said, "Um...I don't know about you guys, but I wasn't thinking about Truth or Dare at all."

"Sure you were, come on. It'll be fun." Pete threw back. "Who's first?"

I looked at Rashonda, hoping she'd say something to put a stop to it.

She didn't. With excitement in her eyes, urged, "Peter, how about you go first."

"Okay, so truth or dare?" he asked Dominique.

"Truth."

"If you had to nickname the last person you had sex with after the sex you had with them, what would it be?"

"Oh, choose another one. That's inappropriate." she said uncomfortably.

I smiled, hoping she'd answer the question. Hell, I was curious too.

Rashonda joined in, "Come on Dom', you gotta answer."

"Alright, alright." she obliged. "I guess her nickname would be Onion."

Pete and I gave each other the side eye that meant we were on the same page about the visualization of her and a "she".

Rashonda asked, "Onion? She must've been thick."

"No, she just cried when she orgasmed. Which was often, with me."

I raised my brow as she sipped her tea like she was Kermit and looked up to the ceiling before throwing a truth or dare back out at Pete.

He said, "Truth."

Apparently nobody wanted to go near the dare section

while out on a nice date.

"You ever ate the...you know."

"The cooch?" Pete asked.

"No, the other one."

Dominique shot a devilish look over to Rashonda to let her know it was payback for making her answer the previous question.

Pete said, "Ooooh, you mean the anus?"

"Yes, that one."

"The litter capsule."

"Okay, if that's what you call it. Yes."

"The fecal chamber."

I interrupted, "I think you get the point P. Just answer the question."

Calmly, he looked off and said, "Nope."

Rashonda shifted in her seat and smiled uncomfortably.

"But I might as well have last night." he continued.

I coughed, without laughing. Somehow. Dominique's mouth dropped. Pete shook his head in affirmation while Rashonda just closed her eyes.

"That's what I get for trying to surprise my woman. A nice little surprise waiting for me."

Rashonda lamented, "I know you did not just,"

"You could've warned me."

"I told you I had a long day! What did you think that meant?"

"Could've mean you were tired. But if you wanted to tell me your catfish was smelling like it was drowning, there's a lot of better ways to make that clear before I put my face down there!"

A few seconds passed by and Rashonda kept her eyes closed. Everyone waited to see what would happen next.

"Rashonda, you alright?" I asked.

"Yeah, I just had to pray. Because when I'm done with him it's going to take Goliath himself to pry my foot up outta his ass!"

Dominique grabbed my hand, pulling me away to another table while Pete pleaded his case to deaf ears.

"I'm so sorry for that," she said.

"Don't apologize. Not your fault. Pete always--"

"Rashonda always," we spoke simultaneously. She joined me in a slight chuckle. "Okay so they're both a trip, huh?"

"Yeah, apparently."

We ignored the commotion at the other table and chatted a while.

Questioned each other about our backgrounds, eyeing each other with subtle admiration, the conversation flowing without a hitch.

She was witty. Fine as hell. Wouldn't have to ask a brother for a dime. Hell, she may even give him a dime every now and then. And she was a freak. I'm sure Onion was missing her like crazy.

My phone buzzed.

Pete: *You good brah? [8:34 p.m.]*

Pete: *I told you. She's hot. [8:35 p.m.]*

Pete: *I know you saw that ass. Hell, I sure did. [8:37 p.m.]*

Me: *Yeah. Can't text tho. Rude. Ttyl [8:53 p.m.]*

Pete: *OK cool. Shonda's getting on my nerves so we need to wrap this on up as soon as possibjklplk/ / / /:fhaseb [8:54 p.m].*

I looked up and saw Rashonda slapping Pete across the back of his head and grabbing for his phone as he tried to explain and defend himself at the same time. She must've been looking over his shoulder and caught sight of that last message he was sending.

"Uh, Dominique, we might better go see what's up with our friends. Looks like they're done eating," I said, nodding over to their table, which went from zero to 100. Real quick.

She slid out of her booth and rushed over to the table. Rashonda immediately started pleading her case as Pete nursed the back of his head.

I went over to our waiter, who was on his way into the back with a few of the plates and slid him two Benjamins for our meals. I didn't do the math, but it should have resulted in a pretty generous tip for his service. Ever since I waited on tables back in college, I had a soft spot for what they had to go through.

Sometimes the people who did tip could be such assholes, and the money wasn't worth it, but none was worse than a non-tipper. You go to work expecting to go through bullshit, but you also expect to get paid for it.

Surprisingly, everyone made it outside in one piece. Rashonda and Pete refused to ride back home together so he went and sat in my car while she sped off and Dominique and I said our goodbyes to each other.

"Next time, we'll leave the kids at home," I said, laughing at Rashonda's tail lights disappearing into the night.

"Is that a request for a second date?" she asked.

"Only if your answer is yes. Otherwise, no. It wasn't."

"Oh, don't pull the *Shy Guy* on me, Mr. Love Expert."

"Okay, fine. I would like to see you again. We can play it by ear over the next week maybe and work it in our schedule?"

"That sounds like a plan. Here's my card. My cell is on the back," she said, reaching in her purse and handing me her info.

"Cool. I'll go ahead and hit your phone so you can have my number too. Guess this is good night."

I reached in to give her a hug. Her body was a lot softer than it looked, and I wasn't complaining.

"Yes, good night. Make sure you drive safe. And don't forget the extra covers."

"The extra covers?"

"For your boy," she said, looking towards Pete sitting in the car. "Seems he may need to crash at your place tonight." She laughed and waved before pressing the remote control unlock button to her own car and driving away.

*****

"All right, bro. So tell me. How fly was that assist?"

"What do you mean?"

"I mean, I just gave you a Magic Johnson slash Lebron James behind the back, no-look assist. I know you didn't slam dunk because clearly you came home with me. But did you lay-up, pull up from three, go left--"

"--Oh, right. Dominique. Yeah, man, she's dope. You picked a good one this time."

He smiled, "And...?" he waved his hands in circles for me

to continue.

"And, you know. She's nice."

His face relaxed back into confusion. "Nice?"

"Yeah. What's wrong with nice?"

"The Golden Girls are nice. The salad that your aunt makes who everyone knows can't cook but tries to let her be involved at Thanksgiving every year, that's nice too. But Dominique isn't just *nice*. She's what happened when God invented ham sandwiches."

"Okay, I guess. I don't know. Wouldn't mind hanging out again, but honestly, doubt we'll go too far. Didn't quite feel that spark. No tingly feeling. And there's always a tingly feeling for *the one*."

He paced around my living room a few times, his right hand on his temple like I'd just given him a migraine.

"Tell me. What was the name of your shrink again?" he asked.

"My therapist?"

"Yeah, you know who I'm talking about."

"Jessica. Or you can call her Dr. Holley."

"Whatever. I think she was right, bro."

"About?"

"You're not over Danielle, man."

I walked into my room. Really not interested in taking that conversation any further.

"You don't have to say it. But you know it just like I do," he yelled after me.

"I'm done with that, P. You're talking crazy now."

"As crazy as a guy who just sat face to face with everything he says he's looking for in a woman, then shrugs her off?

210

Or what kinda crazy you mean?" he responded sarcastically. "You keep looking for that missing something. That missing something is Danielle."

I went back in and stood at the doorway, wrestling with his logic. I hadn't thought about it that way before. I'd already come across countless women, none of them ever seeming to be my type even though on paper they were as good as it gets. Good women didn't seem too hard to find, but I wanted better than good. I wanted right.

"Nah, P., you're trippin'. What's-her-face never even crosses my mind," I lied.

"She doesn't have to cross it. She lives there."

I dropped his covers on the couch and looked at him. He was grinning devilishly. I was annoyed, but curious.

"Okay, cool. You got all the answers. So what do you suggest?"

Pete cracked his knuckles and propped his feet on my table. "I thought you'd never ask."

Emergency

"My uncle, he's an entrepreneur. He has an online business that has loads of people's information. Street address. Email. You name it, it's there."

I asked, "What kind of online business?"

"A porn site. It's called tater tots are hot dot com. It's pretty awesome because the guys, I mean they're little people, so you'd think they'd have really small--"

"Come on, P.,"

"Right. Well, back to what I was saying. His website and hundreds of others took a bid on Myspace's database when it became a ghost town back in '09-ish. Since everyone kept their accounts as sort of a picture album archive of high school photos they never wanted to delete, it was the only way Myspace could keep the lights on. So they sold everyone's information."

"Isn't that illegal?"

"Not really. They changed the privacy policy in the Terms of Agreement page. But again, nobody was active on their accounts. And even when we are, we click that we've read the terms of agreements without reading them. So everyone who's ever had an account, their personal information is still on there."

"Okay, I get all that. But still, that was back then. Hypothetically speaking, if I was to try and find her again, I'd have no way of knowing where she's at right now."

"Yeah, *hypothetically*," he said, making quotation marks with his fingers. "Well, chances are, her home address and phone number hasn't changed. You could always call there and check in with her folks. They don't hate you, right?"

I thought back to Danielle's mom.

"Actually, yeah. They do."

"Some charmer you were."

"Look, now's not the time. I don't know, man. I feel like some kind of creep. Going through all that just to find her and do what? Profess my love?"

"Pretty much."

"It's corny, and you know it. On top of that, I'd probably get my ass locked up and a restraining order. Imagine that headline. *SHAWN FLETCHER, RENOWNED WRITER AND POET HAS ONE MORE TALENT--STALKING*."

Pete laughed, "I mean you can either waste time in jail or waste time out here going on dead-end dates and being miserable. Either way, you're wasting your time. And they always say, if you're going to pick a poison, make sure it's the poison you haven't tried before."

"Who's they?"

"Maya Angelou. Or maybe it was DMX. It was somebody really important, man, just trust me. I think you need to give it a shot. My uncle would gladly help. He owes me one from that one time I let him borrow my old tricycle from when I was a kid."

"Why did he need to borrow...you know what? Never mind. Do not answer that question."

I went back into the room and started my shower water. I looked in the closet, fetched Pete a few bath cloths. He knew where the guest room was from all the other nights Rashonda had left him to fend for himself for a place to sleep.

The thought continued to trouble me the rest of the night. I felt crazy. Like a pyscho, just for even considering going on a manhunt for this girl. For all I knew, she could be out of the country somewhere, a lesbian, anything.

I went back out into the living room one more time. "P.?" I said.

He looked up from his phone back at me, "Yeah bro?"

"Would you do the same for Rashonda? You know, going to find her and all?"

"In a heartbeat, bro. Not because I like, choose to, but I don't think the way I feel about her would give me any other choice. She's all I really want, and when it's real, it's worth it."

"That deep, huh? And it doesn't scare you that maybe you're not perfect enough? Like, if you went through all of that to get her back, you'd just mess it up again?"

He looked off for a second before responding. "The only way I could really, *really* screw up is by cheating. I mean, that part is the hardest for me, because it's kinda involuntary. You don't look at any chick and think to yourself, 'Time to push the horny button so I can fuck up my love life and break my girl's heart.' But, things happen. Then as you grow up, you learn that temporary gratification doesn't stack up to long-term satisfaction. Since I'm at that point, I have faith the rest will work out fine."

I raised my eyebrows in thoughtful agreement. He wasn't always full of such depth, but when he was, he really knew how to make something hit home for me. That's why I confided in him. No matter how different we were, we thought a lot alike, just from different perspectives.

"Rashonda, she wasn't always perfect," he continued. "She started off in a strip club. Not for long though, only until she got on her feet and began her hair styling business. But looking at her growth, man; it's amazing enough for me to want the same for myself, ya know? Like, she inspires me. I'd follow that woman to the edge of the earth and any other planet for that."

"I can dig it, brother," I replied.

"One question though."

"What's that?"

"So, like me and her. We're the same age, right? But if I see an old pic of her when she was a minor, and I think she's smokin' hot, does that make me a pedophile? I mean, technically I was her age at the time and I didn't get a chance to think she was sexy then, so it's not my fault. But for some reason, I feel so dirty."

"A'ight, P., see you in the morn," I said, walking off and shaking my head.

"Wanna see the pic?"

I ignored him and walked off before he asked any more questions about Rashonda. It was ruining the serious moment he'd just had.

Deep down and on the surface, he loved her. As much as he messed up over and over again, there was something about her that never would cut him off.

I guess, in a sense, that was me too. I had always been pretty terrible at letting go because it was too much like giving up. And I was never good at that either.

But this was different. I could keep ducking, dodging, and

denying. Or I could do the craziest, most senseless thing I'd ever do in my life, and find this woman. Find Danielle, and make her mine again.

*****

I reached for my alarm clock, trying to turn it off. As I came to, I realized it wasn't my alarm that was sounding, it was someone at the front door.

Only one person I knew would be knocking down my door when there was a perfectly good doorbell to use, and that was Rashonda. After banishing Pete, she'd eventually come hunting him down. It normally took a little time but she must've been pretty pissed and didn't feel like waiting for him to get a piece of her mind.

I walked into the living room and Pete was already up, grabbing the shoes he left by the couch the night before. "Code red! Code red!" he whispered.

That was what he said when he needed me to tell Rashonda he wasn't there. He only yelled Code Red when he hadn't had a chance to put together a good defense. Code Blue was when he wanted me to stall long enough for him to make an entrance with whatever excuse he had pre-cooked for his dog-house sentencing. But unfortunately this wasn't that time.

"Okay, go get in the closet," I whispered back. "She knows I'll lie for you so she's going to look around a little. Make sure you're in there good."

He ran to the back, in my room. I re-fluffed the couch pillows to help sell the disguise. She knocked again, louder. I swore my hinges were getting ready to come off.

I yelled out, "Who is it?!".

Expectedly she answered, "You know who it is. Open this damn door! I already know he in there!"

I opened it enough to stand in her way. "Oh hey, what's u, Shonda? Good morning rather. You here early."

"Shawn, I ain't got time for this. I need to talk to Peter. Where is he?"

"Not here. He left about an hour ago. Said he needed to get away."

"Peter Winthrop McNeil the third! Bring yo ass!!!" she yelled.

Wait, his middle name is Winthrop? And he's a third? I thought.

"You can call all you want, but he's not here. I told you, he took a cab."

She pursed her lips, "Mm-hmm. Yeah, okay. Yo car is outside and he can't afford no cab."

"I called him one, actually. He told them where to go, figured he was going back home to you."

She pushed through the door way, sniffing around trying to find him. I would've stopped her, but I didn't have my base set, and I needed my base with this woman. She checked the dining room, the bathroom. She even looked in the medicine cabinet. Then she walked over to my room, looked from a distance, but didn't go in. Seemed that was about as far as she felt comfortable.

"Rashonda, everything cool?"

She walked back into the living room where I was still standing by the door and sat on the couch.

"You know, Shawn, I don't get him sometimes. On one hand, I know he a good man who just done made some mistakes, but I also wonder if those mistakes made him. Some of the stuff I get upset about may seem petty, but after a while, it all adds up. Like is it really worth it or am I settling for less by being with him?"

"Don't think too much into it, Shonda. Y'all go through this, but so does everyone else."

"Not everyone. You and Dominique seemed just fine last night."

"Dominique and I aren't a couple."

"But still."

"And everyone is like that in the beginning. Only the good things shine through at first. Then all of the small print you missed, it starts becoming bigger and bolder. But it's normal."

She folded her arms and rolled her eyes, "Maybe I don't want normal...anymore."

"Then turn your normal into better than normal. Talk to him. I'm sure he feels the same."

"I'm done talking."

I felt bad. I didn't want to hear her make a definitive statement on what she was already saying without actually saying it. I just hoped he wouldn't blame my little pep talk for it.

"Okay, I guess. If that's how you feel."

I unlocked the door to let her out and she began grabbing her things.

I looked outside, wondering if my neighbors had been tuning into any of the soap opera without my knowing.

I turned around and Rashonda had stopped right up on me within reaching distance.

"Um, Rashonda, you all right? I mean, I'll tell Pete you came by if I talk to him again before you do."

"I told you already, I'm done talking," she said, her voice and expression much softer now.

"Okay then, fine. So, guess I'll see you around."

She looked uncomfortable for a moment, I thought she was going to break down and cry. But she just kept looking at me.

"Shawn, why can't Peter be more like you? At least you got something going for yourself. I can't do the whole 'nice personality is all I need' thing anymore. That mess is for teenagers."

"Everybody starts somewhere, Shonda. I really feel like you need to talk to Pet--"

"I guess I gotta spell it out for you, huh?"

"What?"

She moved in closer. "So you're going to sit there and act like you're not attracted to me?"

"Wait, what?"

"It's obvious. No need in lying about it now. I mean, I feel the same way and I'm right here." She whispered, "But what you do about that is completely up to you."

She moved in a step closer. I moved back, halfway out the door now.

My heartbeat dialed up to lightspeed. I fully expected Pete to come barging out of the room, to put an end to this. I wasn't sure if he could hear from all the way back in my room or if he was just waiting for a right time. Dammit, it was the right time.

"All right, Rashonda. It's time for you to go home, get some rest. You're upset right now. You're saying some things you don't mean and I don't want you to regret it later."

"I'm grown. I know exactly what I mean."

"Nah, Shonda. I think you need to go. For real."

She stepped closer to me and mirrored me when I tried to dodge her.

"I'm serious," I mumbled.

She trailed her finger tips down my torso before clenching my shirt with her other hand, "That makes two of us."

She's just as strong as she looks. I thought as her heavy ass finger pressed on my stomach.

She stood slightly on her tip-toes, pulling me into her. The smell of her cherry lip-gloss got stronger, our breaths mingled, and her eyes relaxed until they were barely open.

I yelled out, "PEEEEE!!!!"

He came running into the living room and saw Rashonda and me standing in the doorway, no space between us, and my shirt still in her hand.

"Wait, what's going on here?" Pete said.

"I promise, P. It wasn't me."

Without hesitation he looked at Rashonda, "How could you? I mean, I know you were upset, but this...this is dirty."

"So you *were* in there hiding. I knew it," she said. Her eye had scrunched up like Esther from Sanford & Son.

"So you mean, this is just some trick to get me out here?!" Pete shouted.

"Of course it is." she replied. "And it worked. Now, get yo stuff and get in the car. We got some things to discuss."

She turned around and headed back towards the door, but not before winking at me.

It was rather ambiguous, not a clear-cut flirt, possibly a thinly veiled "I win" signal. But either way, it crossed the line between war tactics and plain out manipulation.

She switched her hips as she walked out of the door, her nose so high in the air she would've drowned if it was raining. It all seemed to be a game to her.

But I had bigger fish to fry.

A few hours later, Pete came through on the data base containing Danielle's home phone number. Along with a few sponsored ads within the email from his uncle's website that no one deserved to see, but I digress.

Every time I picked up the phone to dial, my feet got so cold, even my hand shook. My pride told me I was a fool for literally tracking this woman down years after our relationship and all contact had ended, but the fact that I cared enough to even try was proof that that dust was far from settled.

But it didn't help that I was going to have to convince the *other* woman in her life that didn't want me in Danielle's. Her mother.

"Hello?" a woman answered. It definitely sounded like Danielle's mom, Miss Sarah, but I wasn't sure because it was fairly pleasant.

"Yes, I'm calling for Danielle. Is she in?"

"Um, Danielle doesn't live here. Who am I speaking with?" she asked.

"This is Shawn, an old friend of hers. Found this number from a while back and just thought I'd see how--"

"Oh. You." she said, her voice dark now. This was a much more familiar mien for her.

Miss Sarah was something like Aunt Viv from *Fresh Prince*. The original, dark-skinned Aunt Viv. Reserved, calculated, but had quite a mean streak.

She continued, "Young man, unless she's reached out to you personally and asked for you to find a way to get in touch, I suggest you let this be the last time you call anywhere looking for her."

"Miss Sarah, I didn't call to start any trouble. I just wanted--"

"Let me guess. Wanted to talk to her. See if maybe she's been as miserable without you as you are without her?"

"No, ma'am. I just wanted to see how she was doing. I think that's harmless enough for a phone call. Maybe I was wrong. Either way, this is your phone and I'll respect that because clearly I'm not welcomed."

"Not welcomed. Not original. Not genuine. Pick one," she puffed.

I was biting my tongue, but it was starting to hurt, so I let it go. "Miss Sarah, for you to be the so-called adult between the two of us, you're sure not acting like it."

She laughed, "Oh, is that right?"

I wanted to call her a bitch, because that's how I felt. But, there was another way to handle it, and besides, Momma raised me better than that.

"Absolutely. You see, I know where this is coming from. It doesn't come from you hating me. It doesn't come from you wanting to protect your daughter. This all comes from your past relationships. You've always lashed out at the men who did you wrong but used me to do it. Yeah, she told me about them. All of them."

I could hear nothing but her breathing. A pause of at least four or five seconds went uninterrupted before I went on.

"Carl, the one who impregnated you with Danielle's little brother. He told you he was in the middle of a divorce and currently separated. You trusted him, kept the baby, and then raised him alone when Carl and his wife fixed things, changing their number and leaving no trace for you to follow.

"Anthony. He was the one who made you feel beautiful by the way he treated you, showed you off, and took you shopping for clothes just for the joy of seeing you try them on first. But when your mother passed and you gained weight from being depressed, that all changed. His interest went elsewhere to women half your age and weight.

"But first, there was Frank. The love of your life. He was the one man that never did you wrong. Never once disrespected you or ignored you. He was consistent and caring. He wanted children and couldn't wait to start a life with you. But you were so young. You didn't know how to handle someone loving you that way and ended up pushing him away, but not before you had your first child, Danielle. He left you with no viable reason to hate him, and because you couldn't give it to someone else, you harbored that blame and hatred. And now you're trying to give it to me even though I don't deserve it either."

I stopped myself. Didn't realize just how personal I was getting, but then thought about how it was necessary. How she not only deserved to feel whatever she felt from hearing it, but maybe needed to for her own good.

"I...I mean, it wasn't my fault. I didn't know," she muttered.

"I know you didn't. But it's time you stop taking that out

on others."

I heard a shuffle in the background, possibly tissue she was grabbing to straighten herself up and regain her composure.

"Well, young man. You're not the only one who knows a few things. You cheated on Danielle, disrespected her, and she didn't deserve any of that either. What makes you think she wants to walk back into that?"

"I don't think. Actually, I'd hope not. But that's not what I'm bringing with me for her to walk back into."

"And you know this for sure because?"

"Miss Sarah, with all due respect, I didn't call here to explain myself or plead my case for things that happened years ago. I called here to speak to her. That's it. If I did want another chance, and if she was willing to give it to me, I think we deserve that opportunity to get it right or maybe even wrong again. No one stripped you of that and it's manipulative to impose yourself on our relationship to strip us. Even as her parent, you have to realize that she's an adult now. Let her be the judge."

"That's fine, Shawn," she said surprisingly.

I was expecting push-back or maybe even dial tone.

She went on, "But you'd better get here before the wedding. Tomorrow. At one o'clock. After that, any chances of you speaking with her are pretty much vanished anyway.

"What?"

"A wedding. You know. White dress. Vows before God. Till death do them part? If you want to deliver any message to her, you'd better get here before then. I'm not the UPS, I'm not delivering anything. This is her special day and I won't ruin that, but if you'd like to disappoint yourself, I won't stop you. It'll be here at our church in Denver."

Then she hung up.

I was having mixed emotions. On one hand, it seemed like maybe I'd won her over, a battle I'd been fighting since the day Danielle introduced us. On the other hand, I was losing the war because Danielle was getting married.

Fucking...married.

I called Pete and he didn't answer. I paced around my room for a second trying to figure out my next move.

Mind was spinning.

Come on. Think.

I was able to get Stacy on the phone.

"Hey, Shawn," she answered.

"Stacy! I need a flight to Denver International."

Her voice did nothing to match the urgency in mine. "Oh, okay. I don't remember any booking requests coming through though."

"It's not a booking request. It's a...family emergency."

"Okay then, I'll get right on it," she said. "What dates?"

"Tonight. Or the next one out. Just get a one-way ticket for now. I don't know how long I'll be. And I need it quick.""

I heard her opening her laptop. "Okay, let me see. I didn't know you had family in Colorado. Is this distant family or what?"

"Yeah, sorta. I can't think right now, Stacy. Please, just handle this for me."

"Okay, fine."

Her fingers typed around, her mouse clicked a few times. She was a beast in situations like this, always making something out of nothing.

I went into my closet and grabbed my suitcase from the back. Opened it up, set it on the floor, and started raking everything I could into it. A suit, t-shirts, jackets, shoes; everything. I didn't think any outfits through. I wasn't thinking anything at all through. Something was moving me, and it was moving me fast.

I heard Stacy speak again. "It doesn't look like anything is going out tonight. Maybe tomorrow night, but--"

Panic slipped into the room, "That's not good enough. I need to leave today!"

"Well, unless you want to get a private jet, that's all I got. Or you can go tell *Delta* that they need to go a day early."

"Private jet. How much is that?"

"You serious?" she asked.

"Yeah, I am. How much is it?"

"Well, if you only want one way, it shouldn't be that much. But with short notice, it all depends. I can probably find one for today no more than 40k."

"Great. Get it," I said.

I'd never taken a private jet before. Didn't really need to. The normalness of checking in bags, standing in long lines of security, and paying too high prices for airport food; it kept me grounded.

But this was no time for being grounded.

"Okay, found one. I'm wiring the money as we speak. If you can make it to 112 Justice Boulevard by six, you should be fine. Your pilot's name is Eric. He's been flying for twenty years so you'll be safe with him. I suppose you'll need a rental and a hotel. Those details will be in your email by the time you land."

"Awesome. I'll be in touch. Until I get back, no more bookings. No more interviews. No more articles. I have something I have to take care of."

We said our goodbyes and hung up. She was a life saver for sure. But what I was getting ready to do, no one could save me from. It was once again, all or nothing. Just wasn't sure if my all would add up to nothing.

Shit Just Got Real

I got to my hotel, forgetting to eat, which was rare. I was famous around the family for my appetite. At every function growing up, there was always an extra helping or two for me. I even looked down on the other guys in the family who couldn't stack up.

But I needed to get back to the database that Pete had sent so I could try and figure out where Danielle's home address was. My guess was that she may not live with her mother, but she'd be over there eventually.

So, I pulled up the zip file of personal information, browsing, sifting, and occasionally drifting to the thought of Rashonda and Pete.

There was a part of him I wanted to rub off on me, the part that was ready to treat the lady of his dreams right. His ability to let himself be loved. But the other side of that coin was whether or not anyone would want love from the person it was coming from.

Like Rashonda.

Our last exchange had stained my conscious the entire flight. Figured I could probably oust it if I just gave in and dug into her background a bit, so that's what I did.

I went through the Myspace database, but underestimated how much of a task it was going to be sifting through teenager-created nicknames, but eventually I found it.

Rashonda, as her ratchetness would have it, had Trick

Daddy's *Slip-N-Slide* as her page theme song. Early 2000's graphics of glowing money bags and diamond-crested dollar sign HTML followed her screen name, "Rashonda Igetsmoneydontneednonigga Jenkins".

I clicked through a few pictures of finger waves, tinted prescription glasses, and jersey dresses before noticing something strange.

She had on a nameplate necklace that read, "Monica" and down in the comments section, that's what her Myspace friends were calling her. Comments like, *I see you Monica* and *Monica, you betta invite me next time,* which could easily just had been her middle name. But no better way to find out than Google. Of course.

I started with *Monica Jenkins* and the search was too broad. A few deranged middle school teachers having relations with students over in the Midwest and an ex-reality TV show host who'd gotten addicted to cocaine during hard times. Nothing that quite fit the bill for Rashonda. Thankfully.

So I narrowed it down by listing her hometown according to Myspace, Riverdale, Georgia, and then boom. Five different mug shots of Rashonda popped up.

I skimmed over the first few, clicking in and out of the images to check the back story. Looked like mostly white-collar stuff--fake credit cards, embezzlement, etc. Then I checked out her most recent and it was a bit more alarming.

She set up, what the news article referred to as her "lover", to get swindled. Almost got off with 250k but the guy's bank caught it before it was too late.

Nobody got seriously hurt, which explains her short sentencing and the mastermind was never found in connection, but the other girl they caught seemed to have taken that fall for it while Rashonda got out early and the one who they were working for got off clean. I imagine she was just the muscle, and fittingly so.

But I couldn't piece together her motive for dating Pete. He was a far cry from rich, well-off, or hell, even financially stable.

Figured I'd chop it up with him pretty soon and see what all he knew. Wasn't really rushing. It wasn't like she could steal much from him while she was the one paying his rent.

For the moment, I needed to get back focused on Danielle's whereabouts.

I found the address, but two and a half tanks of gas later, I was empty-handed. Apparently, Danielle's mom moved after her kids left the house. Most parents do. A little downsizing to minimize the lonely in the air and lessen the bills to free up travel money. Should've known.

Out all night driving, it seemed like the sleepier I got, the more the sun came out. I had to pop a few pain-killers to dull the pain of my body's sleep-ache. Everything was slowing down but my heartbeat.

Running on nerves alone that this might all just be a big waste of time and money, I pulled into Denny's to try and recharge with some breakfast.

Once I was seated, I noticed a young black father and his two sons sitting behind me. One of the boys was about fourteen and the youngest had to be no more than five.

Just the sight of them as I sat down warmed my heart.

Not because a black man spending time with his children is rare, but rather the very opposite. At church, the men would always walk in proudly with their families. At my football practices, fathers were there to cheer on their son and threaten the coaches when they yelled at them. I'm sure there were many without fathers, but let the media tell it, there weren't any of us who had them.

Seeing it in person was just reaffirmation. Gave me something to look forward to, one day, whether or it was as a father, or reconnecting with my own.

That feeling of euphoria vanished when I caught wind of the conversation they were having.

The oldest son said, "So what you saying is, you want me to work for free. Huh Dad?"

"Work? Cleaning the house ain't work. That's responsibility."

"Well, isn't going to work every day your responsibility as a citizen? Don't you get paid for it?" the son asked.

To me, it sounded like he was getting a little too grown for his britches. If I did have my father, I'm pretty sure he wouldn't have tolerated it. Momma would've been halfway down the aisle, her left hand throwing up the one church finger to be excused and her right hand grabbing me by the tongue I spoke those words with to give me a whooping once we got outside.

"Son, going to work is how I make my living. Not everything in life is about money. I do a lot for free. I brought you and your brother in this world. On purpose. Me and your mother, we waited five years after we got married, until we were absolutely ready to have children so we could do it right.

So now, I take care of y'all. I feed y'all. I put clothes on y'all's back. I make sure y'all get to the doctor every time you get sick. Don't nobody pay me for that. Any of it."

"Wait, hold up a minute. You act like I asked to be here. You brought me into this world. Not me. It's like you buying a car and then complaining about having to put gas in it. That's what you signed up for when you decided not to wear no condom, Dad."

"Son, you watch yo mouth at this table," the father said. He tried to deepen his voice, but the poor fellow didn't have it in him.

"What? It's the truth. So you also bought the house. You signed for it. Then you brought me into it, against my will and now you just transferred the responsibility to clean it to me? That's unfair, Dad, and you know it."

"Well, how about this. It's only fair that you get what you pay for, right? You didn't pay for no house, so you don't get no house. How about you go sleep in the house you pay for tonight so that way you can keep it as unclean as you want. How's that sound?"

I smiled to myself. Good one, Dad.

The little brother must've noticed his older sibling in distress because he chimed in with a finishing move.

"Guess what, Daddy?" he said through a few spoon-fulls of grits.

"What's that, son?"

"Yesterday when you left, my other daddy came to visit Mommy. She was mad at him. They went in the room and she kept fussin' and yellin' 'bout Jesus. I think she kicked him out for messing up her hair because it didn't look the same no more when she came out."

I got up and asked my food to go. That whole conversation was heading nowhere I needed to be when it got there.

The radio stations were a lot different in Colorado than in the South. In a good way. A lot more diversity rather than the seemingly three-song CD they put in rotation on stations back in the Carolinas.

After eating my breakfast, I reclined my seat, put the music on low, and just tried to relax. Since I couldn't find Danielle's mother, I would have to beat them to the church, but I was too fatigued to make the drive at the moment. I needed rest and my car was a familiar sleeping bag. Passersby assumed I was just waiting for someone, so they never bothered to wake me.

But three hours later I was blinking at the dashboard, trying to figure out if my eyes were playing tricks on me, or if I'd really just taken a nap and possibly missed the wedding.

My luck.

I hopped up, put the car in drive, and sped out of Denny's parking lot, apologizing to the Mexican family who had to stop abruptly to miss the front end of the rental.

I glanced over at the time. 11:38 a.m.

That could mean anything. I could only hope that no matter the case, they were on CP time. For once, that would be my friend.

I sped through the city, cross referencing the GPS and the street signs, accidentally running myself into one-ways every now and then.

A long twenty minutes later, I pulled up to the chapel. The parking lot was packed out, they even had parking lot directors steering traffic.

Damn.

In the back of my mind, I pictured how I would look stepping out in my stretched-out deep V-neck sweatshirt and boot-cut dark blue jeans over my Timbs. I wasn't fit for a wedding, but then again, I wasn't coming as a guest.

My hope was that Danielle was somewhere still putting on make-up. Maybe even alone somewhere, though I'd never heard of a wedding that separated a bride and her entourage.

Fear. It crept all over me while I pulled into a spot near the back. I was being foolish. Borderline criminal. I was trying to see her before it was too late, but maybe too late already had happened. I knew from experience that intentions meant nothing once the damage was done, and my actions could cause plenty if I didn't think it through.

I couldn't be that guy. Not again.

My mind chimed in.

Come on, Shawn. You can do this.

I continued to grip the steering wheel, staring through the windshield at the giant doors and the church steps. Visually, I followed them up to the cross-shaped steeple at the very top. Maybe God could give me some guidance.

Maybe God would tell me to stop. Tell me what I already knew. That I was being ridiculous, selfish, and needed to get out while I still could. Catch the first thing back to Charlotte, and get on with my successful and normal life.

This is crazy. Fuckin' crazy. Stay your ass in this car and go home before you make a fool out of yourself.

Nah, fuck that. Come too far to turn back now.

Sweat beads leisurely slid down from the brim of my hairline, most of it stopping at my brow. I closed my eyes and took a deep breath to try and steady myself, but ended up doing the exact opposite.

Before I knew it, my car door was open and I was standing into the cold air as it chilled my eyes into a squint and stung my neck. It was far too cold to be without a coat of some kind, but I didn't exactly plan ahead.

I walked up to the church, trying not to make eye contact with any of the parking lot attendants because I knew they'd ask me who I was. I'd have to think up a lie and hope they believed it.

Look straight, Shawn. Don't look at them. Don't look.

Oh no, they see you. Still, don't look.

I kept walking, now going up the steps to the church. I put my ear to the frigid door, listening to see if it had already started.

The first part was inaudible, but I was able to make out the second half of the sentence being spoken, "...and if anyone feels this couple should not be united in Holy Matrimony, speak now, or forever hold your peace..."

A Terminal Illness Called Living Without You

My heart pounded like HBCU base drummers, and my breath glowed white in the cold air bigger with every exhalation.

I had to do something. This was my chance.

But instead, I froze.

I. Fucking. Froze.

Paralyzed by something. More fear maybe, or just a lack of courage. I don't know. But something was keeping my feet still and my mouth closed.

The preacher continued on while I just stood there.

If I ruined this moment for her, her family would hate me. They may even attack me. Police would come. But more importantly, I'd take away one of the happiest moments of her life.

You can't do that to her, Shawn. You had your chance. Let her have hers.

Nah, scratch that. If she wants a chance, she'll get it eventually. But this one's yours. Probably your only one. Do it. Do it now!

"NOOOO!" I yelled out into the surface of the door.

My fists clenched, my eyes closed...I just snapped. I could hear the crowd on the inside turning in their seats and starting to chatter. The parking lot attendants had all focused on me.

But I didn't care anymore. I had nothing left to lose. This was it.

I reached up and placed the palm of my hand on the church doors, slowly opening them. I was prepared for whatever came with my decision.

One foot in front of the other, I slowly walked in, echoing through what was now a silent building. The church was much bigger on the inside than it appeared from the outside. And the people on the inside didn't look happy to see me.

A few guys standing in the pews seemed to be making their way over. To be manly and protective, securing the women and children. I guess to them I could've been anyone. A murderer, a Satanist, an escaped convict. Who else would interrupt a wedding?

I focused my attention down the center of the aisle. Right at the altar, in front of the pastor.

The groom. He was angry. His groomsmen close beside him. Not exactly welcoming expressions on their faces either.

And then the bride. Beautiful. So elegant. The train of her dress flowed at least six feet behind her like a real-life princess.

But...it wasn't Danielle. Her veil was lifted from her face, and even from what seemed like a country mile of distance between us, I could tell that it wasn't her. It wasn't my baby.

Hol-lee-shhhhhiiiit. I thought to myself.

I must've chosen the wrong church.

I needed to get out of there. If I could stiff arm the door and clear the steps in one leap, I'd have at least a four-second head start on the closest man in pursuit. Cold air and no stretch, could get a Charlie horse, but it was worth a shot. Hopefully the ladies would be so upset they'd get in the way of the angry ass men and slow them down long enough for me to get in the car and pull out.

I turned around to execute the plan and someone said, "Shawn?"

I stopped, looked around for a familiar face, but didn't see one. But that voice, I'd know that voice anywhere.

Danielle emerged from a pew in the middle, in a coral dress, her body still very much so intact and her face just as unbelievable as the first day I'd laid eyes on her.

I'd been praying on this day to come for so long with no real faith it ever would. And now that it had, I was in a state of shock.

"What are you doing here, Shawn? How...*how* did you get here?"

Danielle looked dumbfounded while her mother, behind her, looked on in disappointment.

My words were getting caught in my throat so I cleared it. "Well...I mean, the GPS helped but..."

Her face and everyone else's became annoyed at my obtuse answer.

"Look, it was her. She told me you were getting married," I snitched on Miss Sarah, pointed finger and all.

Older ladies in the church were gasping for air. The brothers all seemed to be still trying to figure out what was going on, including the pastor.

Danielle turned to her mother. "You told him that?"

"No, not exactly. I told him *a* wedding was today. I didn't tell him that you were the one getting married."

I cut in, "You practically did. You said--"

"Mother--"

"I didn't actually think he'd come, honey. That's crazy, only a mad man would come and do such a thing. Even if he were to try, I figured there was no way he could make a flight the same day to get here in time."

"Actually, I didn't." Everyone turned back to look at me. Nervously I said, "I um...I took a jet?"

Danielle walked towards me then stopped short about five or so feet away.

"You did *what?*"

"I said, I took a jet. Rented a car. Googled the church address, and...here I am."

Miss Sarah nervously addressed the crowd who'd been neglected the past few moments. "Um...everyone, I apologize. There's just been a big misunderstanding. But it's all right now."

She looked at Danielle and me, widening her eyes as a signal to go along with it. Danielle came and grabbed me by the hand, leading us to the pew where her mother was.

"Pastor, please...do continue." Miss Sarah said. She smiled and sat down as the rest of the church did the same, all while keeping their attention on me and not the soon-to-be married couple.

The service ended up being rather beautiful actually.

Danielle and I did tidbits of catching up while the rest of the attendees eyed me. It was a love-or-hate stare. I could see those who intended on coming to a picture-perfect wedding that was rudely interrupted and I also recognized those hopeless romantics that always dreamed of something like that happening to them.

After enough fake chatter and lies about me being a distant friend of the family, Miss Sarah went back home while Danielle and I went out downtown to try and catch up and get some clarity on the rest of the day. It was late so the streets were empty, but the streetlamps were still busy with gnats leeching off of the light that revealed the sidewalks.

"So...you're just gonna act like everything's normal?" I asked, walking beside her with a safe space in between us.

Which was difficult. She had on skinny jeans that proved her figure to be everything but skinny in every right way possible. The cup of her ass was still as perfect as I'd left it before, but I wasn't going to dare get caught looking.

"I mean, what am I supposed to do, Shawn?"

"I don't know. Wonder how this all came about. Wonder when I'm going to leave you alone."

"Whoa there. Let's slow down a bit. How about I wonder what you've been up to all this time? Tell me about that."

She looked at me with an assuring smile.

"Well, after graduation, I moved out to Charlotte. Sales wasn't really my thing. Too much pretending to be involved and I'd never been good at that so I stuck with what I knew. My writing."

"It's about damn time."

"What does that mean?"

"Means that I always knew you were supposed to do something with that gift. Glad to know you didn't let it go to waste."

"Well, thanks. Funny thing is, it didn't quite pan out as fast as I'd hoped. I quit my fancy job and things got rough for a little while."

"Yeah, a lot of people take that leap of faith a little too soon. Can cause a rough landing."

"And a fracture."

"I don't see any broken bones from over here, Mr. Private Jet."

We both laughed. The small talk was keeping us occupied but our minds were on something else.

"Well, I'm glad to know it worked out. You went and changed on me. The Shawn I know, the country boy from Deep South Alabama...he wasn't gettin' on nobody's airplane, much less a private jet. To catch a wedding? Something ain't right with that."

"I told you, it wasn't about the wedding."

"But still, you rushed to make sure you got here before it was official."

"Because I respect the vows. Can't go breaking happy homes. The ones that get built right there in front of God himself. Bad karma."

She nodded in agreement as we sat down at a closed cafe's outside seating area. "Yeah, I guess you got a point. Just curious as to what rules didn't get thrown out when you put everything aside to come out here. I mean, damn. A phone call would've--"

"You know Miss Sarah wasn't having that."

"True, true," she said laughing. "Mommy doesn't know how to loosen the grip on that umbilical cord. She means well; she just has one hell of a way of showing it. I think we all do, ya know?"

"Yeah, I do," I said, trying to think of a way to redirect

this conversation away from the obvious path it was about to go.

She looked down at the ground and smiled before looking up at me again, "You know, you kept yourself up pretty well. A bit underdressed for today's occasion, but you got away with it. In my book."

"Young lady, are you flirting with me?" I asked shrewdly.

Her smile bolstered. "Absolutely not, sir. It's not lady-like to flirt, but a secret compliment is about as good as a penny with a hole in it."

I wanted to smile, but my lips were too damn dry. The temperature felt like the sun and earth were worst enemies, so I used body heat as an excuse to get closer to her.

And for the first time in almost five years, I didn't have a single transgression lingering on my mind. Not one. Not the arguments, the fighting, the cheating, the lying...all of that seemed so distant.

Either my conscience was finding refuge in my ability to still make her smile, or the good in seeing her now far out-weighed the bad of everything we'd been through.

My chair was close enough to her now for our knees to touch. My hand met hers.

"I guess some things never change, huh?" she said, look-ing at our fingers locked together.

"Nah, they don't. Like this moment. I swear....I'd give any-thing to make this stay the same forever."

"I like the sound of that." She smiled.

But only for a second.

The happiness on her face subsided and a look of con-cern flushed over her as she gently pulled away from me.

*****

I woke up, Danielle's half-naked body on mine, still asleep after apparently coming up to my room with me.

She was a light sleeper, so as soon I moved my head, she was already looking up to see what was going on.

"Superman?" she moaned, one eye still closed, and the other gazing at me.

"Yes, sweetheart. I'm right here," I answered back. The pet names were back to being involuntary, just a language of affection we'd both missed.

"Okay, you need me to try and make it home? I can probably drive if I just--"

"Nah, you're good. Just get some rest. I kept you out late tonight."

She leaned up and kissed me on the cheek. It was soft. Gentle.

My penis was stiffening from the friction between her legs and mine. I didn't want it to show for fear of ruining what could've been a moment.

She must've felt it rising because her eyes opened and she looked at me, fully awake this time.

"Superman...you all right?"

"Yeah. I'm cool. I mean, I'll be all right. Just give it a few seconds to wear off."

"All right. I know it's uncomfortable, but we're just not.... you know."

"Yeah, I know. We're not there yet. And that's cool. I didn't bring you here for that anyway."

We both just looked up at the ceiling. Things running

through my mind, her wondering what was on my mind.

"Remember when you said that you'd like to make that moment last forever?"

"I do," I said, raising an eyebrow.

"Well, I don't know about forever. But for however long, I say we make it count. For real this time," she said, smiling.

I looked down at her looking up at me, then positioned myself so my penis was firmly pressed against her. You know, so there was no confusion.

There wasn't.

She kissed me. First.

It turned me on. I didn't want to take any chance that she'd get cold feet and feel like she was going too far out on a limb by making such a bold move so I kissed her back. Returning her passion and then some.

She grabbed at my dick which was gorging with so much blood, the grooves of my veins could be seen through my boxer briefs. I was ready.

I flipped her on her back, pouncing on top and kissing lower down to her neck and then between her thighs.

She moaned, exhaling and moving her hands over my triceps.

We were both riding the tidal wave of hormones getting ready to crash into the banks of *too damn long since the last time*.

And then she just stopped.

I kept going, not noticing at first. After a few seconds, I looked up and tried to read her eyes.

"Baby, did I do something wrong?" I asked her.

She looked up at the ceiling, fighting tears. "No, Superman. You didn't."

"Then what's wrong? You sure I'm not moving too fast? We don't have to do this," I said, getting off of her and sliding back to her side.

She lost the fight and tears broke through, fleeing down her cheeks like they were running from the thoughts she wouldn't express.

"Danielle," I said, this time more serious. "What is going on? Please...say something."

"I can't do this, Superman. I want to so bad. I mean, I do. But it's just--"

"Look, don't explain. You don't have to. It's all good. Seriously, I'm not mad or anything. We can just chill or go back to sleep."

Her tears continued to fall into the pillow case underneath her. The disturbed look from earlier was there again.

"Superman...I need to tell you something. I've kinda been afraid to, but I need to just go ahead and tell you this."

"No, Danielle. You don't have to tell me anything. Look, I love you. I still love you, and sex or no sex...that's not going to change. And if it would, I didn't deserve you in the first place."

"But Shawn, that's not the problem."

"I mean, I may not deserve you now, but that's not the point. The point is, sex isn't nearly important enough to tarnish what we could still have together. I've waited and waited, but maybe it's best I just tell you something. Something I've been thinking about for a while. And no, Danielle. This isn't just because we're in the moment. This is for real."

"Superman," she cried.

I ignored her, "Danielle, I want to spend the rest of my

life with you!"

"I have HIV," she said at the same time.

And then we froze. Not sure if I was still breathing. Nor was I sure if she was either. But I know for that moment, nothing moved, not even time.

Maybe my ears are deceiving me, I thought. "Did you...just... say..."

"Yes, Superman. I said, I'm HIV-positive."

My heart sank down into my hands, slipped through, and then crashed somewhere on the floor. My eyes watered up. I've been told bad news before, but this by far was worse than anything I could imagine.

"Baby...I...I didn't know. I'm so sorry."

"You're sorry? No, I'm sorry. I just got caught up in feeling...normal again. I didn't mean to take it this far, and please understand, I would never intentionally put you in harm's way."

"No, this isn't about me. I'm fine. But, I had no idea. I don't even know what to say right now."

"You don't have to say anything. I've been living with HIV the last eight months now. Caught it from my ex. It was a bad choice. He was a bad choice. I don't know what I was thinking trusting him, but I did."

"You say that like this is all some kind of punishment. This was *not* your fault."

"Yet I'm the one who has to pay for it. With my happiness. With any chance for a family. With my life... There's no chance for any of that now."

Her cries became more audible. She couldn't hold it in any longer, and as far as I was concerned, she didn't have to.

I pulled her closer to me, laying her head on my chest so she could get it all out.

She went on about her ex, about how she never really was into him in the first place. She was just going with the flow, and it happened. She kept up a relationship, even with no plans for a future under the guise that we were young and are supposed to have time to make those kinds of mistakes. Which...we do.

But that doesn't mean we'll have more time to live after those mistakes are made.

"Danielle...I'm here for you. You do know that...right?"

"I know," she cried.

It seemed that hearing me reassure her that I was in her corner did nothing to take away the painful reality that she was going to be battling this sickness for the rest of her life or die trying.

I placed my hand on the back of her head gently, rubbing on her ear. The other hand was reached over and holding the back of her shoulder as we laid together. My tears began to form and I didn't want her to be able to see them.

We sat, at least five more minutes. Both of us crying, me comforting her out of her tears while trying to find peace within myself so I could take it all in.

"Danielle..." I said, finally pulling her over.

She looked at me again, "Yes?"

"I still love you."

"I know you do, Superman," she forced out along with a smile.

I leaned down and kissed her on her forehead.

Then again.

Then I pulled her over on her side and kissed her on her lips.

A few times.

I put my tongue in her mouth, locking passionately into another kiss with my hand cupping the left side of her face.

At first she hesitated, but then she relaxed and kissed me back.

I reached down between her thighs, slowly massaging her clit and then I went for the edge of her panties.

"Superman, what are you doing?"

"I told you, Danielle. I love you."

"No, Superman...I can't let you do this. I won't let you do this."

"It's not about the sex. I said I still love you. And I mean that."

"Okay, fine. I get it. But there's a great chance you'll contract the virus and I'll never forgive myself for doing that to you."

"I know exactly what that means for me. But when I said I wanted to spend the rest of my life with you, I meant it. Without conditions.

"Even without a marriage license or some papers saying you and I are now one. At this point, I'm ready to commit to you for the rest of my life. For the rest of *our* lives. That means, you're a part of me. If you're battling this virus, then we both are. And if we die together because of it, it'll still be better than living another moment without you. You will not face this alone, Danielle. Not if I have anything to do with it."

She looked up at me, fear and uncertainty written on her

face. She seemed to believe me, was trying to trust me, but was still holding onto concern for my well-being.

"Superman...but, I just can't. You don't deserve this."

"They say that what you deserve should come before what you want, but what you deserve takes a back seat to what you can't live without. Right now, this is how I feel. Whether it be for a long time or short, I think it's time I make it crystal clear that I want to spend the rest of my life with you. Only you. If you'll have me."

I kissed her neck again. She tensed up, but she didn't stop me.

And I didn't want her to.

It was time I made a commitment, a real commitment, and stuck to it. This was what I wanted. Maybe not exactly how I wanted it, but as far as I was concerned, it didn't matter. She was everything to me, and if that was going to be taken away then I might as well be taken away right along with her. Until then we'd live, fight, and be happy together.

Wedding rings can come off, but there was going to be no divorcing this decision. This was it, and that was just fine by me.

Darker the Berry, the Deeper I Bite

I jumped up, my phone was being obnoxiously loud, damned near ringing off the night-stand table with an incoming call. I felt around for Danielle, but she wasn't there.

In fact, it looked like she had never even been there. The pillow was still perfectly fluffed and the covers not even untucked.

I sat up to see myself still in the clothes from the night before with the exception of my shoes. She must've taken those off for me because I didn't remember. Then everything slowly started to make sense.

My phone rang again, shouting at me with anger because I didn't pick up the first time.

"Hello?" I answered, rubbing my temples.

"Bro, I got some good news. Some really, really good news. You ready?"

"P.?"

"Yeah, man, you don't know my voice? You sound like you just woke up. You just waking up?"

I pulled the phone from my face to look at the time. 10:34 a.m. I never slept that late.

"Um...yeah, I guess so. I think I just had like...the craziest dream ever."

I heard Rashonda's voice in the background and Pete

moving to get away from her. He said, "Hold on."

I put the phone down and hooked it up to the auxiliary cord of the alarm clock radio so I could hear him while I walked over to the bathroom and brushed my teeth.

He came back, "Yeah, man, I was going to ask. How'd that go? You get to see her? You gotta fill me in."

"Yeah, I did." I spat out through a mouthful of tooth-paste. "I think it went well, all things considered. I mean, we talked and stuff."

"Dude, seriously? That's so awesome. Is she there now or what?"

"Nah. I mean we were chillin', but I don't even know if she came back up here. I been so exhausted from all the trav-eling, I can't remember right now but it looks like I passed out on her. Had a weird dream that she had HIV but we were going to...never mind."

I spit again a few times to rinse my mouth out. Looked in the mirror to check for crust. It was there. I must've been sleeping like a rock.

"What are you doing?"

I cut off the faucet, "My bad. Just finished brushing my teeth."

"With what?"

"What you mean, with what? A toothbrush and tooth-paste."

"Be careful, bro. Toothpaste has fluoride in it. That stuff is poison."

"I actually remember reading about that a while back. But I don't know of a good alternative. You?"

"Nah, nothing. I just stopped brushing."

I exhaled sympathetically. Dude was a trip.

Then I remembered everything I had seen about Rashonda. About her criminal past. I needed to bring this up before it was too late.

"Hey, P., Rashonda near you? Like...as in, can she hear me?"

"You're not going to believe this," he cut in with a question of his own to change the subject.

"Believe what?"

"I got promoted to manager over at Bigger Burger. Gonna be making nine dollars an hour now so I can finally buy my own house. Enough room for me, Shonda, and maybe even a little one. Hell, maybe two or three...or four...or ten."

I sighed, "How sure are you that you even really know her like that?"

"If you're talking about the stripping she did back in the day, I don't care. Remember, man, you gotta see her heart. Not her past."

"I get all that, P. but still, there's more to--"

"I'm coming, my Queen-sized Kit Kat!" he yelled away from the phone. I looked at the phone like it was crazy for even passing on Pete's weird ass pet name for Rashonda. "Hey, Shawn, I'll call you back. But just for future reference, I'd like your support on this. Really don't need the negativity."

"I'm your boy, P. You know I support you fully. I just think you'd want to at least know that--"

"Good deal. That's what I like to hear," he said, cutting me off. "Talk to ya soon and make sure you finish telling me about what happened with Danielle. Peace."

"But P.," I responded back as he hung up without hearing it.

Even if he heard me, I don't think he would've listened.

Rashonda's past seemed to be more in her present than he wanted to admit, especially if she was still lying to him about it.

Now that I think about it, she probably thought Pete was a baller. That's why she hooked up with him in the first place. Him borrowing my car. Fronting with his new clothes he always kept the tags on and receipts for, as well as my watches he had leased.

I'm guessing after that fell through, she actually did get close enough to someone with a little money, me, and that's where Dominique came in. That was supposed to bait me in. But that still doesn't explain why she would try herself, though. Hell, I don't know. It was all too much.

I didn't have the mental real estate to stress about that until I got my own business straight.

I hopped in the shower, double checking my penis to see whether or not I had sex. I could always tell the morning after because it'd feel worn out and overworked. I felt like anything less was a disrespect to the beauty of making love anyway.

But it didn't. Still freshly unsatisfied as it'd always been. Confirmation that I'd indeed spent the night alone.

And this time, it turned out to be a good thing.

*****

"Yeah, I'm going to be leaving too tomorrow. Gotta get back to work," I said.

"Okay, so if I do meet you tonight, then what? You're just...gone?"

"Well, I'm hoping we can talk about all that when you get here. eight p.m., sharp. I'll send a driver for you about an hour prior."

Danielle responded, "Okay then. Yes, I'll see you later on mister." Her tone seemed to be smiling through the phone.

Stacy found me a beautiful resort at Colorado Springs. A beach would've been better, but the closest one was about a twelve hour drive so a lake-front vacation condo would have to do.

I wanted a follow up from the previous night with Danielle. Hopefully seal things between us and get a definitive on where she stood. The vibes were great so far, but there was a hint of doubt in every moment we had that stifled my confidence.

Since we'd only met up twice since I'd come in town, spur of the moment and nothing really planned out or coordinated, I decided to switch things up one last time.

I spent the better part of the day planning, working out every detail, and scheduling down to the very last minute.

There was a heat wave, giving me one night out above sixty degrees, and I planned on taking full advantage. I had a table set up in the back lawn complete with an off-white linen cloth, silverware, a pot of lilies, and six-foot tall-fire lanterns for our dinner.

I considered getting a chef to cook, but Momma would have no part of that, being that she took pride in raising a man who could cook for himself (even though I'd never tell her just how bad of a cook I was). But about thirty minutes of recipe writing and helpful tips from her and I was in the condo cooking up a storm.

A little hors d'oeuvres on a bed of ice with cocktail sauce and a bottle of Chateau Montrose imported from France. I knew nothing about it, honestly, but at $300 a bottle, I figured it couldn't be too shabby.

We had this upscale seafood restaurant we went to back in college for special occasions, and none was more special than that night, so for the main course I stuck with the theme and boiled lobster tail, extracted from the shell, coconut rice, lemon peppered asparagus, and of course, homemade biscuits.

By the way, homemade biscuits are a bitch to make. I broke two wooden spoons trying to stir the mix before giving up and doing as Momma recommended and bare-hand combining it.

After dinner, the menu called for some strawberries and squares of pound cake dipped in white chocolate fondue. Originally, I was just going to do a fruit pizza, but the moment I mentioned it, Momma started cussing me out. Daring me to do a "damned fruit pizza on a night like this" and "wishing some man would try to call himself making fruit pizza for me like we twelve-year-olds at a slumber party."

I took her advice.

I pulled out the only suit I had packed, thankful that I packed at least one. It was a favorite of mine, skillfully tailored to fit snug on my six-foot-four, 265-pound frame. I'd always found it difficult to get a suit because of my build. Even after I finished my football career, I was hitting the gym like I was going to line up on kick-off one more Saturday afternoon fishing for highlight film material. My arms were still over twenty inches and my back was broader than most, which made for a headache when dealing with little elderly tailors that barely spoke English.

So the moment I could afford it, I had a few constructed from the ground up, and it was one of the best investments I'd ever made.

With my fade brushed, my tie clip straight, and my shoes shined to perfection, I was ready to start the night.

She showed up promptly at eight as we'd arranged. I could see the driver opening her car door. She didn't exactly dress up, which was normally fine for me. But this was different. I wanted to do it right, and luckily, I'd planned ahead.

The attendants I'd hired walked her into the guest room where a glam squad was waiting for her. Licensed hair and makeup beauticians were brought in, even though she normally didn't wear makeup. I told them to keep it nice and light, not too much, and to insist if she refused, which I'm sure she did. Danielle wasn't into all that, last I checked, but she was game if she could tell I put some effort into the plans.

I finished prepping the food, going over instructions with the waiter who was going to be bringing it out to us, what cues to look for when I was ready.

The violinist had almost fallen asleep from waiting so long, but I couldn't risk him getting there late so I threw in a few extra dollars if he could make it early. We decided on some classic R&B for him to cover, along with *Drunk In Love* from Beyoncé, and of course, *I Ain't Mad At Ya* by Tupac. Don't judge me, I love that song.

About forty minutes went by, and according to the schedule she should've been coming out of hair and makeup and into her dressing room where she would change clothes.

Before I went shopping for her outfit, I browsed online, looking for something that would be her style. That was until I realized that I had absolutely no fashion sense when it came to women's clothing. I had man-taste. That means it went into two of four categories; hot or not, classy or trashy.

And when it came to Danielle, I was biased anyway so I just got a wardrobe stylist which ended up being a life saver.

The stylist presented me with ten options to choose from. Again, overestimating my fashion savvy, so I played it safe and got all of them. Danielle could choose which one she wanted when she got there. Doubt she'd have too much of a problem with it.

Finally, an hour had passed and it was time.

I thought back to days when we were dead broke, splitting packs of Ramen noodles, waiting for my checks to clear from the diner and hers from *Sonic*. It used to make me sick that this girl was everything I'd ever wanted yet had to settle only for what I could afford, which wasn't much.

But she didn't complain. She rode it out. Smiled gracefully every time and didn't make me feel like less of a man because of it. Creativity helped, but I swore to myself that the moment I got my funds together, I'd treat her like a princess. And this was my chance to make good on that promise.

I went to sit down at the table that'd been prepared for us. Then I stood back up, because sitting down would be rude.

I waited nervously for her to come out of the condo. I had in my mind how she'd look, and I was excited for it. But when she actually stepped out, my mind was blown.

Stunning, graceful, and other words I couldn't find because even mentally I became speechless at the sight of her.

Her natural hair was braided into a cascading French roll, exposing her chandelier earrings and almond skin. She radiated from her eyes to her smile, bright enough to turn the moon green with envy.

The slit up the left side of her dress exposed her freshly shaven and cocoa-buttered legs, flexing her quad muscles with every stride.

I was so out of my league.

"Well, hello, handsome. So...what ya think?"

"I can't think right now. Don't make me try," I laughed.

Like I said, I was nervous. Even if I wanted to be smooth, it wouldn't have worked.

"Well, I think what you've put together is quite amazing, sir. You sure did go all out."

"I'm glad you like," I responded.

I walked closer to her and kissed her lips, softly. Didn't want to ruin her lipstick.

I pulled out her chair for her to sit, then went around to my seat, cuing the shrimp, wine, and violinist.

We ate, reminisced, and looked over the water a while. She threw a few pieces of ice at me when I told her about my dream. As if I'd planned it.

"I said it was a dream!" I laughed, still dodging the ice.

"So what? It must've been on your mind or something. And you had the nerve to still try and have sex with me? Even with me having HIV? You're such a horn dog."

She threw another piece.

"Look, it was deeper than that. I mean, we had talked about more, but I don't wanna go into all the detail. Just know, overall, it was a good dream. Okay, not good, but you know, it ended pretty good."

"Just pretty good? I'm just *pretty good* now? You was willing to risk your life for some ass that was mediocre. You're not as smart as you look, boy."

We both laughed, and eventually found our hands together again.

I was full from the entree but dessert was inside waiting on us. Honestly, I couldn't eat another bite and just wanted to lie down.

I grabbed her hand and led her down closer to the edge of the lake. When I sprawled out on the grass is when she stopped following my lead.

"Umm...Shawn, you do know that ground is dirty, right?"

"Yeah, we can always get clean. Come on, get down here with me." I sat up, pushed the back of her knee so her legs would buckle.

She fell down, purposely driving her elbow into my stomach, and said, "That's what you get."

That started a wrestling match.

We tumbled a few times, me wrapping her arms where she couldn't get loose and her still finding a way out and going to cut off my air supply. She was stronger than I thought.

I used my weight to get back on top and pin her wrists to the ground.

I kissed her.

She said, "You win."

"We both do," I responded.

I gave the cue to the waiter to do the last-minute preparations for the room and take the rest of the night off along with the rest of the staff.

We tongue locked for a few minutes, much longer than was necessary. But the taste of her passion was well worth the binge.

"Come on, let's go inside," I said, standing up.

She hesitated. That same disturbed look I'd been noticing came back but only briefly before she reached for my hand anyway.

Sensing her uneasiness, I bypassed it, scooping her from the ground into my arms.

Maybe she was just trying to adjust to me being around again. That disconnect from the time we spent apart couldn't be more palpable, but if it could be mended, then tonight was the night.

I carried her into the room where the fondue was still warm and the music was now playing softly in the background.

No R&B. That was too typical, but the jazz was a bit different. Smooth, grown-up, and still sexy, like us.

I eased off her shoes.

"Superman," she said.

Outside of my dreams I hadn't heard her call me that since we were in college.

"Yes, baby?"

"Why you doing all this? This is all just...too much," she moaned as she took in the room.

I may have gone a little overboard with the room, but life's too short to play it safe. The excitement of finally having someone to do this for was more than I wanted to handle. So I went all out with the Chalet suite, silk linens in the bed, Jacuzzi-style tub in the corner of the room with heated jets already full force.

Ten bags of fresh rose petals blanketed the floor and the comforter. The hanging lamps looked like suspended golden spheres. More bottles of red wine than either of us would ever drink, but it beautifully completed the decor.

I refused to half-step on such an occasion as this. My excitement wouldn't let me. Sex was a possibility, but her feeling complete ecstasy was a must. If this time was the last time I was going to see her, I was going to make it count. I couldn't make her love me again, but I would be one hard act to follow.

"It's not too much," I said. "You just got used to too little. And I think it's time we fix that."

I took off my jacket, then unraveled my tie. I kept on the shirt but loosened a few buttons at the top so just my chest was exposed.

Once she was settled on the bed, I took the bowl of massage oils off the burners. I made sure they were heated just enough to open her pores so I could reach in and evict the stress that had made itself at home in her body. It had no place there and I was going to make that crystal clear.

I started with her neck and shoulders. I don't think she expected the heat from the way she flinched at first, but a soft "ooooh..mm-hmm..." let me know it was still welcomed.

She was tense. Very. Seemed like the moment had a lot to do with it. I remembered her touch like it was just yesterday, but this feeling was unfamiliar. Something was keeping her from loosening completely up with me.

I pushed gently with my thumbs, pulled with the rest of my fingers, and gripped tightly across every bit of exposed skin down to the soles of her feet to try and work it out.

Maybe it was the jazz music. I reached for the remote which I'd purposely placed within reach so I could press the skip button and get to Baby Face and company.

A few moments of silence went by and I asked, "Danielle...you still awake?"

She murmured, "Yes, and that was amazing. Thank you for that."

"We're not done yet. I think we should finish in the Jacuzzi."

"Hmph. You just wanna get me out of my clothes. Don't you?" she smirked.

"What I see in you exposes more than just your body or we wouldn't even be here," I responded. She broke into a wide smile. "But if you're going to play it like that, then fine. We don't have to get in the tub. Close your eyes."

She obliged. I honestly didn't plan for her to resist getting in the tub so I had to think quickly.

I looked around the room and saw three bathrobes hanging on the far side by the closet. A light bulb went off in my head.

I went and grabbed them, pulled the strings off, and came back to the bed.

"Sit up, and keep your eyes closed."

"Okay..."

I strung her wrist to the headboard. That made her look at me again.

"Wait...what is this?"

"This is me making sure I can't see you naked until I make you beg for it." I grinned as I strung her other wrist.

She accepted the challenge by not resisting. I put them just tight enough to bound her without hurting her.

I used the third string to wrap around her eyes.

I took pride in the fact that my demeanor was flexible in the bedroom. At times I could be commanding, and other times simply convincing.

I stepped back to admire her. Still in the dress I'd bought, sexy as ever and tied up. I'd never done anything like that. Heard of it in Fifty Shades but not in real life. But again, playing it safe wasn't on the agenda tonight.

I grabbed the fondue and set it on the table. I fed her the strawberries while I talked; decided to foreplay with her mentally so physically, there'd be nothing left to do but orgasm.

"Everything I'm about to say is completely rhetorical. When I do ask for a response, just nod your head. Understood?"

She nodded, smiling slyly. Chewed the strawberries in her own real-time slow motion, waiting for me to continue.

"Good. Tonight, I need you to do something. It's important, critical even. I need you to forget about anything outside of right now. I need you to find your way to a place where worry and unpleasant memories can't find you. Where obligations aren't allowed. Tonight, I just need you to focus on relaxing and letting me give you some special attention. Is that understood?"

She nodded again.

I dipped a strawberry in the white chocolate, swabbed it across her lips. The moment she tried to bite, I moved it to her neck and licked off the sweet residue.

Her legs crossed. I kept licking, reaching for more strawberries to give her while I did.

While she was responding, a part of her was still holding back.

I spooned the chocolate along her left shin. It was just on the verge of hot but not scalding where it could actually burn her. She gasped when it touched her and exhaled with a moan when she felt my tongue following to clean it up.

Chocolate drops continued to fall, but I couldn't quite get her key to turn, so I kept sucking. And sucking.

I dipped a finger in the bowl, then reached under her dress to the edge of her underwear. I was absolutely sure she would stop me but dared to try anyway, and it worked. She opened her legs for easier access, seemingly trying to let herself be comfortable in the moment. I went right in with every intention of helping her do that very thing.

My taste buds were singing into the surface of her skin and her body was dancing to the melody. The part of her that was fighting to maintain her composure began rearing its head again.

So, I French kissed along her thigh before going to her panties, sucking through the fabric to taste the wetness that confessed her lustful cravings.

Persistence.

As fate would have it, *So Anxious* by Genuine was singing along with what we both knew was on our mind.

"Please, just take it."

"Take what?" I said, purposely being obtuse.

"Me. Take *me*!"

I smiled in victory.

I left her tied to the bed, but slid her panties from her body.

I licked, sucked, flicked, and delved tongue deep into her pussy until my neck was sore. She hadn't orgasmed yet so I wasn't about to stop. I cupped my hands under her ass, then lifted her pelvis off the bed, careful not to let her disengage from my mouth.

That was much better.

She flung her legs over my shoulders and we were in a position I don't even think the karma sutra could explain.

I wanted to be gentle and continue being romantic, but my adrenaline was cascading like a river and there was going to be no dam. If I did have an alter ego, chances are it wasn't human.

I lifted up higher, still licking and sucking like she was watermelon at a summer picnic with one hand and undressed myself with the other. Once I was naked, I removed the string from her eyes so she could see me.

Her attention directed to my shaft like it was a magic trick.

"Well, hello there, sir," she smirked.

She had an air about her I hadn't seen before. Instead of trying to figure it out, I just went with it.

A lot of time had passed. We were no longer just teenagers learning our way around our bodies, but young adults who had just found out and were ready to take it as far as it could go.

I loosened the strings on her wrists so she could do as she

pleased.

That ended in scratches on my back, sheets pulled off the bed, fondue on the floor and the nightstand table pushed over.

I don't even know how that happened.

But with all of that damage to the room, still...no orgasm. Something was wrong.

By the time we were in doggy-style, I was pouring sweat, glistening and panting, and growing impatient.

"What...the fuck....is wrong with you?" I said, speaking more so to her seemingly broken vagina than her.

But it slipped.

"Feed it another berry, maybe that'll work," she responded, her body getting rigid.

I didn't stop stroking. In fact, I went a little harder.

"So, what's that supposed to mean?"

"It means you think a little wine and dine is all it takes to remedy us. That's what." She threw her ass back, hard. A little off target, but I maneuvered just in time to roll with her angle so she wouldn't break me in half.

We caught a glimpse of ourselves in the mirror, neither of us with faces of love making, but now with the expressions of enmity.

I couldn't peel back the layers like I probably should have, but on the surface, she'd just dissed everything I'd worked so hard to put together for the night. She had a habit of doing that. All the effort I put in to make it special. She just spat on it.

I grabbed her waist for more control. My movements were becoming borderline violent with frustration.

"Excuse me, if I don't have a way to go back and undo all the bad, redo all of the unforgiveable...but if a brother is trying his best, the least you could do is appreciate it for what it is instead of stepping on his fuckin' neck."

"Maybe I'm stepping on your neck because I'm having to step over the pieces of my heart you left shattered on the ground," she said angrily.

I stopped. Without the noises of our friction, her cries began to pierce through the room. Softly but undeniable and potent with feelings suppressed for far too long.

I leaned over her, without removing myself. Kissed the back of her neck.

I couldn't say much, but our eyes met in the mirror once again, and it was clear that everything she felt, I shared with her. Not because I went through what she did, but because when you love somebody, what's theirs is yours and that includes the pain.

"You went through so much to earn it," she continued. "just to break it. Somebody was worth it to you. Somebody was worth breaking me."

Shots of agony poured into my stomach. But I remained silent and kissed her again.

"And all the times I wanted to fix me, and put me back together, I couldn't. No one could. And you know who's fault that was?!"

I knew exactly how she felt.

"It was your fault. It was all your fucking fault! Because you...you were the missing piece. You always have been," she cried out.

I slowly grinded inside her. Her cries got louder, but she

didn't pull away from me. She moved her body with mine.

"Don't hold back," I whispered.

I placed my fists over her shoulders just an inch or so away from her ears, caging her in. My body positioned like an ape.

And I kept going. Gently, but firmly. Holding back tears of my own. The emotional osmosis was powerful enough to light an entire city.

Painful cries evolved into pleasurable moans. Traces of hurt were gone and satisfaction was recompensed.

I shoved deeper, using my arms as her bumper so she couldn't run or slip from under me.

I thrusted harder and faster.

As our love sounds crescendoed, that tense, unfamiliar, and disturbed feeling had finally gone away.

That was it all along. She needed to get that out of her system, and when she did, the real her was back again. And I wanted to give her a hero's welcome.

I released her from the constraints of my body to stand on my feet, feeling a bit roguish.

Before she could look at me and see what I was doing, I wrapped my arms around her waist and yanked her off of the bed. Upside down, suspended in the air with her split at tongue level.

I dove in then doggy paddled with my tongue once I was beneath the surface.

Her body squirmed, shivered, and became hot like glowing coals. Memories of what that meant were still fresh and it was only a matter of a seconds now.

She shrilled, "Oh...Oh!...Ohhhh!"

I growled, continuing to feast unrestrained by any etiquette. Kept my arms firmly wrapped around her waist so the jolts in her body wouldn't make her slip away.

With the same intensity, she grabbed my phallus from the very bottom and shoved me to the surface of her tonsils.

It caught me off guard but I held on in spite of it.

Her other hand reached around and grabbed my ass, gripping tightly but not enough to distract me from the warmth of her mouth and the spit dripping down my scrotum. I fought, resisted, mentally pleaded to last a little longer, but it didn't work.

I leaned, back first, against the bed so my legs wouldn't give when I came.

Afterwards, she flopped on the side of me outside of the covers. We stuck to one another like dirt to a dropped lollipop.

"Superman..."

"Baby..."

"I've never felt anything like that in my life."

"Me neither," I said back, still trying to catch my breath. "Oh yeah...my bad for cursing at you. It just came out wrong."

"No need to apologize. Sometimes we all need to be cursed at."

"True."

We both laughed. While I didn't say anything after that, I couldn't fight the thoughts of what was next for us.

But at that moment, it deserved to be left alone. Just good old-fashioned, reconnecting but-we-got-some-things-to-get-straight-first sex rest and recovery.

Let's Break the Rules

7 unread messages.

Pete: *Ay..guess what?* *[11:22 p.m.]*

Pete: *You there?* *[11:29 p.m.]*

Pete: *Bro...hit me back when you wake up.* *[11:35 p.m.]*

Pete: *Never mind that last text, this can't wait. Dude guess what?* *[11:37 p.m.]*

Pete: *Oh wait, you can't guess because you're sleep. Well, we're getting married!* *[11:38 p.m.]*

Pete: *I mean, after she says yes n all. But like right after she does, we're getting married!* *[11:38 p.m.]*

Pete: *Ring's fuckin huge. Cost me a fortune. At least a quarter carot, sterling silver. Wal-Mart's finest man. But yeah...talk to ya tomorrow. Let ya know how it goes.* *[11:40 p.m.]*

I woke up to the messages from Pete, rubbing my eyes several times before admitting that it wasn't just me. This fool really said he was about to marry Rashonda.

I texted my assistant to see if she was up. I swear, that girl never slept. Starbucks was running through her veins with how much she drank their coffee to stay on top of grad school. Tried not to press her too much for that very reason, but this was yet another emergency.

After a few messages had gotten tapped out between us, she found me another pilot to take me back to Charlotte.

It was early, so the sun still hadn't come up, but Danielle's sleep was interrupted by the phone's screen light. Her eyes focused in on my message thread as she came to.

"You stay on your phone," she groaned.

"How you know?"

Eyes still closed, she pressed her lips flat. "Because I know you."

She rolled over out of reach of the glare so she could go back to sleep.

I went into the bathroom to freshen up and started getting dressed. When I came out, Danielle was sitting up in the bed, wide awake and staring.

"What?" I said. Sounded just as dumb as my facial expression.

"I'm too old for these little hit-it and quit-its. And you spent way too much money to be doin' one. So you tell *me* what."

I laughed, walking towards her. "I'm not quitting anything. I have to get back home. Tend to some business. We're not done with anything as far as I'm concerned." I kissed her on her forehead for reassurance.

It didn't work.

She rolled her eyes and sighed, "Yeah, I guess. You dropping me off or do I need to call a ride?"

"Already arranged for your transportation. He'll be outside waiting in about an hour, but you can check out whenever you're ready. He's not going anywhere."

"How does it feel to be so in control? *'He's not going any-*

272

where," she mimicked. "Like the world is in your hands or something. That why you came up here, busting through church doors like you John Travolta or somebody? You think you all'at since you made it, huh?"

"Come on, D. Don't try me like that. I've always had confidence. Just now, with money, it's a little easier to do some things. Other things, I just take a chance and hope for the best. And I'm glad I did." I kissed her again.

This time she smiled.

"So you really wanna do this, huh? Me and you. You serious?"

"Very," I responded.

"How can you be so sure?"

"Well, for starters, I never had a doubt. As a matter of fact, why don't you come with me? Come to North Carolina."

She laughed and looked away. When she looked back at me and saw me not smiling, she stopped.

"Hold on...what?"

"I said come with me."

"And do what?"

"Not be away from me again." I admit, I didn't think before I spoke. I didn't have to.

I'd never been more sure of anything in my life. No insecurities about my ability to love her, consistently and genuinely. No questions about what would happen if I were to ever mess up. I was just...sure.

"That's crazy, Superman. This isn't college anymore. I have a job I have to--"

"Quit your job. And come with me. I took a chance and

came for you. Now take a chance and come back with me. We can get your stuff later and I'll make sure you have everything you need while you're there."

"So you're tryna shack up?"

"I'm trying to shower you with my love until you're drenched from head to toe," I said playfully as I gently brushed the back of my fingers across her mahogany cheeks. "But if it makes you feel better, I can get you a place of your own, name on the lease and everything. As for marriage, definitely don't want to propose to you out of obligation just so we can be politically correct. When it's the right time, we'll cross that bridge."

"And let's not forget there's no guarantee I'll say yes anyway."

"Right. So for now...just trust me."

"That's a lot of trust."

"And we'll need every bit of it to make it last. So, let's break the rules."

I grabbed her hand. She stood up from the bed. The covers slid from her body reminding me that she was completely naked.

I pushed her away from me so she fell back on top of the covers.

"Superman!" she yelled angrily.

I kneeled down, grabbed her legs, and lifted them onto my shoulders.

Had my breakfast early.

*****

By the time we'd gotten off the jet, I'd filled her in on Pete and his whole situation with Rashonda.

She felt like he deserved it for making black women his fetish. She didn't blush at the sound of anyone putting race in the same boat as her character and other things she thought should matter more. Didn't see it like that until she said it, but it made sense.

"So now you're trying to go and do what? Stop him from marrying this chick?" she said, chewing through a handful of dried apples.

"Something like that. Not exactly stop him, but at least let 'em know what's up. I mean, that's the homie. I can't let 'im do that to himself."

"And you said he loves her, right? Like for real?"

"Yea-up. Crazy about her."

"Hmph. You still out here tryna save everybody from themselves."

I looked over at her in the passenger side, taking my eyes off the road longer than I should have.

"If that's what you call it," I said. "I think you'd want somebody to do the same for you."

She shrugged her shoulders. "Yeah, whatever. I think if you keep grabbing people's hand the moment it gets too close to the stove, they'll never learn for themselves why they shouldn't touch it. Then when you leave, they'll just burn themselves anyway."

I didn't respond. Let her have that one while I drove us over to Pete's job.

I pulled up and saw him crouched behind the dumpster, pretending to look busy until he realized it was me.

"Crud, I'd just lit that cigarette. You made me waste it for no reason."

"Told you about smoking 'em in the first place," I said, stepping out of the car.

Without asking or me saying anything, Danielle hopped out too. Her shades on, belly shirt and high-waist jeans. Like my partner.

The way she'd always done when I needed to pay attention in class more, when I didn't have anything and she came to make sure I wanted for nothing. The same instinctive support that had her fueling my dreams from day one was second nature for even the smallest things like hopping out the car and making sure she was by my side. I loved that about her.

"Yeah, yeah. Cigarettes, shmigarettes. They tell us not to put anything in the microwave that has foil or metal on it too, but nobody listens to that. Besides, the way things are going right now, I could use a little help getting put out of my misery."

He looked over at Danielle. Straightened his hat and re-tucked in his shirt.

"You didn't tell me you were bringing company." He reached out his hand. "Hi, the name's Pete."

Danielle looked at me. I spoke up, "And this is Danielle, the one I've been telling you about."

"Danielle? As in....*Danielle*-Danielle?" he said.

I shook my head hoping to God he wouldn't say anything that'd get me and him both slapped.

"Yes, that's me." She smiled and firmly shook his hand.

"Damn, bro. I didn't know you were into black women. I thought you said they were all--"

"P., chill with the jokes. She don't know you yet so she don't know you joking." I turned to Danielle, mercifully. "Babe. He's joking. I promise you, he's just teasing."

"No, no, no," Pete continued. "That's why you asked me to hook you up with my sister. By the way, does she still have the key to your house? I need to wash clothes but I don't want to bother you while you have company."

I laughed out of nerves.

"Superman," Danielle smiled. "I think your friend here is a little jealous of me." She grabbed my ass. "You wish this was your hand. Don't ya, Pee Wee?"

Pete's face straightened back. Danielle reached up and kissed my neck.

"It's just Pete. And no, for your information I do not wish that was my hand. How'd we get on this subject anyway?"

"Man, tell me what's up. You said something about gettin' put out of your misery."

"Oh, right. Man..." His face went back to the perturbed mien he had before. "I don't know, bro. I just don't know."

"Shonda?" I asked.

"Yeah,"

"I was going to tell you before but--"

"She said no, bro. I proposed and she said no..." he looked up at me. "Wait, you were going to tell me about what?"

"Man, I don't know how to tell you this but I'mma just go ahead and say it."

He motioned his hand in a forward circle. "Okay...?"

"Look, she only wanted you for his, money." Danielle blurted out.

She was crossing the line and getting a little too damned

comfortable. I used to like when she finished my sentences. It used to be romantic.

She looked at me. "What? We've been out here too long already for you to just tell him that. I'm hungry, too. Shoot."

"Danielle, why don't you go wait for me in the car?"

She rolled her eyes and walked back like she could care less about Pete's feelings.

"My bad, P. Ain't mean it to come out like that."

"So that's it? I already knew she was with me for your money. Hell, I was in it for hers too. That was our thing. Two completely different people with so much in common. It was supposed to be forever, me and her." He kicked an empty soda can over to the dumpster.

I stood in awe. My face most likely looked more along the lines of perplexed, but it indeed was awe.

"I'm a good guy, Shawn. Don't you agree?" he said rhetorically. "I mean, I'm the same guy who goes to a restaurant and asks for water. Then I go to the soda machine and I actually get water. I'm the guy who drops food, and if I can't pick it up in thirty seconds or less, then I won't eat it. That's me. The good guy. So why is it that bad things happen to us, huh?"

I walked over to him and put my hand on his shoulder.

"Don't trip, man. It'll work itself out. These kinds of things do."

The whole time he was talking, I couldn't help but think to myself; *Maybe he and Rashonda deserved each other after all.*

Hey Stranger

1 year later.

"Yes, sweetheart. I have the face mask," I said, zipping my suitcase.

"Okay, good. Make sure you put it on once you get there. Ebola is spreading like crazy in West Africa."

"But that's in Africa."

"And Africa has air, the same thing the disease is using to spread and the same thing your airplane is flying through. I'd feel a lot better if you'd just take a jet. At least that way you won't have everybody breathing on you."

"Nah, I'm good. It's not spread through the air. I think it's spread through bodily fluids, and besides, we can put that money towards the honeymoon or something."

I could feel her smiling through the phone. "Yeah, I guess. We might as well just take three honeymoons. I don't think two is going to be enough for what I'mma do to you."

"Don't get me all worked up and you know I can't see you for another ten hours."

She laughed. "All right then, Superman. Just hurry up and get back. I miss you."

"I miss you too. I'm done eating out for a while. Please cook tonight, doesn't matter what."

"Sure? Spaghetti's cool?" she asked sarcastically.

"Yes. Even spaghetti will do."

Hopefully she didn't take that literally.

Danielle went ahead and moved in a few weeks into her apartment search last year. Her mother damned near had a heart attack when she found out her precious baby girl was quitting her job to go shack up with the ex-boyfriend from college. And it was partly her fault. Enjoying that truth was just enough petty to last me a lifetime.

As for our relationship, I want to say we picked up where we left off, but we didn't. In our absence, we both had come a long way. Growing closer together while being away from each other. Proof that loving someone isn't always good for your relationship with them, especially when you don't know how to love. Time away can be spent learning how to, learning how it feels to lose it, and then if you're fortunate enough to get another chance like I did, holding onto it.

I walked on down to the lobby to wait for my driver. I had been in Houston for the past week at a writer's conference, connecting with other up-and-coming authors, bloggers, and poets. Giving them the advice no one gave me when I was trying to make it.

Yes, as a black writer you'll only be expected to write about gangs, sex, or church. Otherwise you're doing it wrong.

No, most people don't read books anymore. Most people also don't change their sheets twice a week. That doesn't mean bedding production should cease and neither should you as a writer stop writing.

Yes, until you become successful, everyone will have suggestions on what to change in order to become successful. But the ability to speak doesn't come with a responsibility to be accurate or credible, and you have to keep that in mind.

Some young, others old; all looking for help to keep reading alive when in reality it never died. It's just hard to recognize beyond the popularity of a bite-sized quotable. If the STOP sign had a sentence, most people would crash. Someone caught on to that age-old concept and created social media, and that pretty much changed everything.

My driver finally came. He wasn't late; I was just ready to go. But something about him looked unmistakably familiar.

"Ronnie?" I said, thinking aloud.

He paused a bit as he was opening the trunk to put in my luggage and looked up. When I got a clear look at his face, it was confirmed. That was definitely Ronnie.

"Oh..um. Hey, what's up?" he said nervously.

I went over and forced a handshake. I could tell he didn't want to do it, and normally I wouldn't. But this was an exception. Hadn't seen the guy since we fell out back in college and here he was. My driver.

"Man, it's been a while!" I said, grinning from ear to ear like I'd just reunited with a long-lost cousin at a Fourth of July barbeque. "How you been, dude?"

A look of shame was still on his face. "I been good. You know, just doing my thing or whatever. Decent job, and that's more than what some people can say, right?"

I nodded in agreement.

"How long you been driving? I don't know why, but I never would've expected you to be one. Didn't even know we had that as a major."

"Nah, I mean I majored in architecture. But this is my pop's business. I'm just kinda working my way up. Decided I'd take over for 'im one day and get a feel for it here as a driver."

"Right, I remember you telling me about that. Guess you changed your mind about chasing your dreams n' stuff. Or maybe your dreams changed?" Awkward silence moseyed back in between us. "Either way, that's good, man. Glad to see you doing well and healthy," I said as I handed him my luggage.

I wasn't the type to throw shade on anybody's career, whether it was a temporary job or unfortunate circumstances, but I'd be damned if that wasn't karma. Still thinking back to the conversations we had about him and his dad. It seems like he never got the courage to stand up to him and let him know he had other aspirations.

I can only imagine how that conversation went when he got the assignment to come and pick me up. If he was even allowed to know who he was picking up.

But I had no reason to kick him while he was down. Or kick him at all. I was enjoying my blessings and didn't want to ruin it by being petty. I put in my earphones on the way there, even with no music playing. Figured it might lessen the tension.

We arrived at the airport. I shook his hand, for tipping purposes only, then got on to checking my bags.

It was still early, about an hour left before I was to board my flight. I stopped by a coffee shop to read the news a.k.a. scrolling on my tablet. It was much better that way, clicking from website to website instead of fumbling around with one big origami-like piece of paper.

Only problem was trying to decipher the news and extract what really happened. It's like when something goes down and you want to get the scoop but the only person who was there was someone you know you can't trust.

I split my three sugars and two creamers into my dark roast coffee-- decoding the propaganda of the news to get up on the latest happenings.

I peeked over my article to see a little kid running around, terrorizing people who were trying to catch a last-minute nap or listening to music to pass time before their flights. He was unplugging their laptops, snatching their pillows, and everything.

I got a kick out of it because he reminded me of myself when I was that age. Dark-skinned, scrawny, had a head that he'd yet to grow into, too much energy to contain, but still with the innocence of your average five-year-old.

Difference is, Momma would've been halfway to the county jail for how hard she would've snatched me up. Her whoopings came from a place of love, but I always wonder if there was ever a slight frustration in having to be the one to do it all. You know, because Dad still hadn't come back from the store, and every time I acted out, she was reminded that the responsibility of raising a boy into a man was designed for two.

I continued drifting into thought about whether or not I wanted to meet him. All that I needed him for and he wasn't there that Momma had to sacrifice for so she could come as close as possible to being in two places at once. Not sure if he deserved that privilege to be a part of what was essentially her finished product. It's like someone on your team who skips out on an entire season but is there when it's time to hold up a trophy.

"I know that's not who I *think* it is. Shawn?"

I came out of my stupor then turned around to see where the voice had come from.

"Look to your left....no, your other left," she said.

I recognized that voice.

"Jaz?!"

"That's me!" she yelled back.

I stared for a half second to make sure I wasn't deceiving myself, but there she was. My old friend, the one who'd known me better than anyone in college but had lost contact with since. Right there, in the flesh.

I dropped my tablet then met her for a hug.

"Man, how you been, Jaz?!"

I felt something poking my stomach and looked down to see what looked like a little baby bump.

She met my eyes and smiled, "I been good. And yeah, a few things have changed since last time we spoke."

Her voice still had the same soul with the east side of Atlanta's country accent dripping off every word.

"Well, congratulations to you. I thought maybe you just had a big breakfast," I joked.

"No, not quite. I'm a mommy now. Most people can't believe it and sometimes I can't either. It's cool though, I'm getting used to it. But enough about me, what's been up with you, Mr. Big Time?"

"Please, don't. I'm still just Shawn. Nothing special. I cannot get over seeing you here after all these years! How long has it been?"

"Going on six."

"Right. Time flies. I swear it feels just like yesterday we were trying out your mom's recipes that you remixed. Man, those things were good."

"You still remember those? I mean, I still cook but not as much. I got a maid now."

"And you calling *me* big time?"

"Oh, it's only because my fiancé plays for the Texans.» She flashed her ring finger which had nothing short of a shiny golf ball attached to it. "He says he doesn't like me cooking and cleaning all the time while I'm pregnant. And that's cool too. But I'm actually pretty good at the domestic thing."

"That's what's up. So does that mean you live out here now?"

"Yeah, I moved about two years ago after I finally finished my degree at Perimeter in Atlanta. Just came back from down there, visiting my people."

"Well, don't fault me for saying this, but you look great. Glowing and everything. I'm so happy for you."

Honestly, I downplayed the hell out of that compliment. She didn't just look great, she looked phenomenal. Her hair was cut low on one side, and flowing down the other. And it actually *looked* real, but I was no expert. Even with her baby bump, I could see her body was still tight, curves included, popping nicely under her beige sundress.

She'd come up since the last time I saw her. Like a caterpillar who was just making its way out of the cocoon, except it was a sexy ass caterpillar before it ever went in.

She grinned, "I 'preciate that. And what's up wit'chu? Any kids?"

"Nah, not yet anyway. I'm recently engaged as well, though. Danielle is--"

"Oh, you're still with her? Damn. Y'all wasn't playin',

huh?"

"I guess you can say that. We did split for a while before linking back up. But Danielle, she's good. We live out in Charlotte. No complaints."

"No complaints?" Her face screwed up in disappointment. "That's it?"

"Yeah...no complaints. Why you say it like that though? Something wrong?"

She looked at her phone, pausing to read something from it. "Shawn, I'm sorry but I gotta go. He's here to pick me up and I still gotta find out where this lil' boy done ran off to."

"Who? You got another child?"

She hesitated a moment before answering and her eyes shifted. "Umm...yeah, one more. But it was nice seeing you. Tell Danielle I said hello."

She looked over to where the little boy was running around earlier and screamed out, "S.J.!!! Come back here boy!"

She clenched her sundress away from her feet so she could speed walk and grabbed him. When she did, he looked at me, and a weird feeling made its way into my chest.

Something about his eyes. His nose even.

They were...just like mine. He must've thought so, too, because he didn't stop looking back at me after she walked him off. And I remember that distinct face he was making because it was the same one I made when Daddy told me to wait out on the porch for him. When he said he was coming back for me, but never did.

My heart was pounding and I immediately started doing the math. Jazmin and I had only had unprotected sex one time, which I suppose is plenty...and it was just about six years ago.

And then she moved away. But now she has a son, who's somewhere around the age of...

I pulled out my phone and texted Danielle.

Me: *Baby, I'm gonna be in Houston a little longer than I thought. Flight just got canceled. Will talk later. [1:57p.m.]*

CPSIA information can be obtained
at www.ICGtesting.com
Printed in the USA
LVOW03s1107061017
551437LV00001B/10/P